Amanda911

to Donald Schreiber
healer and rhymester

and to Amanda Carmona
whose life is not an emergency

Paperback ISBN 978-1-7370520-1-2
Hardback 978-1-7370520-2-9
Library of Congress Control Number: 2021939088

Cover and Book Design by Lauren Grosskopf

*Pleasure Boat Studio books are available
through your favorite bookstore and through the following*:
Baker & Taylor, Ingram, Amazon, bn.com &
PLEASURE BOAT STUDIO: A NONPROFIT LITERARY PRESS
PLEASUREBOATSTUDIO.COM
Seattle, Washington

Amanda911

a novel by

Mark Schreiber

PLEASURE BOAT STUDIO:
A NONPROFIT LITERARY PRESS

PART ONE

Down the Well

1

Falling down a well was both the best and worst thing that ever happened to my granddaughter. She was a Disney princess to me, but a comic sidekick to her classmates, who'd never been kissed by a boy—or I suppose by a girl—been asked to a dance, or chosen for any role in a school production that did not conceal her face.

Most people under twenty probably don't know what a well is. Haven't seen one. Probably think it's just something you say when you need to buy time, like *like*, or when someone asks you how you're feeling, although I guess these days everyone says *good* or *OK*, or nothing at all, opting for an emoji instead. Do kids even talk anymore, in the crowded loneliness of their bedrooms? Did Amanda even scream when she fell down the well? Or did she just send a screaming emoji?

So, when millions of kids all over the globe saw the headline, they shared via social media:

Girl Plummets Down Well

More than plenty had to Google *well* to comprehend its meaning.

I'm sure she got at least half a million hits just from image searches that returned a picture of an oil rig in the North Sea. *Geez*, her international peer group must have thought, or words or emojis to that effect. A girl has fallen thousands of feet smack into a tidal wave. I hope she's more Kate than Leonardo.

The headline came from a national reporter whose news organization knew how to hack the local 911 dispatcher. This because they were in Iowa during campaign season and the media, the candidates, and even certain foreign governments were trying every trick in the book to gain an advantage.

911 Dispatcher: What's the address of your emergency?

Amanda (crying): Don't you have GPS?

911 Dispatcher: Please give me your address.

Amanda: I'm at the bottom of a fucking well! I don't think they have addresses in wells.

911 Dispatcher: Are you in a safe location?

Amanda: Helloooooo! Bottom of a WELL.

911 Dispatcher: Do you have injuries?

Amanda: Do you think I could fall down a well and NOT have injuries? I'm not a cat.

911 Dispatcher: I'm sending help right away. What's your name, honey?

Amanda: Don't you have caller ID? Owwwwwww! I think both my ankles are broken! And I'm like in two feet of muddy water. And I just bought these shoes. It's a miracle my phone worked. It really is water resistant.

911 Dispatcher: Is that you Amanda Dizon? It's me, Emma Jackson.

Amanda: Who?

911 Dispatcher: I'm a friend of your mom's. I wanted to go to nursing school but couldn't afford the tuition. And a job opened here.

Amanda (frantically): I'm in a well on our farm. You know where that is? I can't believe you don't have GPS.

911 Dispatcher: Oh, we have GPS. But it's in the script to ask your address. Maybe it's a backup, or to calm you down.

Amanda: It did the opposite. It made me think I'd die here.

911 Dispatcher: Take some deep breaths, babe. Help is on the way. It sounds like you aren't seriously hurt or in danger. Try to think of something else.

Amanda (taking deep breaths): OK. Have you ever gotten any calls from murderers on the job?

911 Dispatcher: You know how many murders we have in Iowa, sweetheart? This isn't Chicago.

Amanda: So, what's the most exciting call you've gotten?

911 Dispatcher: This one!

Amanda: Really?

911 Dispatcher: How many people fall down wells? You think they fall down wells in Chicago? If you survive, you're gonna be famous!

*

The first flashlight down the well was from the cell phone of the national reporter, who beat the fire department by three minutes.

Her photographer was still in the shower, so she took some quick pictures with her phone.

National Reporter: What's your PingPong name, kid?

Amanda: I can't believe these questions today! You're not here to rescue me?

National Reporter: Only from obscurity, babe. I'd record an interview but the acoustics are terrible.

Amanda: I've fallen down a well. I'm hurt and wet and scared. Don't you care?

National Reporter: Of course I care. But I don't have all day. The EMTs will be here any minute, not to mention my competition.

Amanda: My PingPong name is Amanda911. Because my life is an emergency. Get it? Joke's on me, I guess. Why do you want it?

National Reporter: I'm going to link it in my story so people can ask you questions.

Amanda: How long do you think I'm gonna be down here?

National Reporter: And so we can text if you're no longer able to use your voice.

Amanda: Why would I lose my voice?!

National Reporter: Damn. I hear sirens.

*

Throughout modern history there have been numerous cases of children, usually babies, falling down wells, capturing media attention and raising the blood pressure of the nation in which they occurred.

But none has garnered as much attention over so brief a time as my granddaughter's.

Perhaps the most famous antecedent was the case of Baby Jessica, who fell down a backyard well in 1987, in the glacial age of television. It took over two days to rescue her, but to the nation it felt like two years.

From the time of the 911 call it took only 47 minutes for the fire department to rescue my granddaughter, but in the lightspeed internet age it might as well have been two years. By the time she reached the hospital she had two broken ankles and six million PingPong followers.

*

The well was only twenty feet deep, but in the internet imagination it was two thousand. The fire crew had barely lowered a rope with a harness before GIFs were circulating showing a Disney princess clinging to a handsome prince lowered by helicopter above the raging North Sea.

Amanda had started the day with three followers. Now she had two million times that. Not to mention eight million likes for her four posts of her black cat, Luna, taken in the first fifteen minutes after she had created her account. And somewhere between tightening the harness herself around her boney shoulders and digging her bitten fingernails into the fireman's hand, she amassed $23,000 in a MakeItRain account.

*

How did this happen?

First, the reporter was a TV personality and bestselling author as well as the political correspondent for a major newspaper. By posting Amanda's story, with journalistic exaggeration of course, and by including her PingPong link, she created a minor sensation. But what made my granddaughter a major sensation were the presidential candidates, who lost no time reposting the tragedy and rescue on their own pages, exploiting the incident for their own Machiavellian ends.

At the hospital they tripped over each other to photobomb her fifteen minutes/seconds/nanoseconds? of fame.

Even the president couldn't resist, Photoshopping himself with Amanda from her knees up with the captions:

American wells are safe!

and

Drill deeper!

Meanwhile my granddaughter, her left ankle in a cast and her right ankle in a brace, lay in a hospital room that was private in name only.

The candidates were eagerly taking selfies with her, pushing aside her parents—my daughter and son-in-law.

Hey, that's my phone! one of the candidates said, reaching for Amanda's phone while she was busy scrolling through a galaxy of breathless questions.

Is this the new taking candy from babies? another candidate taunted, snapping a picture.

But I left my phone in the library three nights ago and it has a Mt. Rushmore case just like this one—

Snap snap snap. Now all the other candidates were documenting the controversy. Pundits would later claim this as the reason for a three percent drop in his poll numbers.

Amanda awoke from her scrolling trance.

Do you want your phone back? I found it under a table. The librarian said he's a libertarian and doesn't believe in 'Lost and Found.' He restored it to factory settings and said, 'Now you're a capitalist.' It saved my life today, I think. My other phone was a Huawei flip phone. Why didn't you activate Find My Phone? Can I keep it, pleeeeease? I'll tell my parents to vote for you.

The candidate slunk away, while the others signed her cast and took pictures of what would, in half an hour, be the most famous ankles in the world, leading one Singaporean entrepreneur to create a virtual ankle cast app, where anyone could write a message for Amanda, to post and share.

This app led, as might have been foreseen, to a good deal of pornographic Amanda's Ankles posts, and by night's end Interpol cracked a pedophilia ring in Frankfurt that had debased my innocent granddaughter in ways I will not mention. Such are the vicissitudes of our Digital Age that a sixteen-year-old girl raised in a cornfield could be both the beneficiary of enough funds to buy a car and the victim of an international criminal enterprise in the space of twenty-four hours.

*

Where are my shoes?

Indeed, by the time the candidates had all left and her parents were able to get in a group hug, Amanda noticed she was barefoot below the ankle cast and brace.

She shouted at a nurse who was too busy saving Amanda's life to answer trivial questions, like, "Where are my shoes?"

She texted on her PingPong:

Thanks for all the thoughts and prayers and likes and follows! I'm really in shock. I'd love to read all your comments and questions but that would take a gazillion years! So, I'll just reply to a few:

No, I don't have a boyfriend.

Yes, I'm straight.

I'm 16. Stalkers beware!

It happened at 7:00 a.m. Before school.

My parents were already at school.

Their school, where they teach, duh.

How could I not be a virgin if I don't have a boyfriend? Don't answer that!

You think I jumped?

You tell me how to milk a cow.

No, I wasn't with a boy.

No, I wasn't lured.

I have no idea what petroleum tastes like. Do you?

I don't know if I could see the stars from down there. I was too busy panicking.

I know I'm lucky. But I'm bummed about my shoes. Just bought them. Saved my allowance for a month.

Vans. Posting the model now.

Food coming. Yay! Gotta go.

You guys want a pic of my tray? Really? You know it's hospital food?

*

While Amanda eats the most Liked Salisbury steak in the world, let us catch our breath and catch up, because it's going to be a fast rollercoaster from here on out and I don't know when I'll have another chance to fill you in.

Amanda was born on a farmhouse that belonged to my father and then to me. But by the time I divorced my wife and exiled myself to Paris and Bangkok and Buenos Aires to write the Great American Novel, it was no longer a working farm.

Carole, Amanda's mother—my daughter—was a creature that has become almost as rare as the unicorns that graced Amanda's walls—a rural Midwestern hippie liberal. She got her degree in Education but dreamed of reclaiming our ancestral roots and becoming a farmer.

Instead of teaching her the Classics, I should have let her watch *Green Acres*, because she married her own Eddie Albert transplant from the Northeast, a Reagan Democrat with a Master of Economics, and they promptly went bankrupt farming soybeans and had to teach Reading and Social Studies to future baristas at the local elementary school.

I would have bailed them out, except I was teaching English myself at the time to future migrant caregivers in Playa del Sur, Nicaragua for five dollars a day.

The bank sold the land to a multinational corporation for pennies on the dollar, but under the terms of the bankruptcy agreement Amanda's parents got to keep the two-story farmhouse, the crumbling garage, and an acre plot out back, including a moribund well, that for reasons still not explained was never sealed, but that did, to my best recollection, have a hinged wooden cover.

*

Meanwhile my ex, Carole's mother—Amanda's grandmother—out black-sheeped me by discovering that she was a lesbian and subsequently moving all the way to the next town to cohabitate with a series of handbag-renouncing lovers.

Against this tapestry of unwoven threads Amanda entered the world. The name *Amanda* means *worthy of love*. And all of us probably could have loved her better and accepted her for the ordinary child she was. For most of her childhood she wished she could disappear into another world, like Alice down the rabbit hole, or like the heroine in her favorite story, *Coraline*, through a magical door in her house.

*

Her parents believed that LED screens were the new tobacco, and when a tablet her grandmother had given her one year for Christmas broke after falling off the kitchen table during a heated argument over who ate the last Krispy Kreme, Amanda was left with only a Huawei flip phone to connect with the world at large.

Which was why she was at the library that night when she found the candidate's iPhone. She went almost every evening to use the computers and printer to do her homework.

*

Statisticians claim some of us have to be average, there's just no way to work around that. To say that Amanda was average is probably padding her youthful resumé. Her grades were C's, except for her parents' classes in the fourth grade where, mortified and traumatized by pressure both from her peers for special favors and her parents for special effort, she got D's, and counseling.

She had average tastes, following fashions in clothes, boy bands and sugary foods. Unicorns and Hello Kitty, naturally. Rainbows and glitter lipstick.

I found her insipid, to be honest, but hoped she'd grow out of it. During a brief visit to Iowa during her ninth year, we had nothing to talk about. I bought her bubble gum ice cream and called it a day.

*

Her parents expected her to be exceptional, to grow like the corn, and launch out of Iowa like a Saturn rocket. They thought education was the ticket to future success, forgetting that many children of ambitious, educated parents are intimidated by their example and just want to live until they don't anymore.

By the time Amanda had passed out of middle school, after the fortune spent on counseling and tutoring and introductory lessons in piano, violin, electric guitar, ballet and jazz dance, tennis and fencing, they abandoned their dreams of a Marvel heroine daughter to search for vomit in her toilet, OxyContin in her jewelry box, razor marks on her arms. Amanda, in their eyes, became the absence of horrific things that could happen to her.

*

And then she fell down a well. Their well! A peril that had been there forever, within view of the kitchen window, but that no one noticed anymore, if indeed they ever had.

Carole prided herself that though her only child excelled in nothing, at least she was healthy and safe. If she raised her daughter to maturity without addictions, repeated grades, or eating disorders she could count herself among the parenting elite. Her daughter might never be a Marvel goddess, but she herself would be a Parenting Superhero.

*

How many times have I told you to block up that fucking well? Carole shouted at her husband as they raced from school to the hospital.

It was covered up!

Obviously not! You may think our daughter's Coraline, but she can't slip through stone and wood.

When did this become my responsibility? If you wanted it sealed up, you should have sealed it up yourself.

Our daughter could be taking her last breaths and you're triggering me with micro aggressions? Everything is political with you.

She broke a couple bones. The doctor said she didn't even hit her head. Will you slow down please? Or we'll need a family room in the ICU.

*

I'm so thankful you're all right! Carole said, smothering Amanda with kisses.

Robert, the father, crept in for the group hug already described.

I'm not all right, Amanda corrected. But look, I've got six million followers!

Do you need a blanket? Are you cold? Where are your socks?

Where are my shoes? I wasn't wearing socks. And no, I'm not cold. I didn't fall into a frozen well.

I'm so sorry, pumpkin. It's all our fault. I told your father a thousand times to seal up that well.

*

Soon the media pushed their way in, and it took all the doctors on staff to push them back out. But Amanda wouldn't let them expel her classmates, who spilled out into the corridor. Girls who had never made eye contact with her before caressed her cast enviously. And even the cute boys bent down to take selfies with her.

You'll follow me back now, won't you? Promise? said all the teens who had not followed her until just a few minutes ago.

This is huge! You're huge! her best friend, Nicole, exclaimed, draping her *Stranger Things* backpack over the **2 Visitors Maximum** sign. Nicole was a popular girl, already had her driver's license, a trail of ex-boyfriends from school, and a RomeoChat college-age boyfriend she had yet to meet, in St. Louis. But unfortunately, Nicole's popularity didn't help Amanda become popular as well, which was probably Nicole's intent, as I suspect she befriended her in the first place because Amanda was an immobile admirer and in no way a threat. So Nicole strategically compartmentalized her social life between the cheerleader clique and the Diversity Crew, where Amanda had her friends.

You'll be the most popular girl in school! yelled a girl who sat behind Amanda in Science class, yet probably couldn't have told you the color of her hair. (Brown, with vermillion highlights.)

You'll be the most popular teen in Iowa! said an older boy who was a star wide receiver on the football team. Can I have a kiss?

Yes!!!

No!!! her mother intervened.

Countless daydreamed hours, tears, scribbled notes unsent about a boy, about many boys, about that first wondrous kiss, and here it was unprompted, unplanned, without even having to get out of bed, from a star football player no less, a tall and ripped senior!

And her mom had to intercept.

The most popular teen in Iowa? shouted another voice, above the din. By tomorrow you could be the most famous girl in the world!

A hush fell over the room, reached into the corridor filled with friends in waiting, snaked up the stairs all the way to the administrative offices where the hospital CEO had convened an impromptu meeting with the marketing director and the chief physician.

The Montgomery County Regional Medical Center hadn't seen this much excitement since a Republican candidate tripped on the ice during the last election and had his fingers put in a splint in their Emergency Room. But there had been no national media that day, just a local item in the *Iowa Sentinel* the following morning.

Has the Dizon family been given the Premiere Suite? the CEO asked, scanning her medical records on a monitor.

I believe the Premiere Suite is occupied. But she has a private room, said the marketing director.

Well, get her in the Premiere Suite. And let's arrange a media room somewhere. And bring out cots if any of her friends want to camp out in the corridor. Fortunately, we're at only 20% occupancy, so let's take advantage of that.

But we are going to discharge her, said the chief physician.

No, we're not. I've called an orthopedist from Mayo to fly down tomorrow. He's the world expert on ankles.

Don't you think that's overreach? The X-rays show simple fractures. The right ankle doesn't even need a cast. It's just sprained.

Maybe you haven't noticed, but the candidates for our highest office spent the better part of their morning taking selfies with our young patient, and all the world is talking about the girl in the well.

Every five years there's a baby or kid in the well story. Or a cave.

It'll blow over in a day, opined the chief physician.

Which is why we have to act now! chimed in the marketing director.

Where is the CT scan? I don't see it here.

We didn't do a CT scan. She said she didn't hit her head.

Maybe she briefly lost consciousness and didn't know it. How would she know, alone at the bottom of a well?

Physical examination revealed no bruising.

Well get the CT scan anyway.

I don't think her insurance will authorize it.

I don't care. We have the eyes of the world upon us. Or their phones. Get some fruit baskets down there. And staff the cafeteria tonight.

Good idea, said the marketing director. But might I also suggest we order from McDonald's and Pizza Hut? I have budget for it. We can create a slumber party atmosphere.

Done. Now what about our social media strategy?

My assistant has just put Amanda on our landing page. You can see it here.

Good job. Can we get a picture of the well?

Of course.

And what about the TableTennis account? I hear she has a million viewers!

It's PingPong, sir. She has six million followers, and growing.

Well let's see what you've put up there.

Sir, we don't have a PingPong account.

Why the hell not?

Because it's a teen demographic. Mostly food porn and dancing.

Porn?!

I mean pictures of food. Dance videos. Fashion reviews. Our IT guy said we shouldn't have it because it's Chinese and they could spy on us.

Damn our IT. They took away my Huawei phone. If the Chinese colonize the moon because of technology they stole from the Montgomery County Regional Medical Center I'll be the first to salute their flag! Now get out of here and get us a TableTennis page!

*

Amanda was wheeled to the imaging room like a conquering hero, pausing for fist bumps and high fives along the corridor. Nicole, along with Amanda's parents, accompanied her in the elevator.

Why do they want a CAT scan? I don't have a headache. I didn't even hit my head.

It's just precautionary, said the orderly wheeling her bed. We do them all the time.

Not on me you don't!

Maybe you're still knocked out, imagined Nicole. Maybe you're in an alternate universe where you're popular.

Cut it out.

Or you're still in the well and this is all a dream.

Stop it!!!

When Amanda saw the imposing machine with its narrow round opening, she sat up rigid.

Do I have to do this?

Yes, said her father.

Not if you don't want to, said her mother, who had an excessive fear of magnetism.

A young female tech explained the procedure.

I can't do it. I'm claustrophobic.

You were just in a fucking well! Nicole reminded her.

I know, and it was awful.

Man up, said her father, who thought being a feminist meant saying all the bullying things you would say to your son, to your daughter.

Robert, don't be an ass, said Amanda's mother. She was traumatized this morning and this will just give her PTSD.

Carole, the *P* stands for *post*. You can't get post-traumatic stress disorder three hours after the original trauma.

I didn't realize there was a waiting period! Why don't we ask a psychologist?

Why don't we ask your followers? Nicole suggested instead.

What do you mean? asked Amanda.

Give me your phone. You can create a poll.

CAT scan to rule out head injury. YES or NO?

And I'll post a picture. Who else wants to get in the photo?

The tech was not amused and looked impatiently at the analog clock on the wall. We have other patients, so if you don't want to do this now...

But 34,405 followers had already cast votes, comprising a more than sufficient sample size: 76% **yes.**

At least there's no skanky water in this hole, Amanda consoled herself, clutching her phone.

Sorry, the phone stays outside, said the tech.

This is worse than the well! Amanda screeched.

*

By the time she emerged ten minutes later, sweating profusely, the pizza and cheeseburgers had arrived.

This is un-fucking-believable, she exclaimed, walking barefoot on crutches in the cafeteria, surrounded by hungry classmates. Did they bring vanilla shakes by chance?

Honey, you shouldn't walk barefoot.

Mama, it's a hospital. I think they disinfect the floors like every five minutes.

But before her mother could find a pair of hospital-grade slippers an Amazon Prime box arrived.

Vans! My Vans! I'm made whole.

She grabbed her phone and sent Yuji5958 in Osaka several rows of rainbow hearts. It seemed a particularly unusual gesture from an admirer on the other side of the world. But by night's end she would have at least 200 more pairs, making the cafeteria resemble a Foot Locker, and throwing Vans' supply chain into panic mode.

*

Grandma!

Riven by COPD from a lifelong affair with the Marlboro Man, my ex-wife pushed her walker and oxygen bottle through a sea of teenagers in the Montgomery Regional Medical Center cafeteria and sat down, breathless, next to our only grandchild.

Granny, you look worse than me. Do you want to stay? I'm sure we can get you a room.

Let me see your legs. My Lord, poor child! I told your grandfather to fill in that well fifty years ago! This is all his fault.

*

While sipping a vanilla shake that had magically arrived, Amanda paused to answer some more questions from her followers.

No, we don't live in yurts. What's a yurt?

No water buffalo in Iowa. Sorry.

We haven't gotten a hurricane in, I guess, forever, because we're about as far from the ocean as it's possible to be. Don't they have Google Earth where you live?

We have everything here. We're not backwards.

No IKEA. But I'm hoping.

No beaches, no.

No islands.

Volcanoes? Who wants volcanoes?

Skyscrapers? Define skyscraper. We have one.

Megacities? We have Des Moines. Form your own conclusion.

Polar bears? You're thinking of Minnesota.

*

A pair of firemen entered the cafeteria, still in uniform. Amanda recognized the one who had pulled her out. She hobbled over and gave him a hug.

Thanks for saving my life!

I didn't save your life.

I was so scared. I don't know how much longer I could have stayed down there.

I didn't even make a descent. I just pulled up the rope. And I can't even take credit for that, because it was attached to a motor. Although I could have done it myself, skinny as you are.

All the same...

Our chief wants you to take a photo with us out front, in the truck.

Sure. Can I hold the steering wheel?

*

The party continued in the cafeteria, though one group of senior honor students had been kicked out for sneaking in alcohol in Starbucks cups.

Amanda took a moment to answer more questions while a nurse took her vitals.

How did I fall down the well? It was an accident.

I keep telling you guys it wasn't an oil well! And for the thousandth time Iowa is nowhere near the North Sea. Or the South, East or West Seas! Stop asking.

Are there Black people in Iowa? Of course. Duh.

Are there any Asians in my class? Yes. Nipuni is from India. That's Asian, right? And Amy's grandparents came from Taiwan, but she was born here.

Amanda knew this not because she was geographically studious and sensitive to heritage but because Amy and Nipuni, along with Nicole, were the closest thing she had to a group, her three amigas, her three original PingPong friends.

Nicole pulled the phone out of her hand and saw the questions about Blacks and Asians.

Hey, Diversity Crew, you're lighting up the internet. Let's take a picture.

The term *Diversity Crew* had been coined years ago by a student or students, or some said even a teacher, or coach. Some thought it was even by Harding High's first African American principal, or the scandal-ridden principal who had a *Dukes of Hazard* Hot Wheels car on his desk, the orange one with the Confederate battle flag. In any case, it was either a term of shameful prejudice or one of defiant pride. Those minority students, teachers and administrators who had tried, over the years, to eradicate it found themselves stymied by the nuances of identity politics. For what if the original Crew had been forged in the cauldron of resistance?

Any student not white and Christian was lumped in—or belonged to—the Diversity Crew. Present in the hospital cafeteria tonight were Shanda Low (African American); Nipuni Bardalai (not Indian as Amanda had posted but Sri Lankan); Amy Lee (Chinese); and a Dominican boy from another class whom none of them knew.

For a time, last year, Amanda herself had been included (or excluded) because a visitor to the Dizon home spied a statue of Vishnu on the fireplace. But without additional evidence of what the neighbors mistakenly considered Satan worship, the matter was forgotten and Amanda seeped back into the pure soil of Midwestern Americana.

Under other circumstances the representative members of Diversity Crew might have taken offense. But tonight they gathered for a Diversity Crew group photo with pride, knowing most of the teens viewing the post would be Asian or people of color like themselves, and happy to flow on Amanda's contrails, thinking this might be the ticket to their own social media dreams.

*

Perhaps the only person in the Montgomery County Regional Medical Center cafeteria who at the beginning of this singular day lacked social media dreams—and this includes the kitchen staff, nurses, janitors, parcel and food delivery drivers—was, ironically, Amanda herself. Her parents' wariness of electronic devices, coupled with her lack of the kind of skills that would have made her popular online, such as coding or gaming—she had given up Candy Crush at Level 6—dissuaded her from perceiving the digital world as anything but a black hole of envy for kids with only three friends and splotchy skin.

Her mother approached.

Your father has a headache and went to the car, but I can stay over.

Mom, no. I'm with my class. You'll just embarrass me.

How are your ankles? Do you need an Advil? I can get your nurse.

I need a morphine drip, but I'll make do.

Promise you won't get in trouble.

Mama, this is a hospital, not a keg party.

Well at the moment it looks more like Studio 54.

What's Studio 54?

Never mind.

But her mom had a point. Someone had turned off the fluorescent lights. The only illumination came from cell phones, the buffet counter, and *EXIT* signs. Someone had brought Bluetooth speakers and cranked up a playlist from their phone. Students were dancing to Drake and Beyoncé. Some on tables. And to everyone's surprise, neither nurses, nor the night residents on staff, nor security, nor other patients shut down the party.

This wasn't a criminal dereliction of duty but a calculated tactic by the marketing director, who used gift cards from her discretionary budget to get the adults and handful of patients to stay mum.

Her money shot came later that night, when Amanda posed with a nurse and orderly and posted the caption:

Montgomery County Regional Medical Center rocks my world!!!

*

Her mother was about to give some sage parting advice when Nicole raced over, knelt before the seated Amanda, and grabbed both of her hands, mashing their phones together.

Buy me a car, bestie. Please, please, please.

You already have a car.

I have a Ford F-150 with 200,000 miles and no radio. Buy me a Jaguar and I'll drive you everywhere you want until you get your license.

Sure, when I win the lottery.

You won the lottery!

Nicole held out her own phone, or tried to.

Stop shaking, said Amanda. I can't see what you're showing me.

Let me see that! said Amanda's mom, grabbing the phone. What is MakeItRain?

MakeItRain? echoed Amanda, peeking in.

I can't believe you guys! exclaimed Nicole. You never heard of MakeItRain? It's crowdfunding for personal tragedy.

But I only fractured one ankle, said Amanda. The doctor said I can probably go home tomorrow.

But nobody knew that when the story broke, did they? Some good soul lit an account and it rained a hurricane. Now you can post that Iowa does get hurricanes after all. Lol!

What is this figure? asked Amanda's mom. $305,050? Is that the goal?

The goal is ten thousand dollars! Nicole shouted above the music. $305,050 is the amount pledged. So you can easily afford to buy me a Jaguar. I just want a basic one. And you'll have money left over to buy a car painted rainbow colors for yourself, and probably a house with a life-size stuffed unicorn.

A life-size stuffed unicorn?

This can't be legitimate, whispered Amanda's mother.

And this is just day one, said Nicole. Look, someone just pledged fifteen dollars. Now it's $305,065. Let's dance!

But Amanda's mom grabbed her daughter's arm. Can you please give us a minute, Nicole?

She helped her daughter into a wheelchair and wheeled her into the corridor, where it was quiet enough to talk in normal voices, and bright enough to see each other clearly.

She knelt down so that their gaze was level. Are you OK, darling?

Are you kidding? This is the best day of my life!

You suffered a traumatic experience.

The well? I should have fallen down that thing a long time ago!

What were you doing there anyway? Never mind. Listen, this is all nice and fun, and I'm glad all your classmates have finally taken an interest in you, even if they have ulterior motives...

Mom, cut to the chase.

But none of this is real. It's just entertainment. The RainMan account, the six million friends...

It's seven million now! Can you believe that? I've gotten another million followers in like eight hours. How many followers is that an hour, a minute, a second, a half second?

Amanda, darling. Your grandfather always called you his Disney princess. I never liked the gowns and plastic tiaras he sent you. It only reinforces oppressive gender stereotypes. But that's neither here nor there...

Mama, spit it out.

I'm trying to say being a princess has its dark side.

Yeah, for the parents. The princesses are usually orphans.

This is your Cinderella moment. This is your magic ball. You even have your own glass slipper—your cast. But you are going to wake up tomorrow and it will all be gone.

The doctor said I have to wear the cast for eight weeks.

You know what I mean, Amanda.

Who says I'm going to sleep? I'll stay up all night. I'm in a hospital. They can give me any medicines I want. I'm never gonna let this night go.

You have to let it go.

You're making me cry.

Don't cry, darling. I just don't want you to climb out of one hole only to fall down another.

3

Amanda parted from her mother in the corridor, insisting on wheeling herself back into the cafeteria. She was still wiping away tears when Nicole rejoined her.

I'm ready to dance now, said Amanda.

But your cast. I didn't think of that.

Get me a crutch.

I don't know... Listen. I have a better idea. Look around the room. Pick a boy.

What boy?

Whoever you like best. For your first kiss.

Are you crazy! Why does everyone think I'm Cinderella?

What are you talking about?

What are you talking about? I can't ask anyone to kiss me.

Who said you're going to be the one to ask? Did you ask that football player in your room?

I forgot about him! Is he here?

No, he left. But what about a boy from our class? Who is your crush? Gee, I'm your best friend and I don't even know who you like.

I don't even know myself. I've always been too shy to talk to boys. I can hardly talk to girls. My dreams aren't about a particular guy, but general...

There are one, two...seven, eight...twelve...fifteen boys still here. What about Marty?

She waved to Martin Decker, ripped and confident, power forward for the junior varsity basketball team, blond with braces making his sparkling white teeth straighter every day. Dreamy.

But he was your boyfriend.

A lifetime ago. I've moved on. I dumped him because he's a player. But he's a good kisser.

I dunno...

Or if you like nerds, there's Ned. He says he can hack into the voting machines. Bright future there. And Marty's gym locker is next to his and Marty told me he has a giant you know what.

Why is that piece of information important? I thought this was a first kiss!

Or there's that Haitian guy. He's kind of standing by himself. His family just moved here and I don't think he has many friends. But he's cute.

Dominican.

Huh?

He's from Dominican Republic.

Where's that?

Right next to Haiti. That's probably why you said Haiti. But I don't even know his name. I can't kiss someone before I know his name.

Why not? Anyway, we can go over and talk to him first. What do you say?

Martin.

What?

Martin, whispered Amanda.

You little devil. All right.

In the excitement of the moment Nicole pulled Amanda across the cafeteria, forgetting she was in a cast and not supposed to walk without crutches, and certainly not run.

Ow, ow, ow! Amanda screamed, but her pain was muted by the music and the gratifying recognition that she was finally going to receive her first kiss. Martin Decker was so tall and confident and popular that Amanda was afraid to even look at him. But the idea that someone who had dated Nicole might kiss her filled her with delight.

But of course he wouldn't kiss her, she realized as they reached the cashier side of the cafeteria, where most of the boys were hanging out, eating chips and pretzels and asserting their rights to the soda machine, like male lions at a watering hole.

Amanda squeezed her friend's hand in terror. This was going to be the most embarrassing moment of her life. Martin would scoff at her in front of her whole class, including some seniors and a media person or two who had crashed the party.

But before Amanda could speak Nicole cleared her throat and shouted: Music off. Everyone, your attention please. Can someone turn on the lights?

The lights blinded everyone for a moment. The music stopped and even though Amanda was the new celebrity and the reason they were all there, all eyes instinctively focused on Amanda's more vivacious, glam friend.

No lights! Amanda insisted.

It's better for the video.

No. No!

The lights immediately went back off, such was the power of a girl with seven million PingPong followers.

Amanda tried to squeeze away, but Nicole still held her hand. Good thing, because her foot slipped and she would have crashed to the floor. Instead, she bumped against a table and used a chair to catch her balance.

Oh shit, I forgot about your ankle! Nicole cried. Can someone bring Amanda's crutches?

Nicole, I can't do this.

You said that about the CAT scan and you were a trooper. Do you want to take another PingPong poll? Kiss or no kiss?

No.

A pair of folding forearm crutches appeared as if by magic and Amanda righted herself, although now all eyes were fixed on her.

Owwwww.

This time, without the music, everyone could hear her agony, giving Nicole an idea.

Who among you will take away our princess's pain with a kiss?

Under other circumstances Amanda might have appreciated this sweet and metaphorical gesture from her best friend, a vain and immature girl who had been a very poor best friend, who had neglected to show her attention before today and used Amanda chiefly as an audience for her own dramatic adventures. And while it might be argued Nicole was using her still, that her sudden interest was driven more by seven million faces in the dark than by the wan, vulnerable face looking up at her now, I think it not unreasonable to assume there was a dash of goodwill in her effort.

The cafeteria was as silent as the bottom of a well.

Give me your phone, it has a better light, said Nicole, putting her own phone on the table and taking her friend's. For once Nicole was happy to be on the other side of the lens.

Stand against the table and lose the crutches. Like that. Great. Don't move.

Boys?

Still, no one spoke.

You! commanded Nicole, grabbing her ex-boyfriend by his sweater. Pucker up.

One of the reasons Nicole had befriended Amanda was she knew that her boyfriends, including players like Martin Decker, wouldn't play with her comic sidekick. They could all hang out in a bedroom and Nicole could go to the bathroom without worrying about catching them *in flagrante* upon her return.

Had this bit of theater been instigated by a prankster, Martin would have committed felonies to prevent its dissemination to his peer group. But for a viral video, with Likes certain to be in the tens, perhaps even hundreds of thousands—perhaps even millions, who could say?—an invisible girl, like Amanda, was for this night as hot as Cinderella.

Amy Lee, get over here, said Nicole, inspirations coming in waves. For she realized much of their audience would be non-English speaking.

Translate what I say into Asian for our Chinese audience, OK?

Amy knew there was no such language as Asian. For that matter she didn't even speak Chinese herself. But she wasn't about to let those trivial facts ruin her chance for audio fame. So she recited the dim sum menu from her grandfather's restaurant.

Amanda Dizon, at the beginning of this miraculous day you fell into a deep, dark well. Your body was bruised and battered. Bones were broken. You nearly drowned. You had to eat insects to survive until the brave men of the Montgomery County Fire Department rescued you with a frayed rope. Thank the Lord you're so thin. Girls, let this be a warning to you; watch your weight, exercise. For one day you may find yourself at the bottom of a well with only a frayed rope between you and salvation.

Amanda, you were taken by ambulance to this state-of-the-art hospital, the Montgomery County Regional Medical Center, given emergency surgery on your legs and brain scans because you hit your head so many times against the jagged stones of the well. And yet you said no to morphine and Oxy, because you want to be an example to the addicted youth of Iowa and the whole country who are losing their lives to opioids.

By this point Amy Lee had run out of dim sum items and had stopped speaking, but no one seemed to notice. Nicole was rocking it.

So, who will bestow the first kiss upon Harding High's fair maiden and take away her pain?

She prodded Martin. Go, go! But no tongue. Keep it Disney.

Martin Decker bent low and kissed Amanda Dizon firmly, but respectfully on the lips.

Amada felt an electric shock, although it might have been his braces.

Nicole held the camera firm, staring at the viewfinder. But before she could click off, something unscripted occurred. Ned the Hacker hacked the Girl in the Well First Kiss Streaming Event and planted his own confident lips upon our princess.

My God! whispered Nicole, almost dropping the camera.

The Dominican boy swept into the frame next. Not so shy after all! And then the remaining boys followed suit, in single file, as if this were a tornado drill. There might have even been a girl in the mix.

*

In the days and weeks that followed, blogs and newspaper columns would be penned, and panel discussions convened to assert this incident as an ugly example of alcohol-fueled hazing, although the only alcohol that night had entered and exited the hospital in Starbucks cups. Commentators on all sides of the political spectrum would cite Amanda's serial first kiss as an instance of abuse, compelling the Montgomery County District Attorney to bring the matter to a Grand Jury.

But Amanda had stood, or rather leaned, so impassively throughout, in a state of shock, not because this remarkable day was ending, as it had begun, with a trauma, but because the world, which had closed its eyes to her for sixteen years, was finally looking back.

4

When our sweet heroine awoke, she was in motion. But she wasn't being swept off her feet—that had happened last night—or swirling through the vortex of a tornado, like Dorothy in the *Wizard of Oz*, or tumbling in a *déjà vu* trap back down the well, as in *Groundhog Day*. No, she was being wheeled to the operating room in the Montgomery County Regional Medical Center.

She recognized the orderly from the CT scan. He was pushing her. And her parents, one on each side.

What the fuck?! cried Amanda.

Don't be alarmed, said her mother.

Don't be alarmed? Am I dead? I see a white light.

That's just a white light, dear.

Where am I going?

To the operating room.

The operating room!

Amanda reached for her phone.

Where's my phone?

Dr. Patel is going to fix your ankle.

But it's just a fracture! That's what the doctor said yesterday. I'm supposed to leave today.

Yes, dear. But they brought in the world expert from the Mayo Clinic and he says he's pioneered a procedure where you won't have to wear a cast and will only need physical therapy for eight days.

I don't care!

Amanda glanced at the name tag of the orderly.

James, halt!

Whether Amanda's newfound assertiveness stemmed from her millions of followers or a fear of going beneath the scalpel, she could not say.

But James halted.

She sat up straight, her green eyes wide open, the operating room door within view.

What if I hadn't woken up? My God. How could this happen? Don't I have to sign a form?

We signed it, said her mother. You're a minor.

Well, when I'm president that's gonna be the first thing I change!

Nobody knew where that came from. Let's just say it was an expression.

Dad, you refused surgery for your rotator cuff, but you're going to put me under the knife?

Your MakeItRain account has stalled in the $300,000's said her dad professorially. An operation could push it above half a million.

Dad!

I love you as a father, it goes without saying, but I think you should also have the benefit of my economic nous.

Noose? I can't believe you guys. Where are my crutches? Where's my phone?

5

She felt relieved to be back at last in her cozy upstairs bedroom. It seemed a year, a lifetime, two lifetimes since she had been in her room. The last time she had sat here on her bed, scrolling through her phone—or rather the candidate's lost phone—her ankles were not shooting messages of pain. She had three PingPong followers.

Now she had a bottle of extra-strength ibuprofen and nine-million followers.

For the one or two of you out there who haven't heard this most famous of quotes about fame, the artist Andy Warhol once intoned (during the Age of Analog Television) that everyone would be famous for fifteen minutes.

Those pundits, journalists, classmates and parents who thought Amanda's fifteen minutes of fame had been spent were in for a surprise.

*

Honey?

Her mother found her daughter standing by the window, staring out at the backyard. Or rather, on closer inspection, snapping pictures of the backyard.

The grass was turning brown, leaves from the sycamore tree falling through the crisp September air. The wooden garage, to the left of the iPhone frame, looked ready to collapse. The well looked small and innocuous at the far end, a round shadow, a few yards before the fenced-off farmland that had once been mine. Luna, her black cat, was scampering after a squirrel.

I'm sorry about the surgery. We should have asked your permission. But the Mayo Clinic is the Harvard of hospitals.

Doesn't Harvard have a hospital?

You know what I mean. And Dr. Patel flew in on a private jet.

You said you didn't even believe in the MakeItRain account.

Well, your father's the one with the Economics degree, and he said they're legit. And you don't have a college fund.

Amanda turned to her mother with an accusatory glare.

You're not taking my fortune for no college fund.

The money—if there is any money—will be held in a trust until you are twenty-one.

Twenty-one! I promised Nicole a Jaguar.

You what?

Are there really life-size stuffed unicorns? I didn't see any on Amazon.

Honey...

Amanda turned back to the window and looked into the distance.

I was thinking I could buy the farm back and you and Dad could try planting weed this time. But maybe you're right, said Amanda after a pause. It's probably a scam. Or people will come to their senses and withdraw their pledges.

Honey...

Her mother put her arms around Amanda's shoulders.

I want to talk about what happened last night, said her mother. After I left.

You mean the soda machine running out? God, that could have caused a riot.

You know what I mean. I printed some articles from the #MeToo movement I'd like you to read.

Amanda put down her phone and looked her mother in the eye.

Mama, last night was the best thing that ever happened to me. If I ever get raped, I promise you'll be the first to know.

She grabbed her crutches and hobbled downstairs.

In the living room she opened the curtains. News trucks were crowded at the curb.

Snap, snap from the media.

Snap, snap back from Amanda.

Her mother rushed to close the curtain.

The doorbell rang.

Amanda took a step, but her mother blocked her.

Now they know you're here. Why did you let them see you?

Of course, they know I'm here. Where else would I be?

I told them you were sedated.

But I want to talk! No one's ever interviewed me before, unless you count that reporter when I was in the well.

You don't know the media. They're vultures.

Thanks for the advice, Carole Kardashian. You're just jealous because you spent years going to college and trying to grow ethanol and in one day I made more money than you and Dad ever did, and Dr. Evil flew on a private jet to cut me open, and all these reporters want to talk to me. Me!

Is that what you think? shouted her mother. That your dad and I are jealous of you?

I didn't say Dad. Just you.

So, you don't think I have your best interests at heart?

I did until I woke up in front of the operating room!

Owww! cried Amanda. If you have my best interests at heart you can go upstairs and get my Advil.

*

Her mom returned with the Advil, blankets and sheets, and the ragged stuffed unicorn her daughter had slept with since age seven.

She spread the sheets on the sofa, while Amanda watched from the recliner.

What are you doing? asked Amanda.

You're going to sleep down here. You shouldn't be climbing stairs.

No way. I can't post from here.

You're not posting from anywhere today, said her mother, grabbing her phone.

Hey! You can't do that.

I can.

You're a Neanderthal! If you didn't hate social media so much I might have been famous years ago.

You're not famous, Amanda! You're not.

A hush fell.

You're jealous, whispered Amanda. See.

Oh honey, it's like a drug. It's like heroin. I don't want you to crash. This high, it won't last.

Don't you think I know that, Mom! shrieked Amanda, so loud that one of the technicians with a boom mike in his news truck picked it up.

Mama, this is only day two. Day two! Maybe it will last a week or two. Give me that. I'm not going to go into convulsions when it's over. I'm not going to steal car radios. Promise.

You can have your phone back tomorrow, said her mom, disappearing into the kitchen.

Tomorrow?! That's like a decade in social media days. Give it back or I'm gonna go outside and kiss all the reporters!

She tried to get to her feet but cried out in pain.

Her mother returned from the kitchen, bare handed, and kissed Amanda on the forehead.

I have the perfect daughter! She can't run away.

*

The next ten minutes were the most boring ten minutes of Amanda's life. She stared at the drawn curtains, the abstract paintings on the wall, the wedding portrait of her parents, a family portrait taken when she was nine, the statue of Vishnu on the mantle.

She turned on the TV. But her parents didn't have cable. There were only five channels and the reception was poor. Soap operas, game shows. She half expected to find a news story about herself. But what news was there, anyway? Girl in the Well disses private plane surgeon? Her mother was right. The high was over.

*

Her mother had figured out, after much pulling of wires, how to disconnect the doorbell. She had previously disconnected the phones in the kitchen and master bedroom. Yes, the Dizon household still had a landline, which embarrassed Amanda to no end. Her mother had even called the police to keep reporters from trespassing into the backyard.

By mid-afternoon most of the news trucks were gone.

So they were both startled when there was a rapid, repeated knock on the door.

Her mother allowed Amanda's original three followers to enter, Amy and Nipuni shyly trailing Nicole.

Why aren't you answering your phone! Oh, hi Mrs. Dizon, blurted Nicole, breathless.

We've been trying to reach you all day! I was even going to leave school at lunch bell when you didn't show signs of life, but Mr. Barton threatened to give me detention.

I told Nicole you were still under anesthesia from the surgery, said Nipuni, stepping forward.

Yes, echoed Amy, closing ranks. Remember when I had my appendix out and I slept for like fifteen hours afterward?

How do you know about the surgery? asked Amanda.

Nicole showed her a pic of Dr. Patel on the hospital helipad.

I didn't have surgery. I don't need it.

Of course you need it. My Lord! moaned Nicole, sitting on the sofa and squeezing the plush unicorn with rather too much force. Do you know what that could do to our MakeItRain account?

Our!!!

PingPong loves surgery. Do you know how many surgery vids there are? How do you think I learned about Filipino psychic surgery? PingPong!

Nicole glanced at Amanda's hands, her pockets, the seat cushion and coffee table.

Where's your phone?

It's being quarantined for the day, said Mrs. Dizon. And I'm afraid I'm going to have to commandeer yours as well for the duration of your visit.

The three girls reflexively tightened their hands around their mobiles.

Is she serious?

Amanda nodded.

Then I'm afraid we're gonna have to go.

Nicole took a couple quick snaps.

But don't worry, I'll keep you alive online until you get out of jail. Actually, we've already posted some comments on your account and returned follows of some hot guys since we couldn't find you.

How did you get on my account? Did you ask Ned to hack in?

Wasn't necessary. I knew your password had to be *unicorn or rainbow*. You need to change it to something ultra-secure, by the way. The Russians will be snooping around before long. Goodbye, Mrs. Dizon.

*

Luna crept back inside and Amanda hugged her on the sofa in lieu of her cell phone, while game show contestants jumped with joy on TV.

Her father came home from school and, after a brief and meaningless chat about the #MeToo movement, trust funds, and something called the Marshmallow Test, helped his wife prepare dinner in the kitchen.

Amanda popped more Advil and slept.

*

Dinner was excruciatingly quiet and slow. It reminded Amanda of visiting her late great aunt in the nursing home dining room. But at least in the nursing home there were televisions playing.

Not that tonight's dinner was any different from a thousand other meals at the Dizon household. What had changed was Amanda, and the mad rush of PingPong posts, comments, Likes and Shares that had enveloped her over the last twenty-four hours.

Afterward her mother suggested a warm bubble bath and wrapped a trash bag around the cast so it wouldn't get wet.

Ahhh, moaned Amanda, sinking in. This feels so good.

Her mother massaged her legs with a washcloth. Amanda was too exhausted to be embarrassed. Anyway, the suds were covering the parts of her body that mattered.

Nicole had told her that boys get erections all the time. Even in Algebra class they get hard-ons. Why do you think men invented desks? She had showed Amanda snippets of porn. Amanda wasn't much interested. Nicole showed her one of a Unicorn. Unicorn porn. Amanda thought it was disgusting.

Nicole said boys get erections 24/7. Then they get married and need Viagra, haha!

Lying in the bath, Amanda was glad she wasn't a boy. Her life was embarrassing enough without erections. Imagine boys who broke their ankles. Boys in casts. They couldn't let their mothers, or even their fathers or brothers, help them bathe. Too risky.

She wondered if she would take a selfie now if she had her phone. With the bubbles covering her, of course. That would blow up Ping-Pong! Here was a girl who felt self-conscious in a bikini, imagining a bath selfie for millions to see.

And then she closed her eyes and imagined snapping away, and the bubbles disappearing, until her nipples appeared, and then...

And she imagined Martin Decker looking at her body and not being disgusted. Pressing Like.

*

At night her parents turned on the debate, live from Iowa State University.

Amanda recognized the candidates only because they had taken selfies with her and signed her cast. Like most of her class, and to her civically engaged parents' dismay, she wasn't interested in politics. But her phone was in quarantine and there was nothing else to do, so she cradled Luna in her lap and pulled the handle on the recliner.

Blah blah blah?

Blah blah blah blah blah blah blah blah blah blah blah blah blah blah blah blah blah blah blah blah blah blah blah blah blah blah blah blah blah blah blah blah blah blah blah blah.

Blah blah blah blah?

Blah blah blah blah blah blah blah blah blah blah blah blah blah blah blah blah blah.

Blah blah blah blah blah blah blah blah blah?

Blah blah blah blah blah blah blah blah blah blah blah blah blah blah blah blah blah blah blah blah blah blah blah blah blah blah blah blah blah blah blah blah blah blah blah blah blah blah blah blah Girl in the Well...

Fuuuuuuuuuck!!!

Shhhhhh!!!

No one was sure who had yelled the profanity and who had shushed them, although both exclamations might have been uttered by all three. What is beyond dispute is that in the next moment the entire Dizon household was standing two feet from the TV, except for Luna, who had raced away in alarm.

It was the candidate who had lost his phone in the library speaking.

Courage, willpower, and fortitude in the face of adversity, that is the hallmark of the American spirit, said the candidate.

Is he talking about me?! screamed Amanda.

I had the pleasure of meeting her in her hospital room and signing her cast. I think her name is Amanda. In the few minutes we had together we had a nice chat.

All he said was, 'That's my phone!' Amanda recalled.

And seeing that she was going to be bedridden for some weeks, and asking about my new iPhone, I gave it to her. I hope the Election Commission won't consider that a bribe. She is too young to vote, haha.

Liar, he wanted it back! Amanda exclaimed.

The Dizons collapsed together on the sofa.

My daughter...has just been mentioned...by a candidate for president...on national TV! sighed her mother.

Courage, willpower, what else did he say? asked her father.

Still think my Cinderella moment is over, Mom?!

Shhhh. Listen!

Because there was more:

I too had the pleasure of meeting your local hero, said another candidate. If all our youth are as impressive as Amanda Dizon, then the future of Iowa and of our great nation is in good hands.

He said our name! Amanda's father exclaimed.

My name!!!

This Girl in the Well tragedy highlights the need for infrastructure projects in the heartland, opined a third candidate. As I understand it, she fell in while trying to get water for her family because the lead pipes in her district have still not been replaced.

Lord! cried Amanda. Is that true? I mean about the pipes?

Fortunately, Amanda's parents are both teachers and have insurance, pointed out a candidate on the far end. But this is why we need universal healthcare. Think about all the children who fall down wells whose parents aren't gainfully employed.

I referred the hospital director to my friend, Dr. Patel, a renowned orthopedic surgeon, said the candidate on the other end. So, you can say Amanda's life was saved by an immigrant.

Hellooooo! Amanda waved to the TV. Dr. Patel didn't do anything!

Shhhhh.

I had the honor of meeting young Amanda's parents, interjected yet another candidate. Public school teachers, as my colleague alluded to. Fine, upstanding Iowans who know the value of a good education and the dangers of social media, teen sex, e-cigarettes and prescription drugs.

What did you guys tell them?!

I can't believe this! Amanda's mother exclaimed. Say my name! Did I tell you my name? Carole...

He can't hear you, Mom.

I'm sure I told you. Carole!

Relax, Mama. This moment won't last.

6

And where was I? you might be asking by now, the chronicler of our heroine's journey.

I had left Iowa as soon as the ink on my divorce papers was dry, rarely to return. The last time, as mentioned, was seven years ago, when Amanda was nine, bubble gum ice cream dripping down her cone in the chilly Baskin-Robbins at the mall. I remember sitting with my arms folded trying to think of conversation. Writer's block with my own grandchild. It was like a blind date from hell, but with someone who couldn't drive herself home.

Though I'd had the usual problems a father has with his daughter, I had never been lost for words with Carole. She had been full of intellect and ambition, befitting an Archer. (My full name, I might as well tell you now, is Sutherland Archer.) I regretted my DNA has come to this terminus. How thin the double helix has been pulled. As I regarded the rainbow-colored ice cream dripping over her sparkly bracelets, the word *insipid* hammered my thoughts. If she had been a character in one of my novels, the book would only be half a page long:

Somewhere a dog was barking. And in a chilly suburban mall a completely unextraordinary girl was licking ice cream off her fingers and trying to balance the scoop remaining in her half-eaten cone as if she were a circus juggler with a dozen spinning plates above her nose.

It was with a sense of shameful resignation to the possibility of ordinariness, to the triumph of the marketplace over the universe of ideas, that I marked her subsequent birthdays and Christmases with Disney dresses and figurines, stuffed animals and rainbow stickers, sent from distant parts of the globe, where I struggled, as I had for decades, to write a novel of depth and purpose that would secure my place among the pantheon of American writers.

But when I called her *princess,* that was not shameful resignation. Tolstoy wrote of princesses. It could be just as much a term of wistful aspiration as of cartoon vulnerability.

I admit I didn't come back to Iowa after that. Nor did I call as much as I should have, or send as many gifts as I wanted, or search again in my granddaughter for a spark of ambition to kindle. But you must understand I loved Amanda deeply. I did.

*

When my princess tumbled down the well, I was in a hostel on Boracay Island in the Philippines, in the midst of a typhoon. Electricity was down for three days, and even when it came back, the internet was spotty. I didn't even own a cell phone, so it was all the same to me. My laptop was fifteen years old and my only digital account was an email address I checked about once a month, to read accumulated rejection letters from literary agents and publishers.

*

When Amanda woke on the sofa Luna was napping at her feet, the unicorn plush was on the floor, atop her crutches, and her iPhone was back, buzzing incessantly on the coffee table, beside a note from her mom saying:

Grocery shopping. Don't open the door for anyone!!!

Amanda jumped up, banging her foot.

Owwwwww!

She popped a couple Advil and grabbed the phone. Two of the candidates were now following her! Along with nine million others!

Oh my God.

She was startled by a rap at the window. A reporter snooping outside had heard her cry of pain.

She parted the curtains. The news trucks were back. And in the foreground an intrepid member of the media, who looked no older than her classmates, was trying to right himself after having slipped in the bushes.

Oh my God.

She grabbed her crutches and hobbled outside. She stood barefoot on the stone porch, wearing *Beauty and the Beast* pajamas, her hair uncombed, her teeth grimy.

An army of microphones and cameras marched up the lawn.

The youthful reporter reached her first and grinned at her like a schoolboy.

Aren't you a little old for *Beauty and the Beast?*

Amanda realized she was wearing pajamas.

Oh my God!

She turned to retreat, but the door had locked behind her.

No!!!

Is my colleague bullying you? asked a female journalist who had climbed the porch steps. Is that what all those boys did the other night in the hospital cafeteria? Bully you? And worse?

Yes. I mean no. I mean, yes, this guy is bullying me. No, it wasn't like that at the...

She found herself struggling for breath. She instinctively reached for her phone to call her mom, but she'd left it inside.

Everyone was asking questions now:

Were you raped that night?

How much had you been drinking?

Why did you send Dr. Patel packing?

How did you fall down the well?

Will you show us the well?

Is it true you took the cover off the well and that's why you fell in?

Was it a suicide attempt?

Are you under psychiatric care?

Where were your parents at the time?

Had a boy snuck over? Were you hiding him in the well?

Can you take us to the backyard and recreate the events of that morning for us?

*

The voices got more and more distant, even as the bodies got closer. Amanda started to cry. She sat down on the porch step, propped her crutches on her lap, buried her head in her hands, and cried.

The reporters snuck in closer.

Snap snap snap.

*

Amanda! Amanda! Are you all right?

I'm sorry, Mama. I thought I could talk to them. I didn't even get dressed. I wasn't thinking at all. I know you told me not to open the door...

Do we look like your mom?

Amanda uncovered her face and peered up. The three amigas.

Nicole's brown Ford F-150 was parked on the curb where the news trucks had been.

We rushed over as soon as we saw the feeds, said Nipuni.

Worst press conference in history! opined Amy.

And you're here to cheer me up?

What are you doing on the porch? asked Nicole.

I locked myself out.

Don't you have a key in a planter or something?

I didn't think of that!

The Dizons kept an emergency key under an old milk box by the back door. They let themselves in and the three girls raided what was left in the fridge while Amanda scoured the internet.

Oh my God.

What are you doing? Don't look at that, said Nicole, pulling the phone from her friend's hand.

There's time for that later.

They organized a tray with bottled water, orange juice, trail mix, and Cheetos and helped Amanda navigate the stairs.

Once in her room, Nicole locked the door and pulled the shade, in case the media were sending out drones.

How'd you guys get out of school? You'll get detentions.

Let us worry about that, said Nipuni bravely.

Maybe your parents can pardon us, suggested Amy.

They teach at the elementary school. And they think you're corrupting me. They think you're leading me along the road to perdition.

What's perdition? asked Nipuni.

Can you guys be quiet? Nicole shouted, pacing the room. What are we going to do? What are we going to do? What are we going to do?

We?! asked Amanda, sitting at her desk.

The other two girls sat on the bed, tucking in their legs so as not to trip Nicole as she paced.

The room was long and narrow, with the ceiling sloping over the bed. Stuffed animals covered the far edge, where the ceiling met the wall. There was a shelf with Disney figures and another with Lego Friends sets. Unicorn and rainbow stickers covered the door, some in the peeling stage. The only window, which looked onto the backyard, and the well, was covered by a beige elastic shade and rainbow curtains.

There were posters of boy bands on the closet door and a wall calendar with a beaches theme.

A white wooden dresser sat beside the white wooden desk, too old and heavy to be mistaken for IKEA. This was farmhouse furniture, as was the twin bed. A century old, painted and repainted. They would survive a zombie apocalypse.

Atop the dresser was a mirror, a jewelry box, a Huawei flip phone, forgotten now that she had the candidate's iPhone, and souvenirs sent from my travels: a tin Eiffel Tower from France, ceramic tango dancers from Argentina, an embroidered silk coin purse from Thailand, nesting dolls from Russia.

But the room was notable for what was absent: a television and computer.

*

The unvarnished wooden floorboards creaked slightly beneath Nicole's black leather combat boots. She was also wearing black tights, a black miniskirt, a black V-neck top, and a brown leather bomber jacket. Heavy metallic loop earrings contrasted with her soft, light skin and shimmering blond hair. We might also mention the angel tattoo on her left forearm and her silver tongue stud.

Nipuni was a dark-skinned Sri Lankan who preferred brightly colored print dresses. She wore a nose ring, as did her mother and grandmother. She craved a mandala tattoo on her back shoulder, but her mother said: Not until you get your Ph.D.

Amy was a petite, finely boned girl who adored stilettos. But today she was wearing lilac Nikes, ripped jeans from Forever 21, and a pink nylon windbreaker over a tank top. She wore blonde highlights in her raggedly cropped black hair and a Pandora bracelet with half a dozen charms.

Amanda, as has been duly noted, was wearing *Beauty and the Beast* pajamas.

*

Hello? Amanda are you up there?

Yes, Mom.

Are you hungry? I'll make lunch. Come down and you can see what I bought.

Nicole had stopped pacing.

She doesn't know, whispered Amy.

No thanks, Mom.

Is that Nicole's truck outside? Did she skip school? Are there boys up there?

Always, Mom.

Footsteps on the staircase.

Amanda opened the door. Inspect away, said Amanda.

It's dark in here, observed her mother. Why is the shade drawn?

She opened it. Iowa sunshine streamed in.

We were worried about drones with zoom lenses, said Nipuni.

Amy pinched her.

What did you say? asked Amanda's mother.

Nothing Mrs. Dizon, said Nicole, trying to steer her out of the room. Do you want some Cheetos?

Amanda's mother noticed all the food.

You know I don't like you to eat up here. We could get mice.

That's your priority at this moment? asked Amanda. That we don't attract mice?

And why are you still in your pajamas?

Amanda started to tear up, but Nicole blocked her mother's line of sight.

I'm glad everything's all right. I was worried because the news trucks were back this morning when I went out. I told them I was driving to the police station.

Good work Mrs. Dizon, said Nicole. You put the fear of God into them!

*

Nicole resumed her pacing.

Amanda went to the window and gazed out.

Shouldn't you get away from there? asked Amy.

Let her be, said Nipuni.

So, what are we gonna do? asked Amy. I don't want to sound selfish or anything, but I think they might have noticed we're AWOL from Harding by now. And why are you still in your pajamas?

That's it! exclaimed Nicole.

Amanda took out a pair of jeans from her dresser, but Nicole grabbed them away.

Where do you keep your pj's?

As Nicole suspected, Amanda had more sleepwear in the closet. Lots more. Fairies, Hello Kitty, Minions, and Disney princesses.

Perfect.

She tossed a *Tangled* to Amy, a *Frozen* to Nipuni, and took *Brave* for herself.

You want us to do what with these? Nipuni asked.

Shoes off, urged Nicole. Hop to it.

She closed the curtain and turned on the overhead light and the desk lamp.

These bottoms are too small for me, said Nipuni, struggling to put her legs in.

Just wear the top then. We'll shoot from the waist up.

Shoot what? Amanda wondered.

Nicole waited until they were properly attired. Then she posed them sitting on the bed, got in the frame, and snapped a photo with Amanda's camera.

The other three leaned over to read what Nicole was texting for the caption:

Late upload. Sorry you all couldn't join us for our princess slumber party, but as you can see my room is rather small.

Send? Nicole asked.

I guess so.

No! said Amy and Nipuni in unison, but it was too late.

Why did you do that? This is soooooooo embarrassing, said Amy.

I don't know what you're trying to accomplish, said Amanda, other than all of us looking like six-year-olds.

And Hello Kitty isn't like for six-year-olds? asked Nicole. And don't women of all ages use Hello Kitty stuff?

Are you sure you got me from the waist up? asked Nipuni, looking for the photo on her own phone.

Look, explained Nicole. One guy's pants ride down so you see his underwear, he's a dweeb. But a million guys do it and it's hip hop. We're turning your embarrassment into fashion. Check out the Likes pouring in.

The girls scrolled through comments:

Wish I was there.

Invite me next time.

So cute!!!

I have the Tangled pj's too.

OK, I get it, said Amanda. I was on the porch in pajamas not because I'm an immature moron who forgot to get dressed and brush her hair to meet the national media, but because we had a cosplay slumber party last night.

They all fist bumped in triumph.

But wait, said Amanda. That explains my clothes. But what about my breakdown? Amy, you were right. That was the worst press conference in history. And my God, what happens when my mom finds out?

At that very moment a shriek, a wail, a howling like a she-wolf in distress reverberated throughout the farmhouse, echoing, no doubt, even in the depths of the well.

Any other questions? asked Nicole.

*

Shortly after they were all gathered at the kitchen table, Amanda's father arrived home, slamming the door so hard the glass panes rattled.

I'm going to kill those sons of bitches—

He saw her friends and stopped in his tracks.

Girls, can you leave, please. We need to have a family discussion.

They're family too, said Amanda, reaching for their hands. And they're helping me enormously.

It's her life, said Amanda's mother, perhaps forgetting that the day before she had threatened to confiscate their phones.

It's my curb, my lawn, my porch, my daughter.

Dad, I think the curb belongs to the Roads Department.

He was too wound up to sit down. Amanda's mother was taking deep breaths.

I'm sure it looked a lot worse than it was, said Amanda. It wasn't the media's fault. No one bullied me, no one made me cry. It was a first day of school kind of thing.

Grown men and women don't push microphones in your face the first day of school, said her father.

Well, if I'm going to be famous, I'm gonna have to get used to it, same as kindergarten. Yesterday you told me to man up, Dad.

You're not going to be famous, dear, said her mother.

She's already famous, muttered Amy and Nipuni.

I'm already famous, echoed Amanda. You don't know the digital world. You come from the generation of television, when you had to get on *Oprah* to be famous. Well, look at my cast. The name of probably the next president of the United States is written there. And the real president in the White House tweeted about me. People all over the world know my name: Amanda Dizon, the Girl in the Well.

My Lord, said Nicole, scrolling rapidly. Look at these comments. People are totally behind you:

Fuck the media!

Asshole reporters!

If you had a gun you wouldn't have this problem!

Leave our hero alone!

We share your tears, Amanda!

Idiots, can't you see she has PTSD? Leave the poor girl alone.

So much love, whispered Amy.

Which only reduced our heroine to tears once more.

*

I've got an idea, said her mother. Let's all go out to a nice restaurant before the paparazzi return.

I've got a better idea, said Amanda. You two go out to a nice restaurant and my girls and I will go hang at the mall.

You can't go to the mall, you'll be mobbed.

I'll wear a hoodie.

Her mother didn't say yes, but she didn't say no.

The girls went upstairs to change. Amanda grabbed a hoodie, but she had no intention of going to the mall.

Route 23, she said when the four of them had squeezed into the F-150's cab.

That's the edge of town, said Nipuni. What mall is out there?

The auto mall.

Route 23 was a six-lane road lined on both sides with auto dealers.

Are you looking for a car? asked Nicole, for once slow on the uptake.

Pull in there. Park where it says *Visitors*.

It was a Jaguar dealership.

*

I'll leave it to you to imagine the look of shock on the faces of the jaded, middle-aged salesmen with their Christmas gift ties, their high school rings, their gold-plated cufflinks, their musky cologne, when they saw three high school girls step out of a dusty brown Ford F-150 with 200,000 miles to its name and enter their pristine showroom, where the least expensive of their vehicles cost north of forty thousand dollars.

Three sales associates paused their coffee cups midway to their mouth, and stared. The leasing manager, a woman, rose from her desk in the back. A fourth salesman, who was either very diligent at his job, a highly curious individual, a pedophile, or some combination thereof, strode over, his polished shoes clicking on the highly polished floor.

His eyes absorbed all three, but fixed on Nicole, naturally.

How can I help you girls? Aren't you supposed to be in school?

Nicole saw only the cars.

This is the one I want! And they have it in red!

The girls followed her to an E-PACE compact SUV.

Caldera red, said Amy, reading the Dealer Specifications. Gosh. It's $46,500!!!

Nicole opened the driver's door.

Hey! shouted the salesman, who normally couldn't wait to introduce himself to visitors as Barney and offer a firm handshake, but in the case of the three high school girls had no intention of doing anything other than kicking their pickup truck butts out of his jungle within the next thirty seconds.

One of the perks of being a beautiful, popular girl was that you learned at a very early age how to ignore people who bothered you. The less attractive of the sex, like her three friends, when encountering an obstacle in human form, stopped to listen, nodded and smiled, apologized profusely, and approached or retreated on request. Girls like Nicole grabbed the leather-wrapped steering wheel with both hands and shouted, Vroom, vroom!

Please come out of the car!

Nicole was too busy adjusting the seat to accede to his request.

The other salesmen were observing from a closer distance. The Leasing Manager ignored her ringing landline.

Amanda cleared her throat. She was pretending she was on stage, in the role that was her life. She told herself this man was not going to make her cry. She had strength in numbers.

Excuse me...sir. We'd like a test drive.

His eyes bulged.

Don't worry, I've never had an accident or even a ticket, said Nicole from the cockpit.

The salesman peered closer at Amanda.

Hey, aren't you that girl...?

The Girl From The Well, said another associate, stepping forward. Look, there's her cast.

The Leasing Manager hurriedly typed into her computer and then joined the associates, who were kneeling on the highly polished floor, trying to decipher the candidates' signatures.

Amanda saw the Leasing Manager whisper into Barney's ear:

Psst psst psst psst psst psst psst psst psst MakeItRain account...

Barney straightened up and walked over to Nicole.

I don't think I properly introduced myself. My name is Barney.

And he enjoyed the soft flesh of her hand as he shook it thoroughly.

So, you and your friends have your eye on this car?

Yes, mister.

And you like the red color?

Caldera red, as I understand it.

We have black too, said Barney, eying her black outfit from t-shirt to boot heel.

We want the red, said Nicole, and rolled her tongue along her upper lip.

Nicole was wearing bright red lipstick, had I mentioned that? I don't think it was caldera red, but the salesman was now staring at her lips as if his job depended on assessing the degree of similarity.

Don't quote me here, but I'd venture this brief but potent exchange was the most seductive encounter Barney had experienced in years, perhaps ever.

If you could just let me make a copy of your license, said Barney solicitously. I'll round up those keys and we can be on our way!

*

The girls were saved potential embarrassment and perhaps even trauma when the Leasing Manager, who had been groped more than once en route to her prestigious desk, and knew well the frailties and transgressions of men, intercepted Barney as he opened the passenger door. We can't accuse Barney of inappropriate behavior on this point alone, however eagerly he had rummaged for the keys. No luxury car dealer in the country would let a sixteen-year-old take a test drive without being accompanied by an associate.

In any case, the SUV seated five, so the girls piled in back while the leasing agent gave a consolatory pat to Barney and buckled in next to Nicole, who was in a state resembling heat.

*

At the first green light the girls shrieked, as though they were on a rollercoaster. The leasing agent was worried Nicole would floor it, but Nicole was a cautious driver. She wasn't attracted to the car for its horsepower but for its sexual and social power.

Ordinary people envy beautiful people. Beautiful people envy beautiful people with beautiful things. Nicole dreamed of being the girl who drove a Jaguar, not the girl who drove a pickup truck with 200,000 miles.

Can I play the radio?

What's your station? asked the Leasing Manager.

At a red light the Leasing Manager checked the MakeItRain site on her cell phone, reading the fine print this time. It all seemed legit.

You don't have your license yet, Amanda? asked the Leasing Manager, turning to the object of all that rain.

I'm supposed to take the test soon. But this car isn't for me.

The leasing agent nudged Nicole.

I wish I had a friend like that!

This is my reward for being her friend when no one else would, said Nicole, rather blithely.

What about me? asked Nipuni.

What about me? Amy wondered.

I take it you plan to pay for this car with funds from your MakeItRain account, Amanda?

Yes, ma'am.

Have you discussed this with your parents?

They're completely on board, lied Amanda.

Because they might want to put the funds in a trust. That's usually what happens when a minor comes into a large sum. But if they do choose to create a trust in your name, we might be able to structure this as a lease, with the trust as collateral.

Really?!

Can I roll the window down? asked Nicole, accelerating smoothly. I want to feel the wind in my hair.

The Leasing Manager pointed out the controls, and cool wind flowed over the brand-new leather, and through Nicole's corn-colored hair.

Can you take some pics of me while I'm driving, please? she asked the Leasing Manager. With my phone.

The Leasing Manager, who was hardly a Boomer, being still in her thirties, a digital native, suddenly felt ancient among this new species of American female, skipping school, test-driving Jaguars, confident and sexy, exploiting themselves for the first time in history, rather than being exploited by the patriarchy.

Is this for your PingPong, Amanda? the Leasing Manager asked, trying to demonstrate her hipness to the culture.

Notice how something as insignificant as a girl with nine million followers paired with a girl with corn-fed beauty could turn a power dynamic as old as commerce on its head.

Here was a Leasing Manager, a college graduate with a platinum card and a mortgage, who had only deigned to rise from her desk—a desk in an office, mind you, not a cubicle—because the sight of four high school girls entering her realm was a novelty that broke up the tedium of a slow September day.

And now she was the odd girl out, trying to impress these shrieking teenagers that she belonged in their—their!—car.

But her efforts were a face palm fail, as she lost the camera app and found herself on the settings page.

Oops...

Here said Amy, getting her back in focus. She clicked away.

It's for my own Instagram, answered Nicole, belatedly. This is such a dream!

Watch the road!

Now get Amanda in the pic, said Amy, pushing her friend into the frame at the next red light.

No, said Nicole.

Why not? asked Amanda. For the first time in her life, she actually wanted to be in a photo. No matter her stringy hair, her splotchy skin, her awkward grin, the Jaguar was a speeding Photoshop.

Amanda leaned over the console.

It's not your brand, said Nicole.

What's a brand?

We all have a brand. It's like an image, explained Nicole, whose father was a brand manager at John Deere.

I never had one, said Amanda.

You're the comic sidekick offered Nipuni.

Yeah, agreed Nicole.

Except you're not funny, said Amy.

You're the Girl in the Well, added the Leasing Manager, who knew a thing or two on the subject. You're the Every-Girl who became a hero.

What's an Every-Girl? I have no idea what you're all talking about. Can't you just take my picture?

Look, said Nicole. I'm glam. I'm suited for this car and lifestyle. Unfortunately, I have a father who would rather save for retirement than buy me a decent set of wheels. But you...you didn't get ten million followers—

Nine.

Ten. Look at your damn account, would you? You didn't get all these millions of followers because you're glam and drive a Jaguar. If you start trying to be that person you could lose them. Capiche?

You have to be true to yourself, concluded Nicole.

But I hate myself.

You don't hate yourself. You're an ordinary Midwestern girl who fell in a hole and came out a hero. You have to be a role model to girls like you everywhere.

But I'm not even a role model to myself.

7

When Amanda woke and parted the living room curtains the following morning, she was surprised to find the street empty. She almost felt sad to see no news trucks. She had had a dream last night of standing on the porch holding an actual jaguar on a leash, wearing a silk dressing gown open to her cleavage—in the dream she had cleavage—answering admiring reporters' questions with the flair of Marilyn Monroe.

But the candidates had left and the national media had gone with them.

A note from her mother:

No media, yay! So I've decided to teach today. Your phone's in quarantine till I return.

Ahhhhhh!

*

I guess Mama was right, Luna.

The cat stared inscrutably from the recliner.

Amanda was wearing a red silk kimono I had sent her from Tokyo. No more Disney pajamas, perhaps forever.

Her mother had relocated Amanda's toiletries to the ground floor bathroom. She brushed her teeth, washed her face and brushed her hair. She wasn't going to make that mistake again!

But without her phone and without any news trucks outside, there was no reason to get dressed, was there?

She went into the kitchen and poured herself a glass of orange juice, and made Honey Smacks with almond milk.

The pain was much better, and she was getting adept at hopping around on her right foot, without crutches.

She noticed the flashing answering machine. The corded landline had been disconnected, but not the answering machine.

You have 160 new messages.

Holy moly!!!

Hi, this is Brad Fisher from Fisher Capital Management. Please give me a call to discuss your financial future.

How does everyone know about my MakeItRain account?

Hello Amanda. I hope you are recovering nicely from your terrible fall. My name is Claire Stevenson and I'm the Features reporter for the Des Moines Sentinel. I'd love to do a story on you.

Hello Ms. Dizon. This is Michael Dunn from the *New York Times*. I'm writing an opinion piece to run in tomorrow's edition and I'd like a quote from you. Give me a call before end of business day, Eastern Standard Time.

She looked at the time stamp. Yesterday.

Damn.

More financial planners. Media people she hadn't heard of. A few perverts she hurriedly erased.

She fast forwarded to today. Her mother could sort through the other messages if she wanted.

Amanda, hi, this is Brenda from the Leasing Department at Hobert's Jaguar. I talked to Barney, your sales associate. We normally don't hold cars without a deposit, but he has a soft spot for you guys, and I persuaded him to hold the caldera red E-PACE for a week. Just have your parents call me or stop by nine to six, any day except Monday, and I'll be glad to run through your leasing options.

Erase! Erase!

Good afternoon, Amanda. I hope you're getting around all right on that broken leg of yours. If you're feeling up to getting on a plane and in and out of taxis, we'd love for you to come to New York. My name is Jennifer and I'm a producer for *Just Us Girls*. The ladies want to see that cast of yours in person and give you a big hug.

Oh my God oh my God oh my God!!!

She picked up the handset but there was no dial tone. She remembered her mother had disconnected the phone and looked for the cord. Then she pressed the New York number for the producer, but nothing happened. She scrutinized the dial pad. She had never used a landline before.

She realized she had to press *TALK* to get a dial tone.

Hi, this is Amanda Dizon, the Girl from the Well, calling back for Jennifer.

How are you doing, Amanda? Thanks for calling. I imagine you're pretty exhausted after your ordeal and trying to keep connected with your eleven million followers.

Eleven?!

We'd like you to come to New York Sunday for the Monday morning taping. How does that sound to you?

It sounds—

Amanda in her nervous excitement had walked back into the living room, forgetting she was on a landline.

She stared at the decapitated handset.

Oh no. Oh no!

The phone rang.

I can't answer it now. I'm such an idiot. First the pajamas, now this. Then she realized her parents had a phone in their bedroom. But could she reach it in time? We all know how impatient New Yorkers are. After four rings the producer hung up.

But fortunately Amanda noticed the redial button.

Yes!

Sorry we got cut off, said Jennifer. I was asking if you'd be interested in being on the show.

Of course. I love *Just Us Girls*. But I'd have to ask my mom if we have the money for the plane tickets.

We would pay all expenses, of course, for you and your mother, including business class airfare. If they have business class in Iowa.

Then yes! Super.

Great. I'll have my assistant call you tomorrow to arrange the details. And if your mom could be available to talk as well.

Click.

Oh my God, said Amanda.

*

She reached for her phone like a phantom limb to text Nicole. Where could it be?

She looked in her mother's nightstand and scoured the cabinets in the kitchen.

I'll just go to school, said Amanda out loud.

Without thinking, she returned to her parents' bedroom, picked up the phone and looked for the Uber icon.

Damn! How did people exist with just landlines?

She put on the outfit her mother had laid out for her—flared jeans, a black Iowa Hawkeyes sweatshirt, Hello Kitty socks, and half a pair of Vans—grabbed one crutch, some quarters from the kitchen, and hobbled to the bus stop.

*

She arrived one period before lunch, so she went to her American History class. Her three friends didn't have this class with her. She only knew a couple of the students here by name: Ned and one of his gamer friends. But they had never shown any interest in her, until, that is, Ned had kissed her at the hospital.

The teacher, Mr. Cargill, seemed not to know she existed. It was still the first quarter of the school year, of course, so she had neither distinguished nor embarrassed herself in his estimation. But he had never called on her or even made eye contact.

Yet before she could take her seat in the back row, a wave of murmurs rose to applause and she received a standing ovation.

And rather than bringing the class to order, Mr. Cargill rushed over and helped her take her seat and prop her crutch against the desk.

We were told you'd be out for two weeks, said the American History teacher.

Or forever, now that you're rich and famous! said a female student to much laughter.

Don't get too uppity for us peons, said another girl.

Amanda wanted to assure them that the thought of leaving school or looking down on her classmates had never occurred to her. But she merely grinned awkwardly and asked her neighbor to borrow a pencil and paper because she had forgotten her backpack.

*

Naturally, she couldn't concentrate at all. Didn't hear a word the teacher said. When the bell rang her paper was covered with unicorns and rainbows, and a drawing of the Statue of Liberty. Well, that referenced American history, at least.

Ned sidled over to her.

Hey, said Ned cautiously, suddenly shy.

Hey.

I wonder if you can do me a favor and not call me *Ned the Hacker* anymore.

When did I call you *Ned the Hacker?*

On PingPong.

That doesn't sound like me. It was Nicole. She was helping me post that night.

Oh. Cool.

Sure thing.

Because *hacker* has negative connotations. Like *thief.*

Well, aren't hackers thieves? But not in the real world?

No. A hacker is just someone who likes to manipulate other people's code.

That doesn't sound righteous.

Well, if you accidentally deleted your homework you would want a hacker to retrieve it, wouldn't you? Hackers are like cops. They can be good or bad.

But I think most hackers are bad, aren't they? And the vast majority of cops are good. At least in Iowa.

The important thing is how the word is perceived, said Ned. So, from now on can you call me *White Hat Ned?*

From now on?

I'd be grateful.

You don't even wear hats.

It's just what people call good hackers.

My mom would say that's kinda racist. Why can't good hackers be black hats, ya know?

I'm not a sociologist, just a code geek.

White Hat Ned patted her shoulder, smiled, and took his leave.

*

Amanda found her friends in the cafeteria, but not together. She was the glue that bound them, even before her plunge into the well. Because by the normal order of things Nipuni and Amy were relegated to the neither glam nor brainiac set, while Nicole settled naturally with the cheerleaders and honor students.

So it was today, with Nipuni and Amy eating quietly together, while Nicole was entertaining Harding High's social elites with Jaguar pics and Barney's business card.

Amanda sat at Amy and Nipuni's table. When Nicole saw her, she left her group to come over. This was not lost on our heroine. It was like a film reel in reverse, because in the past Nicole would always leave Amanda's side to join the popular set.

Maybe she *had* fallen through the well into an alternate reality.

A hush fell over the cafeteria as all those present became aware of their famous classmate. Then the myriad conversations and clanking of dishes resumed.

What are you doing here? asked Nicole.

My mom confiscated my phone again. It was the only way I could talk to you guys.

That guy Barney from the dealer texted me, said Nicole. I think he wants to date me.

Oh God.

I'm joking. It was totally professional. It's not like he sent me dick pics or anything.

Nipuni and Amy laughed.

He's not half bad looking. I'd do him for a Jaguar.

Amy spit out her iced tea.

Nicole! exclaimed Amanda. Does everything have to be about sex with you? I'm three days out from my first kiss and everything with you is a porno.

It's just a joke.

It's not funny. Men can be dangerous. You saw how Brenda practically tore the keys out of his hand.

Maybe *she* has the hots for me, said Nicole. Women can be dangerous too.

Anyway, you're not going to have to look at dick pics or sleep with car salesmen old enough to be your father. I'm going to buy you the car like you wanted and like I promised. They said they'd hold it for a week and by that time I hope to persuade my parents to let me use the MakeItRain money.

Are you guys talking about money?

It was White Hat Ned, making a cautious approach to the girls' table.

If you want a car, you're gonna have to flip burgers for it, said Nicole. Charity ends with her best friend.

What about me? said Nipuni.

White Hat Ned took an empty chair.

Are you very computer literate, Amanda?

Nicole made a face.

Are you kidding? she asked. Amanda's parents don't even have cable.

What kind of setup do you have? I mean, desktop, laptop, tablets?

Did you not hear me, Hacker Ned? said Nicole. Our classmate wouldn't have even a smart phone except some doofus candidate dropped his in the library.

You're kidding? Not even an old desktop?

Squat, said Nicole. Her bedroom could be from the Middle Ages.

You need a home office. ASAP.

A home office? asked Amanda. What am I, an accountant?

Don't you follow YouTubers? Instagrammers? Don't you know what an influencer is? They don't get where they are with just a phone, even if it's the latest iPhone. You need a laptop. You need a desktop with terabytes of memory. You need a large monitor, preferably two or three. You need a keyboard and an ergonomic chair. You need professional grade cameras and an external mike, studio lights, a backup phone in case yours goes down the toilet, a tablet or two for good measure.

How can I afford all that?

You're buying your friend a car and you're asking me how you can afford tech gear? What I'm talking about is twelve thousand tops, but you don't have to get everything now. A laptop with an external camera and mike would be a good start. Less than 2k.

But I don't know anything about computers.

I can take you to Staples.

Sounds like a date! teased Nipuni.

I don't know, said Amanda. Everyone says this is all going to blow over in a few days.

You need a computer for school anyway, said Nicole, finding herself allied with White Hat Ned against her better interests. And when you go to college.

This is not going to blow over, said White Hat Ned. Not if you use your bedroom for something more than masturbating to boy band posters.

Amy spit out her tea again. Gross! she exclaimed.

I don't...I never..., said Amanda.

How do you know she had boy band posters? wondered Nicole perceptively. Have you been in her house?

We know a million things about her life since she fell in the well. Most are probably lies. But so much of her is out there. Like the pics of her room from the slumber party. You can see the posters on the closet door.

Boy, you were paying close attention, said Nicole.

You didn't see anything of me below the waist? asked Nipuni. Tell me you didn't see anything.

Being an influencer is a business, said White Hat Ned, ignoring their jokes.

But I'm not an influencer.

Ned shook his head in frustration.

There are bloggers with five hundred subscribers who call themselves influencers. There are chefs with one YouTube video that got over 20,000 views who call themselves celebrity chefs. There are life coaches who spend money to buy fake Likes so they can speak at conferences on how to be an influencer.

Really?

But if you don't get your act together and treat this like a business, it *will* go away, and people will forget you.

But I thought only celebrities like Kim Kardashian make a lot of money on social media, said Amy.

What is a celebrity? asked White Hat Ned, rather philosophically.

Does Kim Kardashian sing or act or dunk basketballs? The way I see it, someone with millions of followers is a celebrity. Here...

He rummaged through his backpack and pushed a Google Chromebook tablet across the table.

Start with this. I hardly use it. The password is IloveVista, capital *I* and *V.*

I couldn't possibly...

I'm walking away, said White Hat Ned.

Hey, how do we know she can trust you? asked Amy suspiciously, taking the tablet for safekeeping.

Because I'm White Hat Ned.

*

Amanda was so stunned by this new information that she completely forgot the reason she had come to school in the first place—to tell her friends she was going to appear on *Just Us Girls.*

She walked like a zombie to her afternoon classes, scribbling *influencer* and *Amanda Kardashian* over and over on borrowed paper.

8

Nicole gave her a ride home. Amanda would have invited her inside except there was a police car in the driveway.

What did I do? exclaimed Nicole.

You?! This is my house. Go on home. I'll text you later.

Amanda crept up the walkway, imagining any number of disasters, all attributable to her. The candidate had changed his mind and wanted his iPhone back. Or there was classified information on it and the CIA had asked the local cops to get it back. Or Nicole had posted something obscene on her account, in which case Nicole had been right to think this was about her. Or a PingPong serial killer had broken into the house and slit both her parents' throats.

Amanda gulped.

At least there was no yellow police tape over the door. Not yet.

She peeked inside.

Her parents were standing in the living room, talking to an officer. A white hat officer, she hoped.

Amanda! her mother screamed. Where have you been? Are you all right?

I will be all right if you don't suffocate me, said Amanda, tearing herself away from her mother's arms.

We were worried you'd been kidnapped, or jumped down the well again, said her father. Your mother told you not to leave the house.

I went to school to...

Amanda realized she had forgotten to tell her friends about being booked on the *Just Us Girls* show. And now was certainly not the time to tell her parents.

Why would you go to school? You're supposed to be off for at least a week.

Because you keep confiscating my phone! said Amanda in her own defense. And why did you say *jump* just now, Dad?

I didn't say *jump*.

I can't believe you think I'm suicidal! Holy moly. I told you it was an accident. I—

So, I think this wraps things up for me, said the white hat officer. Little lady, I suggest next time you run away you leave your parents a note.

Kids run away from school, pointed out Amanda. Not *to* school.

By the way, do you think I can get a picture of you for my son? He's a follower.

Is he cute? asked Amanda, startled by her boldness.

He's ten, answered the officer. But we think he's adorable.

*

Her mother suggested they go to a quiet Chinese restaurant where they could talk things over without being seen, and because she was too frazzled to cook. But Amanda shrewdly remarked that PingPong was a Chinese app and going to a Chinese restaurant, even in Montgomery County, Iowa, might be like walking into the dragon's den.

Get it? said Amanda. China? Dragon's den!

So they went to Olive Garden and asked for a table in a back empty room.

I had one of the candidates in last week, said their waitress. So don't you worry, I know how to deal with the riff raff. No one will bother you on my watch. Can I start you guys, I mean the adults, with a bottle of Chianti?

I'll have a vodka martini, said Amanda's mother.

That sounds like a good idea, said her father. Double.

Can I have a virgin piña colada? asked Amanda.

It was rare for the Dizons to eat out, and when they did they told Amanda cocktails were overpriced, even without the alcohol. But now that Amanda had a MakeItRain fortune and a future business in her bedroom, her parents felt empowered to splurge.

*

Amanda looked down at her lap, as though there were a screen there.

Mom, do you have my phone in your purse?

No. And even if I did, we don't allow phones at the table.

Well, the rules are gonna change. America's a democracy. I get a vote.

That makes one vote for and two against, said her mother.

Then I'm expanding our family to include my followers. That gives me eleven million and one votes to your two. Or maybe by now it's twelve million and one.

They're probably all bots, said her father. Not real people.

Oh, suddenly you're the technology expert. You don't even know what a bot is.

It's a fake person, said her father.

A robot is a fake person. A mannequin is a fake person, argued Amanda. A bot is... Well, I don't know what a bot it, actually. But my followers are real, thanks for your support. And if I had my phone, I could poll them as new members of this family whether they think the No Phone at the Table rule should be abolished.

The drinks and salad came. Amanda gulped down her colada as if hoping the bartender had mistakenly added rum. She grabbed a breadstick, glad to have something in her hand. She rapped it against her plate like a drumstick.

She noticed her parents peering at her over their martinis, looking at her the way psychologists look at a new patient.

What?!

Honey, are you alright? asked her mom in a tender voice.

My ankle's fine. I haven't even taken any Advil today.

I don't mean your ankle.

I should have left a note, OK? I'm sorry. I have a lot on my mind. But everything's OK. It's not like a PingPong stalker got our address and slit all our throats.

Her parents stared.

I'm joking! Look at you. You think I'm crazy. You...

And then she saw the police car in their driveway and rewound the film to when her parents came home and didn't see her in the kitchen or living room, and called upstairs, then went upstairs.

Where would they look for her next, before calling the police from the bedroom landline?

You looked in the well, didn't you?!

She burst into tears and hobbled into the bathroom.

Her mother followed.

I told you it was an accident. Why don't you believe me?

I believe you.

Then why did you look in the well?

It was your dad.

But the cover was back on, right? I haven't been there. I've been pretty busy since I got out, you know. And anyway, if Dad thinks I jumped then why would I try again when I only broke my ankle the first time? I could just jump out my window. He's always saying how irrational teenage girls are, but your behavior sounds major irrational to me.

I know.

I don't drink anything stronger than virgin coladas. I don't take drugs. I don't even take all the Advil I'm supposed to because I hate swallowing pills. I don't smoke or vape. I don't cut myself. Understand?

Yes.

Her mother handed her towels as Amanda washed her face.

How about we go scarf down some pasta? said her mother. I don't know about you but I'm starving.

Restore to factory settings? said Amanda.

Restore to factory settings.

*

Amanda took advantage of her parents' guilt to order another piña colada. And to ask if she could borrow two thousand dollars for a computer.

Can't you get a laptop for five hundred? asked her father. Assuming we allow you to have one?

Amanda shot him a look.

Which I don't see why we won't, he added sheepishly. Assuming you use it for schoolwork as well as social media.

It's for a home office, explained Amanda.

Maybe we can all go look for one next week, offered her mother.

White Hat Ned is going to take me to Staples tomorrow.

Who?

Ned, a tech geek in my American History class.

Is he one of the boys who kissed you?

Mom!!! Anyway, I'm going to pay you back. So, can I have your credit card?

A home office is for a business, said her dad. What business exactly are you going to be doing?

I'm gonna be an influencer, said Amanda proudly.

Her parents looked at her the way psychologists look at a new patient.

*

It was still light out when they returned home. They parked in the driveway—they never used the garage—and went in through the back.

Darling, did you forget to lock the door? Amanda's mother asked her father, finding it unlocked.

Ahhhhh! screamed Amanda, spotting a man sitting at the kitchen table, facing them.

He was overweight, balding, with a blond walrus mustache and a genial smile, which he offered up immediately, rising nonchalantly to his feet.

What the— exclaimed Amanda's father.

Amanda's mother had screamed at well. But all their exclamations were silenced by the sight of a worn briefcase lying flat on the kitchen table and piles of paper covering Mr. Dizon's cloth placemat.

Also, all the kitchen lights were on, despite the remaining daylight streaming through the uncovered windows, as if to signal the intruder's intent to be seen. Either that or he had been busy working and needed the extra light.

Forgive me for letting myself in, but I didn't want to loiter outside in the event reporters were about. My name is Manfred Cole, attorney-at-law, said the lawyer, extending his business card to the family.

Get out of my house! shouted Amanda's mother protectively. Or I'll call the police.

Just as beautiful girls are practiced in the art of ignoring insignificant people who get in their way, so are lawyers desensitized to people who threaten and scream.

So instead of fleeing before being hit with a saucepan, Mr. Cole sat back down and searched for his silver pen in the stacks of papers.

In the matter of your MakeItRain account...

Amanda's father slammed the intruder's briefcase and grabbed him by the lapel of his wrinkled suit jacket.

Wait! shouted Amanda. What about my MakeItRain account?

Please, everyone, have a seat.

What nerve, telling me to sit down at my own table! shouted Amanda's mother.

Mom! Shhhh. Sit.

A tense moment ensued. But Amanda sat down and her parents followed suit.

So, mister...whatever your name is, said Amanda with an assertiveness bolstered by several hundred thousand dollars in the cloud. What do you know about my MakeItRain account and why do you care? If you're trying to sell us insurance or scam us, I should warn you my father's an economist, even though he teaches fourth grade.

Mr. Cole looked directly at Amanda, then at her parents, then back at the girl.

You mean to tell me you don't know? Your account has been invalidated.

Amanda gasped.

I knew you were a con artist. I should report you to the Bar, if in fact you are really a lawyer, said Amanda's father, reaching for his lapel again.

Wait!

The lawyer pulled out an iPad and anxiously tapped *Settings*.

Can I have your Wi-Fi password?

We don't have Wi-Fi, said Amanda.

You're kidding. You don't have Wi-Fi?

I know. Right? said Amanda.

Well here then, he said, rummaging among his papers. Here.

The Dizon family looked at a printout of a screenshot of Amanda's MakeItRain home page. Partly obscuring a photo of Amanda being pulled by the firefighter from the well was a box with the words:

NOTICE: THIS ACCOUNT HAS BEEN INVALIDATED

Amanda let her head fall to the table with a dull thud.

How could you not know? asked the lawyer in a state of considerable surprise.

My mom confiscated my phone, cried Amanda, looking up again. I haven't seen it all day. And my parents don't even have HBO.

But how could they take her money away? asked Amanda's mother, forgetting that she had never believed in the site's validity in the first place.

It's because Amanda didn't have surgery, explained the lawyer.

That's all? Then I'll have it, said Amanda, whose fear of losing a fortune exceeded her fear of going under the knife.

I'm afraid they might perceive that as gaming the system, seeing how you changed your mind subsequent to their decision, said the lawyer. Not that I would recommend unnecessary surgery in any case. But I believe we have other options.

This doesn't make sense. Their business model is based on commissions from gifts, said Amanda's father. If they don't release the funds to Amanda, they don't get their percentage. So, I don't understand their motivation.

You're right, agreed the lawyer. And last year I'm sure this wouldn't have been an issue. But lately there have been several high-profile scandals about people illegally profiting from crowdfunding companies. Therefore, they've tightened their oversight to stay on the right side of the regulators.

But I looked at the site myself, and did some research, said her father. It's for disaster victims and personal injury.

Did you read the *Terms and Conditions?* asked the lawyer. Even lawyers don't always read *Terms and Conditions.* I was going to show you on their website. Good thing I made printouts...

Amanda grabbed them from her father's hands. She tried to read the small print.

This makes no sense.

Her father took it back.

...Necessitating surgery, as defined in paragraph 32, he read. Or inpatient hospitalization in an accredited hospital, as defined in paragraph 33, for a minimum of three nights...

I'll go back to the hospital for two more nights, said Amanda. I loved it there. We can go tonight, can't we?

I don't believe any of that is necessary, said the lawyer. As you pointed out, Mr. Dizon, the company wants to release the funds. They have obviously made this precipitous decision based on their own legal advice, without considering the ramifications from a public relations perspective. I think there is certainly scope for arguing Amanda's case meets the intent of their business, if not the letter of the law, which after all isn't law but merely their own *Terms and Conditions*, which by these very *Terms and Conditions*, they are permitted to change at any time.

So what do we have to do? asked Amanda's mother, feeling relieved that there was hope once more for her daughter's college fund.

Just sign this *Client Agreement* and I'll file a formal appeal with MakeItRain tonight.

He pushed a single-page agreement across the table and held out his pen for either of the adults to take.

This straightforward agreement retains me as your exclusive legal representative for this matter, said the lawyer when neither parent looked at it. No retainer or any fees are due from you for my services. I receive a one-time 33% commission on any MakeItRain monies awarded for Amanda Dizon, account number MIR0005593745.

But that's over a hundred thousand dollars for a couple hours' work! Amanda's mother realized.

I appreciate the information you've given us, said Amanda's father. But I think we'll go to our own attorney.

Suit yourself, said the lawyer. He stuffed all his papers back in his briefcase, but slyly left the *Client Agreement* and pen on the table.

He stood.

But if you look again at the *Terms of Service,* you'll see the company refunds the donors twenty-four hours after invalidating an account. Once that happens you have no recourse to obtaining those funds. I trust you are able to reach your attorney tonight.

He walked toward the back door.

Sign, Dad! Mama! Wait! Sign it damn it!

*

They walked Mr. Cole to his well-traveled BMW, parked innocuously down the street. He handed out more business cards, this time one for each of them. Amanda read it like Scripture.

I'll be in touch tomorrow, said the lawyer. I'm confident they will release the funds, although these things can take time.

Excuse me, said Amanda's mother. But how did you get into our house?

Key under the milk box, answered the lawyer. You really should find a more secure hiding place with all the attention your daughter's receiving now. There are a lot of nefarious people in this world of ours!

9

Amanda tossed and turned all night, several times nearly falling off the sofa. Nightmares uncountable. Her American History teacher marking her test INVALIDATED. Driving a Jaguar with Barney, who caresses her leg, but no it's Brenda, the leasing agent, and they crash into a cell phone tower and then she's in court and the judge is wearing a black hat. Her father chasing Luna after she breaks a vase, a patrol car in the driveway come to take the unlucky black cat away. The phone ringing and ringing and Amanda trying to talk but the headset is decapitated. Walking interminable aisles at Staples with her three amigas, looking at laptops that cost a million dollars.

This last one woke her suddenly.

Whew!

She heard an engine in the driveway. And in a rush of adrenaline and cortisol her mind cleared away all the garbage it had been storing and recalled, really, the only thing she must, must do this Friday morning.

Mama!

Forgetting everything she had told herself she would never do again, she rushed out the front door without dressing or brushing her hair or teeth. And forgetting to brace the door.

But this time she was wearing a stylish, womanly kimono, not kids' pajamas, and there was a key under the milk box—or was there?—and anyway her mother had a key, if only Amanda could stop her.

Mom!

She had not taken her crutches and hopped down the porch steps, tumbling onto the grass.

Fortunately, her mother heard her cries and stopped the car.

For Heaven's sake, Amanda! screamed her mother, coming to her aid. Are you hurt? What's the emergency?

You can't go to school! I forgot to tell you.

Tell me what? asked her mother, thinking the worst.

We have to go to... Owwwww! Owww, my ankle!!!

To the hospital? guessed her mother.

To New York City! Eeeeeeeeeee!!! Owwwwwww.

*

Her mother cooked Amanda Canadian bacon and scrambled eggs and poured herself another cup of coffee.

Normally her parents drove to school together, but her mother's first bell had a special event scheduled, so she went in late. Or was about to when Amanda collapsed on the lawn.

By the time Amanda filled her in, having to give the same information over and over, and say *I don't know* a dozen times, it was nine o'clock.

And who knows what's on those other messages I didn't have time to check? said Amanda. And look, there's over two hundred now. You really need to check them, Mom.

Me?

It's not my phone. Look, it's after nine. The show could call any time. We should go into your room so we can hear the phone. And when are you going to fix *this* phone?

I'm not the one who broke it, said her mom.

*

Amanda sat on her parents' bed, scrolling on her no-longer-confiscated phone, while her mother paced.

She had thought she would have to argue like a defense attorney to convince her mother to let her go to New York, but her mom's only concern was that the producer would cancel, or that Amanda had misunderstood the request, hence all her questions.

Maybe *you* should call, said her mother.

You think?

Is this the only contact info they have for you? Yes, I think you should call.

Damn, I don't have the number. I pressed redial last time. Did you make any calls since then?

Of course. The police, remember?

Shit.

But the phone keeps a record of previous calls, pointed out her mother.

I guess landlines aren't completely medieval, said Amanda.

She lifted the handset and was scrolling through the menu when it rang. She dropped it, but fortunately the floor was carpeted and nothing broke.

Hello, sorry about that.

Is this Amanda? Hi, I'm Jennifer's assistant...

*

Amanda's mother took her back to the hospital to have her ankles checked. Amanda prayed she wouldn't need surgery, even if it helped secure her MakeItRain account. She didn't even want to have the cast removed, since it had the candidates' autographs and had become her glass slipper. She even entertained the silly belief that as long as she wore it her magical new life would continue.

Fortunately, the X-rays revealed no new fractures. She didn't need surgery or a new cast. However, the doctor warned her to be more careful, to keep taking ibuprofen to reduce the swelling, to wear the right ankle brace when active, to sleep with her legs raised above her heart, to use her crutches, and not to put any weight on the left ankle.

Promise, agreed Amanda with a huge sigh of relief.

Her mother asked if she could use a computer and printer at the nurses' station, since the Dizon household lacked such technology. She used it to check her email—a rare event—and print the itinerary and business class plane tickets from the *Just Us Girls* show.

Then her mother drove them to the city mall to do some shopping.

*

She took Amanda to Nordstrom and bought them both pants suits, although you would have thought her mother was the one appearing on TV, given all the time she spent consulting with the sales associate and trying on different designer outfits, while Amanda sat on a loveseat checking her PingPong.

Are you really sure about this? asked Amanda as they got their hair done and matching mani-pedis at an upscale salon. I don't mind taking my clothes back. I've never worn a pants suit before. It seems kind of strange. And I don't want all the money you're spending to be a reason I can't get a home office.

Don't worry, said her mother. We consider it an investment. And you don't have to pay us back.

Really?!

Because as suddenly and unexpectedly as Amanda's world had exploded with rainbows and glitter, so had her mother's lofty dreams for her come true. My own dreams, as you have probably surmised by now, had been cruelly thwarted, as had my daughter's (Carole) and son-in-law's (Robert). No profitable farm, no distinguished professorships. And a granddaughter (Amanda) who, to the deep dismay of us all, didn't have any dreams to be derailed.

And in the blink of an eye, they had business class tickets to the Big Apple and a slot (at least Amanda did) on the *Just Us Girls* show. *And* a lawyer who was going to secure that college fund. *And* a lucrative—according to White Hat Ned—business as an influencer, although Amanda's mother was still trying to wrap her head around that.

*

They finished in time to pick up White Hat Ned from school. Nicole had cheerleading practice and Nipuni and Amy band practice, so it was just White Hat Ned in the back seat of Carole Dizon's Camry.

White Hat Ned had hoped the Staples excursion would be chaperone free, both for romantic and budgetary reasons. But after Amanda grunted, "Mom, don't embarrass me," two or three times after her mother injected unsolicited advice regarding tech she knew nothing about, her mother backed off, and trailed the pair at an embarrassment-free distance.

*

Her only other action was to dutifully insert her credit card at the cashier. The haul, as White Hat Ned promised, was well south of two thousand dollars: an HP all-in-one desktop computer; an external microphone; a motion-detecting video camera; a wireless mouse; a surge protector; a handful of flash drives; a mesh-backed ergonomic chair with adjustable arm rests.

*

Don't close the door, said Amanda's mother after helping her daughter up the stairs, while White Hat Ned carried the computer and then the chair.

I know. Three-inch rule, said Amanda, having heard this on some TV show.

Three feet, said her mother, inserting a door stop.

White Hat Ned set up the home office while Amanda scrolled through her followers' comments.

You can always upgrade to an iMac Pro when the ad revenue starts coming in, said White Hat Ned, attaching the last of the cables.

Where's the Chromebook? he asked.

Ummmm.

Fortunately, White Hat Ned was too busy tethering his cell phone to the computer to create a Wi-Fi hotspot to inquire further about the tablet he had gifted her.

Are you ready for me to drive you home, Ned? asked her mother from the bottom of the stairs, worried that her daughter had gone from future spinster to teenage mother in the space of a week.

Mama, this isn't like plugging in a microwave. We've gotta install software and get accounts, said Amanda, meaning White Hat Ned would have to do all these things. And we might need your credit card again, and I need my savings account info, if you can get that please.

Her mother eagerly complied and even offered to order pizza.

Can you make that two, or three? asked Amanda. The girls are coming over.

*

As soon as Amanda saw Amy marching up the stairs, she pulled her aside.

I need my Chromebook. Ned asked where it was.

It's with my brother, said Amy.

You gave away my Chromebook to your brother?!

No, silly. I asked him to check it for malware. I know Ned wants to get in your pants and he may have given you a tablet that videos you without your knowing. Maybe he's a perv, or maybe he wants to get compromising photos so he can blackmail you to have sex with him.

Are we living in the same universe, Amy? asked Amanda. True, he kissed me in the hospital. But we've hardly ever talked before that. And Nicole told me he likes Victoria Robinson.

He likes you too.

I'm never gonna see that Chromebook, am I?

Nope.

*

This is a disaster! yelled Nicole upon seeing Amanda and her new office. Stop taking pictures of the chair!

Nipuni was twirling in the ergonomic chair, taking selfies.

Pun, those are for your own accounts only, ordered Nicole. Don't tag Amanda.

Why? asked White Hat Ned. This shows she's a professional, not some Podunk country girl.

We don't want people thinking she's cashing in on a tragedy, explained Nicole. This is too professional. The chair is OK I guess, as long as you don't draw attention to it. She has millions of followers who like that she's a Podunk country girl. Capiche?

I'm a Podunk girl? asked Amanda. I don't even know what that means.

It's not good, said Amy.

It was good enough to get you thirteen million followers. You're the Girl in the Well. You're the girl who doesn't live in a megacity. You're exotic because pretty much all your followers live in cities. But they can also relate to you because you're not a model or child of celebrities.

Lord, went on Nicole, look at your hair! This is a disaster. A disaster!!!

What do you mean? asked Amanda.

For the first time in her life, Amanda felt good about her appearance—her hair, her nails, her wardrobe. She was a young woman, stylish and put together. The beneficiary of hundreds of dollars in salon and clothing charges. And now she was being told by her best friend, a Ph.D. in hotness, that her Gen X mother had led her astray.

And this! cried Nicole, extracting the cream-colored pants suit from its vinyl Nordstrom's bag. Are you trying to be Hillary Clinton?

She ran her fingers through Amanda's long hair, which had never been more shapely or controlled.

They colored over your highlights? Your followers loved the red. Don't take any more pics until we can get this fixed, OK?

What about my mom?

I'll deal with her, don't worry, said Nicole confidently. If she doesn't come around, I'll have my dad talk some sense into her. I'm sure he'll agree with my brand strategy. Besides, think of the money she'll save. Your suit must have cost over five hundred dollars!

*

White Hat Ned ate his pizza at Amanda's desk while creating Dropbox and PayPal accounts, as well as an Apple Pay account on her iPhone.

The girls ate cross-legged on the bed, their heads abutting the sloped ceiling.

I don't think it's a good idea for your mom to give Ned her credit card, whispered Amy into Amanda's ear.

I don't know what you have against him, said Amanda. He's helping me a lot. I could never do any of this. Besides, my mom gave him the second card, the one they give me when I have to buy something without them. It only has a limit of three hundred dollars.

Oh, good.

Whose pink duffel bag is that? asked Amanda.

There was a pink Adidas duffel behind the computer box that she hadn't noticed until now.

We stopped on the way over to get clothes and stuff, said Nicole. The fake slumber party was such a hit I thought we'd have a real one. You have a couple sleeping bags or an air mattress, right? Otherwise, I can go back home and get some.

Can I stay too? asked White Hat Ned, who only felt emboldened to make such a suggestion because he was staring at a blue Dropbox logo and not the faces of four sentient beings, each of whom he considered to be girlfriend material.

But before Amanda could say yes—because practically speaking there was so much work still for him to do dropping boxes and paying pals and what all and whatever, and because, well, just because—Amy shot him down.

Dude, if you get slumber-party zoned, which means simultaneously friend-zoned by four rockin' girls, as well as the host girl's mother, it could shrivel your dick for decades, at which point you'll be an old man and will need the blue pill. You might die a virgin.

Who said I was a virgin?

Pleeeeeease...

Hey, don't tease him, whispered Amanda, remembering Amy's earlier admonition. He might change into a black hat.

10

At 1:00 a.m. Amanda's father drove Ned home, interrogating him during the ride, not about his strength of character and intentions toward his daughter, as was customary for fathers of teenage daughters to do during their first interview with a potential son-in-law, but rather about 5G and clouds and bots and Bitcoin. By the end of the journey, he proffered the possibility of—assuming his daughter's venture as an influencer was a success—retaining him as a paid consultant, if not promising his daughter's hand in marriage and a dowry of mutual funds.

*

The girls were wakened by the sound of a truck. But it was coming from the backyard, not the street.

Amanda, get over here, called Nipuni from the window. Look!

The girls all squeezed together, pushing the rainbow curtains to their limit.

A dump truck was on the grass, dumping...concrete? rocks? gravel? sand? into the well.

Come on, said Nicole. We need to document this.

*

The girls quickly dressed, helping Amanda into a pair of old jeans and sneakers and giving her a hoodie to cover her hair.

Amanda's father was standing to the side of the truck, watching the contents of the dump truck spill into the well. Whether it was sand or gravel or rocks or concrete, it made a lot of noise, so that Nicole had to shout into the phone as she recorded the conclusion to Amanda's traumatic episode.

Amanda's father was visibly startled when he saw Amanda, as if he thought she was going to jump in.

Stay back! yelled her father, as Amy and Nipuni ran to the well and tried to look over. But Amanda needed no such warning. Feeling overcome with a sense of terror, she stood at a distance, forcing Nicole to record her from behind.

It isn't easy returning to the scene of the awful disaster that trapped my poor friend and nearly snuffed out her youthful life, commented Nicole. See, she can't go nearer, but neither can she look away. But at least she can rest assured no other child will befall the same fate.

*

Nicole had a spirited discussion with Amanda's mother over breakfast, ending with Amanda in possession of the platinum card, as long as she agreed not to spend more than the pants suit cost.

Your mom had the right idea, said Nicole in the truck. She just botched the execution.

So they returned the suit to Nordstom, then went to H&M for a pair of distressed jeans and to JC Penny for a maroon plaid flannel shirt.

You can't get any more Midwestern than a plaid flannel shirt, said Nicole approvingly.

What about overalls? asked Amy.

OK, after overalls, you can't get any more Midwest than a plaid flannel shirt. They probably don't even sell these in New York!

*

They then went to Nicole's salon in a nearby strip mall, where Amanda got her vermilion highlights back. And then to meet Amanda's mother at a day spa to splurge on a microdermabrasion treatment.

Amanda's mother had agreed on the condition that she would be present. But after reading the brochures and asking the esthetician a battery of questions, Amanda's mother decided to have one herself as well.

The procedure involved wearing goggles and having very fine crystals sprayed over the face and vacuumed off, along with dead skin cells. It didn't hurt, but it wasn't Amanda's idea of a day spa, which in her mind meant getting a neck massage in an aromatherapy room and having cucumber slices put over her eyes.

Afterwards her face looked even pinker than before. However, the esthetician said her skin tone would return to normal by tomorrow, rejuvenated, healthy and glowing, the splotchiness a thing of the past. And if not, the spa offered a five-treatment package for the price of four.

Tomorrow, said Nicole, after church, we'll go to Babylon Skincare for makeup, the last piece in the Amanda makeover puzzle.

After church? asked Amanda.

*

I had raised Carole to be respectfully insubordinate to all authority, especially the spiritual kind. And her husband came from the non-Irish-Catholic part of Boston, where the *Social Register* passed for Old and New Testament.

So Amanda's parents raised her with a vague sense of spirituality rather than dogmatic certainty. They enrolled her in a Christian preschool because it was close to their home, but the only time they set foot in a church was when invited to weddings. Their daughter's incurious personality, which troubled them no end, was a blessing when it came to religion, for they weren't sure how to answer cosmological questions in a way that would lead her neither into insufferable bliss nor existential despair.

Amanda regarded religion as fashion, art and entertainment. Silver cross necklaces didn't bring to mind a horrible execution. Beautiful old stone churches were no different to her than other beautiful old buildings she liked to look at, such as the historic post office. The nativity was a doll house, Christmas a time for fireplaces and presents, Easter not a resurrection but an egg hunt.

She had gone to Nicole's United Methodist church several times over the course of their friendship, mostly because she craved Nicole's esteem. But Nicole, not being evangelical, didn't press her to join, and though Amanda liked the choir, and the young pastor was kind of cute, Nicole's father had the worst body odor she'd ever smelled and she was always made to sit in the middle.

She tried to put Nicole in the middle today, but the father sat in the middle instead. How could a tall, handsome man, well-dressed, with a good job and a knock-out daughter, not know that he smelled like a manure pit? Amanda was well aware of the phrase: *He thinks his shit doesn't stink.* But what about everybody else? What about Nicole? However, Amanda was too embarrassed to raise the matter with her best friend, and the whole thing was as much a mystery to her as the phenomenon of divine miracles that was the subject of the sermon by the rather cute pastor, who by coincidence said, We are blessed today to have in our congregation the subject of a miracle herself!

All eyes turned to Amanda, and her eyes turned to everyone else.

Amanda, Our Girl in the Well. Can you please stand up?

Me?!

She rose with trepidation. Were they going to ask her to speak? She hadn't even been baptized. Were they going to do something Godly to her?

But after a grateful round of applause and a Praise the Lord! from the rather cute pastor, no more was asked from her.

*

After church they drove to the mall, this time specifically to Babylon Skincare, where Amanda was overwhelmed by the shiny counters of chemicals, colors, scents and creams designed to make the female sex attract a mate—or a hookup, or another member of their own tribe, or visually ace a job interview. There wasn't just one reason to wear makeup, any of the Babylon Skincare sales associates would tell you. But Amanda had not thought of any of these reasons before today. The extent of her makeup universe had been glitter lipstick from Target.

Her mother did not wear makeup, except for lip gloss and eyeliner. She had not even worn more than that to her own wedding at the City Hall. So Amanda had been raised to think makeup was unimportant unless you were the kind of girl who was already pretty enough to merit being looked at, which she didn't think she was.

But today she got a crash course in foundation, mascara, eyeliner, blush, lipstick and perfume—although they wouldn't buy perfume here but, almost as an afterthought, a bottle of discounted body spray at the Victoria's Secret on their way out of the mall.

Amanda enjoyed having the young women at Babylon paint her face and ask her to look at herself in the magnifying mirror that sat on the counter.

But the comprehensive makeover tutorial was just for education and fun. After fifty minutes Nicole informed her naive friend that her look needed to be fresh. And the TV show's makeup person would get her ready for the camera.

So they just bought lip gloss, blush, eyeshadow, and standard size velour eyelashes, which they applied on the spot with the associate's help.

Can I get foundation too?

No.

This is so sweet of you, said Amanda, handing her mother's platinum card to the sales lady. But how come we never did this before? All the years we've been friends and you never took me here.

Nicole simply smiled in response. What could she say? That the thought had never occurred to her to help her friend improve her appearance, let alone invite Amanda on her quarterly buying trips to Babylon Skincare? The fact was that Nicole never cared before, or even wanted her splotchy friend to shine.

*

It was dusk and the dump truck was gone.

Amanda gazed out her window at the fading light, at the soybean field in the distance, beyond the barbed-wire fence, at the well no one would ever fall into again.

She sat in her mesh-backed ergonomic chair and played with the keyboard, although the monitor only displayed the desktop. The Wi-Fi people would not arrive until tomorrow.

But by that time she would be in New York.

New York! She had traveled with her parents many times before, on vacations. To Disney World once, to Virginia Beach several times, to Boston to visit her father's distant relatives one Christmas, to St. Louis and Yellowstone, and to Chicago many times.

But never New York. And never to be interviewed on a television show. She got butterflies just thinking about it. How would she feel when she was actually on the set?

*

Her father used a personal day the following morning to drive them to the airport. Her mother could have driven them herself and left her car in long-term parking—it was only for two nights—but her father regretted that he wasn't going himself and this was the least—or the most—he could do.

Speaking of personal days, Amanda's mother had already used hers. But the principal was as excited as everyone else by the attention Amanda had brought the county and even offered to sub here and there for the Dizons if needed—a fact I'm sure their students would not have applauded, had they known.

Have a good time, said her father, giving Amanda a big hug. Don't fall down any wells.

I don't think they have wells in New York City.

Don't fall down any manholes then.

Don't forget to feed Luna, said Amanda. Don't give her away.

Amanda believed her father hated the cat, despite his protestations to the contrary. It was a stray she had found in the fields and she had pleaded with her parents to let her keep it.

You look good, said her father, as if looking at her for the first time.

Amanda grinned proudly, showing her crooked teeth.

Maybe after you get back we can see about braces or aligners, or whatever they're called these days.

Really?! exclaimed Amanda. She had been asking for Invisalign for years.

She gave her father another tight hug.

*

Guess you're too big for Iowa now, said the TSA agent with a smirk, after looking at her name and the destination on the ticket. (Being sixteen, she didn't need ID.)

Don't worry, said her mother. We're coming back Wednesday.

So what's in New York?

She's going to be on *Just Us Girls* tomorrow!

My wife watches that show. Guess I'll have to watch it too. Just be careful, ladies, said the TSA agent, handing back their documents. People in New York aren't as friendly as they are here.

*

Have you ever flown business class before? asked Amanda as the smiling flight attendant took her crutches and showed them to their seats in the second row.

Once, when I was about your age. Sutherland won an award and he took me to the ceremony. I don't know if they gave him business class or if your grandfather upgraded himself, but it was great.

You never told me that!

Would you like something to drink? asked the flight attendant.

Can I have a virgin piña colada?

The flight attendant smiled, and while the unfortunate hoi polloi were still stuffing their carry-ons into the tiny overhead bins in economy, she returned with Amanda's drink in a real glass and a vodka martini for her mother.

I can't believe there are people who live like this all the time, said Amanda. Did you ever want to be rich?

The really rich fly in private jets, said her mom.

Do you think I will be rich someday?

You mean like in a week? joked her mom.

I don't know if I want you to be rich, said her mom more seriously.

Why not?

There are two kinds of people whom I wouldn't want to be: the very poor and the very rich.

*

At LaGuardia Amanda saw a man in a black suit holding a sign with her name on it. And she didn't have to hunt for their luggage. It was taken off the carousel for them and carried to a waiting limousine.

Wow.

Amanda hadn't posted anything from the plane because she remembered what Nicole had said about luxury being bad for her brand.

But now she posted pics of the skyline as they drove into Manhattan, and a separate post asking her followers to watch her on *Just Us Girls* tomorrow at 11:00 a.m. Eastern Standard Time.

They were driven to the Marriott Marquis in Times Square, and a bellhop took their bags to registration.

They rode the atrium elevator to the fortieth floor, where the bellhop opened the curtains, revealing a stunning view of Midtown.

Wow!

She watched her mother tip the bellhop.

You're gonna have to teach me how to tip, said Amanda after the bellhop left. For when I'm traveling on my own.

That won't be for some time, said her mother, somewhat nervously.

The phone rang.

Amanda looked at the red light on the landline as if it were an alien object.

Her mother answered it while Amanda snapped pictures of the CNN building.

That was Jennifer's assistant, said her mother. She wanted to make sure we got in OK and confirm tomorrow's schedule. She also got us tickets to *Hamilton*!

What's Hamilton?

Really? asked her mother in despair. You don't know the blockbuster musical? Tickets are hundreds of dollars, if you can get them.

Amanda shrugged. Can't we see *Frozen*?

No!

*

Under normal conditions Amanda's mother would have taken her to the Metropolitan Museum of Art, the Brooklyn Bridge, a stroll through the East Village and a visit to the World Trade Memorial.

But since she wasn't supposed to walk much, and needed to save her energy for tomorrow, she suggested going to the 86th floor observatory on the Empire State Building.

They almost didn't make it out of Times Square. Her mother hated Times Square, except for the theaters. But the very things she detested—the crowds of out-of-towners and foreigners, the massive, bright LED signs, the tawdry souvenir shops—were the very things that attracted her daughter.

I want to go in here, said Amanda, pulling her mother into the nearest shop.

She loaded up on trinkets for her friends.

*

Amanda wasn't as impressed by the Empire State Building as you might think a girl from Iowa would be, where the tallest structure in Montgomery County was a grain silo. But Amanda had visited the SkyDeck of the taller Willis Tower in Chicago, and even lain face down on the glass ledge.

Afterward they took a taxi to Central Park, where her mother splurged on a carriage ride to spare Amanda from walking.

Then they returned to Times Square for dinner.

What do you want? asked her mother.

There's an Olive Garden.

We can go to Olive Garden back home!

So she took her daughter to a deli, where they witnessed two homeless men get into a fight, wrestling on the floor before the manager broke it up and pushed them back outside.

The diners, many of them Asian, seemed to consider it performance art and applauded at the end.

This doesn't happen at Olive Garden, said Amanda acerbically.

*

She fell asleep twice at *Hamilton*, but found her second wind back in the room.

I got one of these for Gramps, said Amanda, holding up a tin Statue of Liberty. He's always getting me souvenirs. I thought I would get him one.

That's sweet, honey, said her mom. But I think he already has one.

What time is it in Asia now?

Asia, why?

I want to call him. Can we? We can use the phone for free, right?

I didn't speak to my granddaughter often. Not as much as I should have. As I've already mentioned, I never could find words with her, and she was shy in return. The last time we had spoken was when I called to wish her luck in the new school year.

I suppose we can try, said Amanda's mom unenthusiastically. I couldn't get through to his hostel the day you fell in the well. There was a typhoon I was later told.

Such is life for people off the grid. One person without a mobile phone is bad enough. But if the other person doesn't have one either, then they might not speak to each other for months.

Of course, that was largely intentional, at least on my side.

Amanda's mother was surprised the hostel answered.

Boracay Island was twelve hours ahead of Manhattan Island, so I was just eating breakfast: a piece of toast, a banana, and coffee thick and black.

Carole: Sutherland, have you heard?

Me: Is something wrong?

Carole: So, you haven't heard. Well, yes and no. Remember that well out back? That you never filled in?

Me: I remember a wooden cover.

Carole: A wooden cover wasn't good enough. You should have sealed it up. Because Amanda fell in.

Me: When?! Why didn't you tell me? Was she badly hurt? You should have contacted me at once.

Carole: I tried to. Why don't *you* have a cell phone?

Me: Why don't you have a cell phone?

Carole: She broke her ankle, but she's OK. She's actually great. Her accident garnered national attention and she's become an internet sensation.

Me: What's the internet?

Carole: I'm serious. There's an app called PingPong and she has millions of followers. And now we're in New York, at the Marriott Marquis.

Me: I hate the Marriott Marquis. Worst service I've ever had at a Marriott. Now the Marriott in Bangkok...

Carole: Are you listening to me, Sutherland? We're in New York because your granddaughter has been invited on the *Just Us Girls* show. I don't suppose you can get it in the Philippines?

Me: Developing countries are backwards because of their rapacious elites, not because of their lack of access to mind-numbing American television.

Carole: Wait, she wants to speak to you.

Amanda: Gramps!

Me: How'd you fall down that well?

Amanda: It was an accident.

Me: Of course it was an accident. You didn't jump in, did you?

Amanda: I bought you a Statue of Liberty. You can put it on your dresser, like I have the Eiffel Tower you sent me on my dresser.

Me: I certainly will. How is your ankle?

Amanda: Fine.

Me:

Amanda:

Me:

Amanda: I guess I gotta go. Love you, Gramps.

Me: I'll be watching you, princess.

*

Amanda raided the minibar and checked her PingPong feed while her mother took a hot bath. Then they watched television until her mother said they needed to hit the hay.

I'm wired, said Amanda. I've got all this nervous energy. How am I supposed to sleep?

Her mother improvised.

Swallow this with a full glass of water, said her mother, placing what looked like a white capsule in her palm.

There were two queen beds, but Amanda got in bed next to her mother and cuddled up to her.

I'm afraid.

You survived the well. You're a very brave girl. And I'm very proud of you.

Amanda got up and went to the window and parted the curtain. The night view of Times Square and Midtown New York from the fortieth floor was magical. A million blinking lights below on signs and video screens advertising the world's most famous brands. Streams of taxis, buses, police cars. Thousands of energetic tourists from all over the planet.

I have the world at my feet, said Amanda. It's exciting. And, also scary. But I'm not going to jump. I'm never gonna jump.

PART TWO

On the Treadmill

1

The green room wasn't actually green. That was just a term used for the waiting room guests before going on television shows. Once upon a time I'm sure there was a green waiting room, but this one had black leather couches and chairs, gray carpet, yellow walls. It could have been anywhere, except the people in it were famous.

Or famous to some groups. Amanda didn't recognize the elderly lawyer who was here to promote his book, or the bald psychologist here to promote his book, or the retired actress here to promote her book.

I wish I had a book, said Amanda, feeling like she had appeared on exam day without a #2 pencil.

Gramps should come on this show, said Amanda. He's a writer.

These guests have books people want to read, said her mother. My proud daughter.

The other guests were busy with their phones, or assistants, but in time each came over to Amanda and graciously said a few words.

Her mother asked the retired actress for her autograph. The actress obliged, but Amanda cowered in embarrassment when her mother continued to talk and talk and talk when it was clear the actress wanted to be left alone with her phone.

Amanda ate carrots and celery sticks from the buffet table, and poured herself a Mountain Dew from a can. A monitor suspended from the ceiling in the far corner of the room showed the empty glass oval desk where the hosts would sit with each guest in turn like the best of chums.

Salvatora Morani entered like a tempest, bringing the room to life. One of the three hosts, she was an Italian media mogul who dressed for the talk show as if it were the Oscars, in sequined gowns and glittery jewelry, her dyed raven hair curving down her shoulders like storm clouds.

Welcome to the show, darlings! said Salvatora in a loud, highly accented voice, and swept among them for big hugs and kisses.

When she came to Amanda, she urged her to sit back down.

Poor girl, rest your ankle, said the media mogul.

Amanda's mother said how much she admired Salvatora's efforts to empower women in male chauvinistic Italy.

Blah blah blah blah blah blah blah blah blah blah blah blah blah blah blah blah blah blah blah blah blah blah blah blah blah blah blah blah blah blah blah blah blah blah...

Mama!

*

The green room emptied one person at a time, leaving only assistants. First to go was the retired actress, then the lawyer, then the psychologist.

Amanda and her mother watched the show on the monitor and nibbled on snacks.

I'm so nervous! whispered Amanda into her mother's ear. Do you think I could have another pill? It won't make me sleepy, will it? Just to relax?

Her mother gave her two this time.

*

Finally, Amanda was led to the edge of the set, where the first thing that struck her was the studio audience, which looked smaller than on TV.

The show had just gone to commercial and a face she knew from countless comedies smiled upon her. This was Shandra Murray, the only one of the three hosts who had been an original member of the show.

Are you OK to walk? Otherwise, we can seat you first.

Amanda?

If it was possible for Amanda to be both staring at the beloved celebrity and looking around at just everything, then that's what she was doing.

The comedian took her hand. Sweetheart?

Mmmmm, said Amanda.

I know you're nervous. I hate when people ask if I'm nervous because that just makes you a hundred times more nervous, right sweetie? So, I'm gonna assume you're already plenty nervous. But I'm gonna be right here with you, and we're gonna do something that will put you right at ease and break the ice.

What?

So, rules. Don't say *fuck* or the *n* word.

I never say the *n* word, said Amanda.

Well, you're from Iowa, so I had to make sure. Last rule, have fun. OK?

Mmmmm.

Suddenly the audience applauded and Amanda heard her name called by Salvatora Morani.

She looked at the audience. All their eyes were upon her.

Then she found herself walking into the hot lights with the comedian's arm around her.

Instead of having her sit at the table like the other guests, a chair was wheeled around in front, and she was helped to sit down. The crutches were leaned conspicuously against the table, and the comedian raised Amanda's left foot—the one with the cast—onto a footstool.

How does that feel? Are you comfortable?

Mmmmm.

Can we get a closeup of the cast? asked the comedian of her cameraman. So we can see the signatures of the presidential candidates? That must have been a very special moment for you, Amanda?

Mmmmm.

Is there room for us to sign too?

This was Trish Dalton, the country singer with a million gold albums and a million ringlets in her wheat blond hair.

Sign?!!!

A Sharpie was produced and the three famous ladies took turns bending beside the footstool and adding their names to those of the potential president's.

The audience applauded. They cut to commercial. After three minutes the Applause sign flashed.

Shandra: We're back with Amanda Dizon, the Girl in the Well. Do you mind if I call you that, sweetie? Being African American I'm particularly sensitive to how we all address each other. So, no offense taken?

Amanda: Mmmmmm.

Shandra: I'm sure you've been called worse. I wouldn't want to be a teenager these days, with all the bullying that goes on in school and social media. But now you're a big success. That's the best revenge, agree? Tell us what that feels like?

Salvatora: Slow down, Shandra. We haven't even asked her about the tragedy.

Shandra: You Italians!

Apparently, the comedian had forgotten her earlier statement about being sensitive to how we all address each other.

Trish: How'd you get down that well, darlin'?

Shandra: You didn't jump, did you?

Amanda: Why does everyone keep saying that? No! I swear.

Shandra: Give me a fist bump, sweetie. You know that if you ever feel like ending it all, there are resources available...

Salvatora: There are rumors you were assaulted. Pushed down the well by a boy. Or a man.

Amanda: No!!!

Trish: How many days were you down there? How did you sleep?

Amanda: It was only a few minutes.

Shandra: Listen to her, everyone! Such modesty.

Trish: Could you see the stars? I heard tell that from the bottom of a well you can see stars in the daytime.

Amanda: I don't know. I was crying so much I couldn't see anything. And then the reporter flashed her phone light in my eyes.

The comedian offered up a high five.

Salvatora: We will be back after a short break to learn about Amanda's sudden rise to fame.

*

The Applause sign went on and off. A flurry of activity surrounded Amanda, as the hosts moved about, drank water, had their brows dabbed for perspiration or their hair brushed.

Shandra asked Amanda if she was having fun yet.

I can't believe I'm talking so much, said Amanda, feeling proud of herself. I thought I would be tongue-tied.

Her mother knelt down to her and said how great she was doing and asked if she needed anything.

Mama! said Amanda in terror. Scoot back to the green room!

*

Shandra: We're excited to have the Girl in the Well. Or as her millions of PingPong fans know her, Amanda911.

Salvatora: So, you're an entrepreneur.

Amanda: What's that?

The audience laughed at what they took to be the teenager's modesty and wit.

Salvatora: Were you digital savvy from a young age?

Amanda: I thought I'm young now?

Salvatora: You're certainly young to have amassed so many followers. And you don't even have a gold record yet, like our talented colleague.

Trish: I'm a far piece from sixteen, though. Tell us how you did it, darlin'.

Amanda: I fell in a well.

Shandra: Lots of people fall in wells. Or get lost in caves, or the woods. They don't get millions of fans.

Trish: Did your parents teach you computers?

Amanda: We didn't even have a computer.

Salvatora: Yet here you are a digital entrepreneur. Are you part of a hacking community?

Amanda: My boyfriend is a white hat.

Shandra: Our country needs more heroes like you, sweetheart. Especially teenage girls on social media. There's so much hate out there these days. But fame can be a double-edged sword, you know that?

Amanda: Mmmmm.

Shandra: But you have three experts here, and I'd say between us we know a thing or two about the problems and perils of fame. Is there anything you'd like to ask us?

Amanda: Nope. I'm good.

*

It was late night in the Philippines. I had tipped a bartender at a sports bar to tune the satellite TV to *Just Us Girls*, pissing off a group of Aussies watching a cricket match.

Amanda's courage to appear on live national TV filled me with a profound pride. She wasn't saying much, but she was in the arena, something I had never achieved.

The conversation, as expected, was insipid. I wouldn't have given longer answers than hers, so banal were the questions. But at the end she was given the opportunity to ask the three hosts about the one subject they were truly masters of: fame. A phenomenon, a way of life, that if this rabbit hole she'd fallen into was not a flash-in-the-pan, would be something my granddaughter would have to get her head around or be herself decapitated. And she asked nothing.

Insipid.

I caught the bartender's attention and ordered another rum and Coke.

*

As Amanda and her mother were leaving the studio after the show, a fashionable young woman thrust a piece of thick paper in her tracks.

Great show, Amanda! said the woman. I'm Marnie from Spitfire Cosmetics and this is for you.

Amanda took the thick pink paper and looked at it blankly.

Turn it over, said the young woman from Spitfire Cosmetics.

Pay to the order of...

Amanda realized it was a check.

Pay to the order of Amanda Dizon.

$10,000.00

The largest check Amanda had ever received were the fifty dollar checks her grandmother gave her every Christmas.

What is this? asked Amanda's mother, taking the check to examine it herself.

It's ten thousand dollars, said Amanda, grabbing the check back, nearly tearing it in the process.

Thanks! said Amanda to the young woman from Spitfire Cosmetics.

You can't take that! exclaimed her mother, trying to take it back and actually tearing it in the process.

Mama!!!

That's all right said the young woman from Spitfire Cosmetics. We can print another, or just transfer it to your bank.

I have a PayPal account now, said Amanda with pride and relief.

People just don't give people money for nothing, warned her mother.

They do for the homeless. You gave money to three homeless people yesterday. For nothing.

You're not homeless, said her mother. And this is a big corporation. Why don't you ask her what she wants?

It's quite simple, said the young woman from Spitfire Cosmetics, unperturbed by Amanda's mother's undisguised hostility. We just want to help raise your spirits after your terrible ordeal and show our support. Our sole request is that you create a post that states Spitfire Cosmetics are the best cosmetics in the world.

I just went to Babylon, admitted Amanda. I've never used Spitfire Cosmetics.

That's no problem, said the young woman from Spitfire Cosmetics. We can send you samples. Or even have a representative come to your home for a consultation.

Nice try, said Amanda's mother, pulling Amanda away, as though the woman were a pedophile.

*

Rather than basking in the afterglow of her appearance on *Just Us Girls*, Amanda sulked in the limo to the airport.

I can't believe you tore up ten thousand dollars! said Amanda.

They want to you to lie, said her mother.

She said they'd send me samples. I'll use them, why not?

And what if you don't like their products?

For ten thousand dollars I'd put dog shit on my face! screamed Amanda. For the wife of an economist, you sure don't understand the value of money. No wonder you lost the farm.

*

Two virgin coladas in business class and several requests for selfies from fellow passengers restored Amanda's mood, and when her father met them in baggage claim that evening, she breathlessly recalled their adventure.

Mr. Cole, the rumpled lawyer, was sitting on their front porch steps when they arrived home.

Couldn't find the key this time? asked Amanda's mom snarkily, letting him in.

He helped carry their luggage.

Congratulations on your appearance on *Just Us Girls*, said the rumpled lawyer. I'm sure it will be the first of many interviews. You have a likable countenance.

Thanks, whatever that means, said Amanda.

Do you always show up at clients' houses? asked Amanda's father. Don't you have an office?

Personal touch, said the rumpled lawyer. How else can I compete with the slick law firms in Des Moines?

My mom tore up a check for ten thousand dollars, said Amanda. Can I sue her?

I'm afraid not.

I have rights.

I'm afraid you don't. But I have good news, said the rumpled lawyer. MakeItRain has agreed to release the funds. I just need Mr. and Mrs. Dizon to authorize a bank account.

Amanda jumped up and down and screamed. Even her parents were not displeased.

I still can't believe this is happening, said Amanda's father as the rumpled lawyer opened his laptop on the kitchen table.

You want our Wi-Fi password? asked Amanda proudly. We have Wi-Fi now!

After the lawyer left, Amanda asked her parents if they could pick up Nicole and go to the Jaguar dealership.

No! said her mother.

Why not?

Really? wondered her mother, alarmed. You've just come into a small fortune and the first thing you want to do is buy your friend a car?

Yep.

Oh Amanda, said her mother, throwing her arms around her. I don't know if you're too sweet or too gullible, or too much of each. For years I've wanted you to change, and now I'm afraid all this attention is going to change you too much.

Can we go tomorrow?

*

Amanda hobbled up to her new home office. The monitor blinded her with its light. After staring at phone screens all her social media life, it was like an IMAX.

But she wasn't sure how to record on it. She lay down on her bed for just a minute, but fell into a deep sleep that would last till morning.

Her friends stopped by, but were not allowed to disturb her.

She now had twenty million followers.

2

Amanda wished to go back to school, and her parents agreed.

Everyone welcomed her warmly. Hugs, selfies, shrieks of excitement.

Before American History class began, White Hat Ned took her hand and kissed her on the lips.

Hey, what are you doing? exclaimed Amanda, both shocked and delighted.

She noticed that White Hat Ned had his arm around her shoulder. She shrugged it off. This was getting weird.

Is this a prank? asked Amanda, looking around for hidden cameras or something. But the other students seemed absorbed in preparing for class.

White Hat Ned smiled at her, confused himself.

I'm not being punked or whatever? asked Amanda. You can't just go around kissing people and holding their hands.

I'm not kissing people. I'm kissing my girlfriend, said White Hat Ned.

Girlfriend?!

You said I was your boyfriend.

When?!

On the show.

I did not!!!

Are you denying it?

There's nothing to deny. I remember mentioning you. But I didn't say you're my boyfriend. Why would I do that? You're not.

White Hat Ned took out his phone, and after a bit of navigating and fast forwarding, showed his new girlfriend the clip.

Amanda stared. Those aren't my words. You hacked that! You... black hat!

*

She didn't see her friends until lunch. They surrounded her with a group hug and asked a million questions about flying business class and New York and the show and what the hosts were really like. Amanda opened her backpack and gave them the souvenirs she had bought on Times Square and told them her mother had torn up a check for ten thousand dollars.

So, go to Babylon Skincare and ask *them* to give you ten thousand, said Nicole. And if they won't, say you'll use Spitfire, or someone else's makeup.

Nicole, you're brilliant! said Amanda.

Have you seen your boyfriend? asked Amy with a sneer.

Where is he? wondered Nipuni, scouring the cafeteria.

He's not my boyfriend, said Amanda.

Then why did you tell all of America he was? asked Nipuni.

I didn't...

Amanda covered her mouth with both hands.

Oh my God! Oh my God! Oh my God!

But why would I say that if it's not true? asked Amanda, looking pleadingly at her friends.

It's your subconscious talking, said Nicole. What's the big deal? He likes you, right?

Here he comes, whispered Nipuni.

White Hat Ned was fast approaching their table, carrying his lunch tray.

But I don't know what to do. I'm not ready for a boyfriend.

I had boyfriends when I was six, said Nicole. You'll figure it out.

Hi ladies, said White Hat Ned, possessed of a swagger he didn't have before.

Amanda blushed and looked away.

Martin Decker, Nicole's ex, happened to be walking past at that moment and observed her fraught embarrassment.

He winked at her.

*

At home that afternoon she received a FedEx letter. She opened it to reveal a gold envelope.

What is it? asked her mother, stepping onto the porch.

It's an invitation to a New Year's festival for influencers in Turkey! Can I go?

Let me see that, said her mother. It's Turks and Caicos, not Turkey.

What's that?

They're islands in the Caribbean.

Even better! I'll be on the beach in winter! Sand in my toes and piña coladas! Can I go?

Possibly. I have to research who these people are and what they want. But it could be a nice trip for us, said her mother with a bright smile.

Us?! You can't go, said Amanda.

The invitation states it is for two persons, said her mother.

It also states no mothers allowed!

Her mother thought her daughter was being serious, because her daughter usually was. She re-read the invitation, which said no such thing.

We can't let you go on your own, said her mother.

New York was OK for you to go, said Amanda. But this is a festival for cool, popular people. Fashionistas. Hip hop artists. Mista Sista is headlining. Nobody is taking their mother!

You're still angry I tore up the check.

You couldn't even stay in the green room!

Well, it's over three months away said her mother. We have plenty of time to discuss it later.

*

Fortunately, Harding High had a liberal electronic device policy. Or unfortunately, as this created a conflict of interest for Amanda, who found herself overwhelmed by the demands of both social media and school. It had been difficult enough paying attention in class before.

Students were allowed to bring phones, tablets, and laptops on campus, but it was up to each teacher to decide whether to allow their use in the classroom. Mr. Cargill, in American History, was one of those who did not. So White Hat Ned resorted to the primitive method of passing notes to Amanda.

You need three email accounts. Personal. Business. Public.

I don't use email, Amanda wrote on the back and sent through a courier system of four students.

Time to start. You need a website. I can make a WordPress site for you, White Hat Ned wrote on another scrap.

Amanda drew a smiley face and sent the scrap back.

You need to learn simple tricks for photos and videos. Like time lapse. I can teach you.

Thanks!!!

You need to learn video editing. Sometimes you should make professional-looking videos. Or you'll want to excerpt a scene from a longer video.

Too much work!

Not really. You'll need a photographer too.

No.

Why not?

Nicole says I can't look too put together. I need to be fresh. And photographers are expensive.

Then at least get a good camera for times you want great pics. You need to think of this as a business.

I am.

You should form an LLC.

???

Limited Liability Corporation. It protects your personal assets from business debts and lawsuits.

I'll ask my dad.

You need a lawyer.

I have one!

And which battle would that be, Ms. Dizon? asked the American History teacher.

The Alamo? guessed Amanda, not having heard the classroom discussion.

Mr. Cargill frowned. The students snickered. A cheerleader friend of Nicole's was caught videoing and her camera was confiscated for the remainder of the class.

*

This is a bad look, said Nicole, watching the Alamo video, sent to her privately by the cheerleader. I think even the Chinese know the Alamo wasn't fought during the Civil War. Are you prepared to promise her a hundred dollars not to share the video with anyone else?

She's blackmailing me?

Not yet. I'm going to bribe her first.

Amanda nodded. But before Nicole could hunt down the cheerleader, Amanda grabbed her arm.

I got my parents to agree. We're getting the car tonight! We'll pick you up at seven, OK?

Nicole let out a scream and gave her friend a suffocating hug.

*

Nicole was waiting outside when the Dizons drove up.

Where's your father? asked Amanda's father.

He has a meeting, said Nicole. But if he needs to sign anything, he said I could bring it home.

They would discover that wouldn't be necessary. They were greeted by Jennifer and Barney, who shook all of their hands warmly, a far cry from their first encounter.

They went into the leasing agent's office, where driver's licenses and insurance cards were passed over her glass table. She was anxious to get this lease consummated, as the month of September was drawing to a close and she hadn't yet met her quota. The MakeItRain funds showed as deposited in the Dizon's account and their credit check displayed a score in the high seven hundreds, their bankruptcy having been under an LLC they created to buy the farm and therefore not affecting their personal borrowing power.

Everything seems to be in order, said the leasing agent. Now I'll just guide you through these forms, Mr. Dizon.

She laid a tablet on the table between them and started to explain the first form.

Amanda doesn't have her license yet, said Amanda's mother. But she'll be taking the test soon.

The leasing agent smiled.

And Nicole, her friend, will probably be driving the car sometimes as well.

Amanda's mom felt like she was skirting the edge of the law, but the leasing agent would have dropped the keys into Nicole's palm if the teenager asked to drive it home.

The lease is in your name, Mr. and Mrs. Dizon, said the leasing agent. Who drives it is up to you. I suggest you check with your insurance company about your coverage. I assume you'll be putting your daughter on your policy. And her friend is under her father's policy, as I recall from the test drive. But this isn't an issue for us.

She proceeded through the rest of the forms and shook their hands gratefully.

Barney will now show you the car, and answer any questions. I believe it's already been washed.

*

They dropped Nicole off. She thanked them profusely. But they did not leave her the car.

We'll let her have it Saturday, said Amanda's mother. I want to drive it tomorrow, make sure there aren't any kinks.

Right, Mom, said Amanda cynically.

*

Amanda was glad the next day was Friday. School was too distracting. Not only classes, but the time between bells, and lunchtime. She could barely walk past a row of lockers without someone requesting a favor or putting her in their selfie.

Maybe you should be home schooled, suggested Amy at lunchtime.

Can I do that?

It's up to your parents. They'd have to teach you.

That didn't work out well when I had them in class, confessed Amanda.

I'd miss you in American History, said White Hat Ned, joining them.

And I'd miss you in gym, said Nipuni.

Lots of influencers and teen stars are home schooled, said Amy.

But what would your followers think? asked White Hat Ned.

Who cares what her followers think? asked Amy. It's her life.

Well, it really isn't anymore, said White Hat Ned.

What did you say? asked Amanda. She had been reading the comments about a photo she posted of Luna that morning.

Here, I created a poll, said Nicole, showing them her screen.

Should I stay in Harding High or be home schooled?

I bet you they vote home school, predicted Amy.

I bet they say Harding, predicted Nipuni.

Why do you still let Nicole post on your site? asked White Hat Ned.

She's a big help, said Amanda. I don't know what I'd do without her.

But what if you get in a fight sometime? She has your password. She could destroy you.

I could destroy you, said Nicole to White Hat Ned. With or without your password.

You have my password too, White Hat, said Amanda.

Well maybe I shouldn't, said White Hat Ned. Maybe no one should. You're too trusting. Maybe you should change it and just give it to your lawyer.

Look at these comments, said Amanda. They love my Luna!

*

After school Amanda and Nicole drove to the mall and strode confidently into Babylon Skincare.

Can I help you? asked an associate.

Yes, said Amada. I'd like to know if you'd give me a check for ten thousand dollars.

Me? asked the associate with a big grin.

She means she wants to inquire about getting a sponsorship for her PingPong page, explained Nicole.

I don't have anything to do with that. You'll have to ask corporate.

Where is she? wondered Amanda, glancing around the store.

I mean in New York. Or L.A. Wherever the headquarters is.

Do you have their number? asked Nicole.

I can ask my manager. Or you could go on our Facebook page and send a message. That might be better.

Great idea! said Nicole.

*

On a padded bench in the mall, they sat down to compose a message. Nicole thought it best for Amanda to do it in her own voice and style:

Hi Babylon Skincare Corporate. One of your competitors gave me a check for $10,000, but I tore it up because I'm using your products. Really my mom tore it up because she doesn't want me to lie. Will you please send me a check for $10,000? Thanks so much!!! Amanda Dizon (The Girl in the Well)

*

She received a response within the hour.

Hello Amanda! We at Babylon Skincare appreciate your loyalty to our products and would love to talk to you. Please send us your phone or Skype number and some convenient times to call.

*

Lord, are those your parents! cried Nicole.

Sure enough, Amanda's parents were riding down the escalator, carrying a big Apple bag.

The girls ran to surprise them.

Guess what? exclaimed Amanda. Babylon Skincare wants to talk to me!

What's in the bag? asked Nicole.

Your father has finally allowed me to join the 21st century, said Amanda's mother.

Allowed?! wondered Amanda's father.

We each bought a phone, so we can now stay in touch and keep abreast of your PingPong. And we bought a MacBook.

You bought me a MacBook? exclaimed Amanda.

The MacBook is for me, said her father.

*

They celebrated their new acquisitions over dinner at the Olive Garden.

Maybe Olive Garden will send me ten thousand dollars too, said Amanda, tapping a breadstick on her plate.

She sucked on the breadstick thoughtfully.

Nicole snapped a picture, then thought better and deleted it.

*

When Amanda got home, she searched for the copy of Mr. Cole's card and found it on the floor behind her desk.

I hope it's not too late to call, said Amanda when the lawyer answered. This is Amanda, The Girl in the Well.

Hello Amanda, what can I do for you?

I want to be an LLC. And I want Babylon Skincare to pay me ten thousand dollars if I post they are the best in the world.

3

Amanda was awakened by the doorbell. Her phone read 9:15 a.m.

She thought it was a reporter or salesman. Who else would ring this early on a Saturday morning? Certainly, her friends slept later than this. Amanda, for her part, had been up till 4:00 a.m., reading and responding to comments.

Amanda? shouted her mother from the bottom of the stairs. Did you call Mr. Cole?

*

Scrambled eggs, bacon, toast, orange juice and coffee were quickly assembled on the table by Amanda's parents, who then joined their daughter and lawyer at the table for a business breakfast.

Forming a limited liability company would be a simple matter. The lawyer told them he would do it at no charge.

That's generous of you, said Amanda's father sarcastically. Considering you pocketed six figures for a few hours' work on the MakeItRain appeal.

People who want to understand money become economists, shot back the lawyer. People who want to make money become lawyers.

And he broke a piece of crisp bacon.

The LLC would have to be formed in her parents' names, as Amanda was a minor. But she could be a partner.

We just need a name for it, said the lawyer.

How about Dizon Enterprises? offered Amanda's father.

Amanda made a gesture of vomiting.

Archer Dizon Multimedia? suggested Amanda's mother, putting her own surname into the mix.

I want to call it Amanda911, said Amanda. Next!

*

The lawyer explained to Amanda that the LLC would have a bank account into which she would deposit her income and on which her parents and she could write checks.

Can I get the checks in plastic so my mom can't tear them up? asked Amanda snarkily.

Speaking of plastic, said the lawyer, I'm sure the bank will offer you a credit card with a favorable interest rate. Although I see no reason for you to incur credit card debt. As for paper checks, yes, while I still use them myself, and I'll bet your parents probably do too, your generation does all its financial transactions digitally. This will no doubt be more convenient for you. But you need someone to consult with for internet security.

White Hat Ned has his eagle eye on this, said Amanda confidently.

Who?

A school friend of hers, said Amanda's mother.

Oh yes, the boyfriend, said the lawyer with a smile.

But surely, we shouldn't keep all the money in a bank account, said Amanda's father.

If you are happy with your bank, stay with them. Request a business private banking account with a personal representative. A great perk, if you've never had it. Maintain the minimum balance to avoid fees, but transfer anything above ten to twenty thousand to your brokerage account or other investments. I assume, as an economist, you have investments?

Times have been hard, admitted Amanda's mother. We just have our retirement accounts.

I'm afraid I can't help you with that, said the lawyer. Although my sister-in-law is a financial planner. I think I have her card somewhere.

He rummaged in his thick, torn wallet for his sister-in-law's business card and passed it across the table.

I can help you with taxes though, said the lawyer. But being an economist, I'm sure you know more than I do.

The lawyer smiled humbly, and perhaps cleverly.

But if you don't want to dirty your hands with that, I don't mind including tax planning and preparation in my portfolio of services. Are you good with record keeping, young lady?

What's record keeping? asked Amanda.

Ha ha ha, laughed the lawyer. Well, you'll want to stay on top of that, as you'll have a lot of deductible expenses. Home office, utilities, computers, phones and other equipment. Business-related travel and meals. And since your life is literally your business, I think you have wide latitude here. Could I have another cup of coffee please?

But none of these things are the reason I came over here first thing on a Saturday morning, said the lawyer after taking a sip of his refilled mug. After all, the LLC filing and discussion about banking, investments and taxes could have waited until Monday.

Is there a problem? asked Amanda's father with a worried expression.

No, no, no assured the lawyer. It's just getting our hands around the sponsorships. Fortunately, I have a thirteen-year-old daughter, and she gave me a tutorial on the social media landscape. I spent several hours on PingPong—I'd be honored for a follow back—and I watched half a dozen YouTube videos about the life of an influencer.

Most influencers can't afford lawyers to review and negotiate sponsorship contracts, said the lawyer. They not only spend many hours a week pitching for business and going back and forth with sponsors over what is expected of them, but they make lots and lots of little deals, for instance bartering a free meal in a restaurant for a good review. That's probably unavoidable if you've only got five thousand followers.

But you have twenty million followers. Which means you don't need a hundred sponsorship deals. You don't need to haggle over free meals or allow sponsors to repost your testimonials on their own sites.

He reached into his briefcase and gave them each a copy of a sponsorship contract.

This is a template contract I drew up, said the lawyer. Normally, influencers sign the company's contract. In Amanda's, or I should say Amanda911's case, the company will sign our contract.

And I suppose you want 33% for this too, like the MakeItRain appeal? asked Amanda's father, feeling cheated.

No, I only want fifteen percent.

I'd rather pay per hour, said Amanda's father. What's your hourly rate?

I won't do an hourly rate, Mr. and Mrs. Dizon. I think my offer is in all our best interests.

But we'll be paying you much more this way, pointed out Amanda's father.

You should hope so, agreed the lawyer. But fame is fickle. What if Amanda loses her followers? What if a sponsor fails to pay, or sues for breach of contract? You can hire another lawyer, by all means, said the lawyer with one hand poised threateningly on the lid of his briefcase. But when your daughter calls him on a Friday night with an urgent request, she is going to get voicemail.

Dad, shhhh! said Amanda.

She looked hopefully into the lawyer's gray eyes. Do you think Babylon Skincare will pay me ten thousand dollars?

Oh, answered the lawyer. I think they will pay you much more.

*

The three amigas arrived in Nicole's Ford pickup just as the lawyer was leaving. And White Hat Ned arrived minutes later in his mother's Subaru.

After admiring the Jaguar in the driveway, they went inside and finished what was left of the breakfast while discussing the video shoot.

The video was Amy's idea. A lot of Amanda's Ping-Pong comments and questions concerned not just Iowa and the American Midwest, but Amanda's house specifically. Was it hundreds of years old? Was it painted red, like barns they had seen in movies? Did she have to go outside to pee? Were there ghosts?

Asians living in megacities found it particularly difficult to get their heads around the idea that she didn't know exactly where her family's property ended.

How many square meters is your property?

No idea.

*

Our flat in Hong Kong is nine square meters. How big is your house?

Are we talking about area or volume? In either case, no idea.

*

Can you play cricket in your back yard?

We have lots of crickets in summer.

So Amy came up with the brilliant idea to do a video tour of the house.

Nicole took over the project from there. She had stayed behind the camera until now, except for some selfies Amanda posted together with her friends. But this was an opportunity to get in front of the camera and, she hoped, boost her own PingPong account, which only had 338 followers.

White Hat Ned's father owned an actual video camera, and White Hat would serve as photographer. Amanda's parents would join the group, to give historical background and make sure no identifying information was revealed, such as their address, or valuable items that might attract burglars.

Valuable items like what? wondered Amanda. The most valuable thing we have is the statue of Krishna.

Vishnu, corrected her mother.

And I don't think there are any Indian burglars in Iowa, so we're safe.

Actually, they weren't safe, as White Hat Ned would tell her later. Anyone could take a screen shot of their home and do a reverse Google Image search. And the press or one of their classmates had probably already posted their address somewhere.

Your parents should have left the well open, said White Hat Ned. As a burglar trap.

*

Before shooting, Nicole asked that the Jaguar be parked down the street, and she moved her F-150 prominently into the driveway. She didn't want viewers to get the impression Amanda came from money.

Hi everyone, said Amanda, reading from a cue card introduction Nicole had written. So many of you have asked about where I live, so I wanted to give you a tour. This is my front yard, and this is our house. I live with my parents, Carole and Robert.

Amanda's mother and father smiled and waved, standing beside her, enjoying the novelty of their first social media video shoot.

And these are my friends: Amy, Nipuni and Nicole.

Nicole dropped the cue cards and made her first entrance into a major video, doing a cartwheel on the grass.

And White Hat Ned, my boyfriend, is behind the camera, added Amanda, blushing.

*

We're going to go inside now, said Amanda, walking slowly so that White Hat Ned could keep her in frame.

This was part of the three minutes of advice White Hat Ned had given her about making videos. To date all her photos and videos had been either reposts from professional media, such as the original video taken of her at the bottom of the well, or clumsy, unedited videos from her and her friends' phones.

This would be the first polished work, containing all three phases of a proper video: preproduction, production, and post-production. The planning and cue cards were the pre-production; the shooting itself the production; and White Hat Ned's editing would be the post-production.

But we can't let this be a slippery slope. That had been Nicole's admonition earlier at breakfast. You didn't get twenty million followers by following the rules, said Nicole. If you Hollywoodize everything you could lose every last follower.

*

This house was bought by my grandparents about a hundred years ago, said Amanda's mother after they entered the living room.

My great grandparents, added Amanda. Mama you have to be clear. People won't understand who you're talking about.

Yes, Amanda's great grandparents. They were farmers. The house then went to their son and his wife—my parents, Amanda's grandparents. Is that clear?

No, said Amanda. I'm getting a headache. Maybe someone can draw a family tree like *Game of Thrones*.

Do people really care that much about this family? asked Amanda's father.

They don't care about your family, said Amanda, not meaning to be rude. But there's a lot of interest in Iowa and how come I live on a farm if we're not farmers.

That's because Amanda's grandfather went to college and got a Ph.D. in English, said Amanda's mother. He and my mother, who was a schoolteacher before becoming a housewife, didn't want to farm.

Mama, you're making this too confusing. Tell them Gramps was a famous writer.

He was never famous, dear.

His name was Sutherland Archer. Look him up.

Not was, whispered Nipuni. He's still alive.

This house is very boring and not at all like most of you think, explained Amanda. We don't have outhouses or barns or stables or pigs and sheep. We don't have giant tractors and grain silos. The most interesting thing we have isn't even American. My Indian friends will be interested to see this statue on the fireplace—it's Vishnu. My Gramps brought it back from India in the days when he had money.

Not to mention lax customs regulations, remarked Amanda's father.

It's caused us a bit of trouble in the community because some people think the god Vishnu is Satan worship, admitted Amanda.

It's an idol, not the real God, said Nicole with an air of authority, drawing a derisive stare from Nipuni.

And look we have cable TV, continued Amanda. But for my whole life, until a few days ago, we only had five channels. And they didn't come in good. And we didn't have computers. Can I show them the landline?

They went into the kitchen to view the landline on the wall. And while they were there Amanda opened the cabinets and refrigerator to show her followers what they ate.

This probably isn't interesting to you guys, said Amanda. I know it's not interesting to me.

Here's the dining room, said Amanda. Except we hardly ever have more than two people over, so we always eat in the kitchen.

And here's my parents' bedroom. Don't ask me what goes on in here. I don't want to know. But you can see from the bookshelves that they read a lot. Look, here are some books about farming, and about bankruptcy.

Where is Gramps' book? asked Amanda.

*

Sorry it takes me so long to go up the stairs, said Amanda, being helped by her friends. But I've still got the cast on. Maybe we can edit this or make it go fast speed, like people do on YouTube? Now you're going to see my new home office, and where I sleep.

And make out, added Amy.

Edit that! exclaimed Amanda.

First here's a guest bedroom. If any of you ever visit me this is where you would sleep.

Edit that! said Amanda's mother. You can't invite strangers to visit.

Twenty million strangers! said Nipuni.

Aren't we at twenty-one yet? asked Amy. We seem to be plateauing.

We? asked Amanda's father.

And here's another bedroom, said Amanda. But there's no bed. Just boxes and more books. As you can see, we don't get many visitors. And here's my bathroom. God, I guess I should have cleaned up first. Don't film that!

Welcome to the party room! said Amy in Amanda's bedroom, as White Hat Ned panned around. Let's look in the closet.

Hey! shouted Amanda. Don't listen to her, friends. I've never had parties here, or even guests except for these guys. Oh, I had the slumber party, but that's it. I never was popular. And as you can see, this room is built for work. It's a home office, added Amanda, having become enamored of the term and using it whenever she could.

White Hat Ned motioned to the window.

Oh, and this is my view, said Amanda. The other bedrooms are bigger, you might have noticed. But I took this one because I prefer the view out back and the other rooms look onto the street. In a moment we will go outside for a closer look. The backyard. Our sycamore tree. The filled-in well. And the fence where our farm used to be before my parents screwed up. I'm hoping they'll grow hemp next time.

Edit that, whispered Amanda's mother.

*

After a tour of the back, including a meeting with Luna, who was scampering around the garage, they called it a wrap and went inside for lemonade.

White Hat Ned said he'd better get home to start editing, and his mom needed the car back. The girls hoped to hang out, but Amanda's father said they had a college visit.

Amanda shrugged. This was news to her.

Nicole, of course, had come not only to make the video, but to claim her vehicle. She feared Amanda's mother would change her mind, or never intended to let her drive it in the first place. But Amanda's mother motioned to the key fob on a hook. Nicole traded it for the keys to her F-150 and shot off as fast as an actual jaguar.

So where are we going? asked Amanda, sitting in the back of the Camry, absently scrolling on her phone.

A recruiter from Iowa State invited us for a tour, said her father.

A tour of what?

Of the university, silly, said her mother.

You're going back to college? asked Amanda with surprise.

You! It's for you, said her father impatiently. Can you stop being dense for once!

Don't shout at her, said her mother.

I can shout at my daughter if I want! shouted Amanda's father.

No, you can't, said Amanda without meaning to be subordinate, but just stating a law of the cosmos, like gravity or the speed of light.

That would piss off my followers, said Amanda.

*

Iowa State University was located in the city of Ames, population 67,154. The student enrollment was almost half that. The campus was designed for strolling, with wide lawns crisscrossed by wide footpaths. But because of Amanda's cast the recruiter had thoughtfully arranged for a golf cart to whisk them around.

He introduced himself as Mr. West. He gave Amanda an information packet and then handed her an Iowa State Cyclones cap to wear.

Red and gold just aren't my colors, said Amanda, tossing the hat onto the front seat of the cart.

Can I have one with the Hawkeye on it?

It seemed the tour might end before it started. They were about to get in the golf cart, but Mr. West and Amanda's parents froze. Mr. West struggled to contort his grimace into a smile.

You know, the black cap with the yellow icon of the bird? persisted Amanda. Or it can be a yellow hat with a black bird.

Are you UI alumnae? guessed the recruiter, looking in horror at Amanda's parents.

UI was the University of Iowa. The Hawkeyes. Bitter rivals of the Iowa State Cyclones, 138 miles away by road in Iowa City. A veritable megacity compared with Ames.

My dad says the Big Twelve Conference is for dweebs, said Amanda.

The Big Twelve was an athletic organization of major schools of higher education, including Texas, Oklahoma and Kansas universities, among others. The University of Iowa, on the other hand, belonged to the Big Ten, which included Ohio State, Michigan, and Penn State, among others.

Amanda's father was shaking his head in vast embarrassment.

I have a question, said Amanda. Have you guys ever beat Oklahoma at football? I mean, like ever?

She let the ensuing silence play out for several seconds, deeply regretting none of this precious scene was being documented.

Finally, she grabbed the cap and put it on.

I'm just joshing you! said Amanda. Ha, ha, ha! I was born in this state, for crying out loud. You have to be deaf, dumb and blind not to know when the Hawkeyes and Cyclones are playing football. The whole state shuts down. Even on our old TV, which only got five channels, the game came on crystal clear.

*

Amanda's parents sat in the back and Mr. West drove across Union Drive to the Golden Loop, presided over by the Campanile, a brick and terra cotta bell tower built in 1897, that served as the university's signature landmark and symbol.

Can I take pictures? asked Amanda.

Please do, said the recruiter.

It was a beautiful autumn day, the leaves on the sycamore trees vibrant shades of ocher and crimson. As they drove on, Amanda was impressed by the neoclassical buildings with their Corinthian columns and carved pediments, although she didn't know anything about architecture, only that she liked these old buildings better than the modern structures like the unadorned Design Building.

The campus was quiet, since it was a Saturday and the football team was playing in Kansas. But many of the students who were on the grounds recognized Amanda and some came over for selfies.

Are you planning to take the PSAT? asked the recruiter.

What's that?

Are you joshing me again? asked the recruiter.

My dad thinks I'm dense. So you tell me.

Amanda's mother elbowed Amanda's father. See what you get?

Though I have to admit I didn't know what *dense* meant until just now. Thank God for *Urban Dictionary,* said Amanda, glancing at her phone.

So, the PSAT... said the recruiter.

Tests make me nervous. My parents are bugging me to take it. But I don't want to.

But that's the point of the PSAT, explained the recruiter. It's practice. So that you won't be nervous when you take the SAT.

But if I'm nervous taking the practice test, doesn't that just make me practice being nervous?

None of the adults were quite sure how to answer that question.

I hope I'm not wasting your time, said Amanda.

Not at all, said the recruiter. In fact, a student's SAT score is just one of many factors we consider in her application.

If you consider PingPong followers, I guess I've got a shot, said Amanda, glancing back at her phone.

4

Amanda was wakened by a loud noise. It was her phone ringing. She reached for it under her pillow.

Only six people had her number. Her parents, her three friends, and White Hat Ned. And her friends never actually called her; they always texted.

But here was Nicole, calling.

Oh, I'm so sorry, sorry, sorry...

Amanda could almost feel the tears, so earnest was her friend in her mysterious remorse.

Amanda shivered herself awake. The phone read 2:15 a.m.

I'm so sorry, sorry, sorry... It's the end of my life!!!

Suddenly Amanda understood without Nicole saying another word. The Jaguar.

*

Amanda was still wiping the sleep from her eyes when she trailed her parents into the Montgomery County Police Department.

She expected to see her friend in handcuffs or behind bars, so she was relieved when Nicole rushed over and threw her arms around her, sobbing.

Amanda cried, too, the way people cough when other people are coughing. But in truth things weren't so bad in Amanda's eyes. Nicole wasn't in a hospital or a jail cell.

I screwed up...

At least you're not dead. Did the airbag go off? asked Amanda.

Nicole showed her fresh bruises around her eyes.

Don't be so sad about the car, said Amanda. I can buy you another one.

Get away from my daughter, exclaimed Amanda's mother, pushing Nicole away.

She stared at her daughter as if she were an alien. And you—that's your reaction to your supposed best friend wrecking your unbelievably generous gift? Buy her another one?

Yup.

Amanda smelled Nicole's father before she saw him, and the mystery of why his body odor made her want to puke but didn't bother anyone else in the room occupied her thoughts almost as much as the damaged Jaguar.

I had no idea you bought her a car, said Nicole's father anxiously to Amanda's parents. I never would have consented to this, I want you to know.

So you lied to us, Nicole? Amanda's mother asked in a voice of rage.

That's why you weren't at the dealer for the lease signing, said Amanda's father to Nicole's father.

You shouldn't have agreed to letting our daughter lease an expensive car for her friend, said Amanda's mother to Amanda's father.

But you're the one who argued it's her money and that it's only right to let her spend part of it, said Amanda's father in his defense.

You didn't have to agree! shouted Amanda's mother.

Amanda was getting a headache from the bright fluorescent lights, Nicole's father's body odor, and her parents' shouting.

I don't understand, said Amanda softly to her devastated friend. You're such a careful driver. How could you crash into a tree?

Where's the car? asked Amanda's mother.

Towed away, said the officer in charge. I'm afraid it's totaled.

You didn't even have the car for one day! shouted Amanda's mother at Nicole.

If Nicole's father hadn't been there, and if they hadn't been in a police station, Amanda's mother probably would have ripped out Nicole's beautiful blond hair.

You couldn't wait a week before totaling a forty thousand dollar car? screamed Amanda's mother. You had to destroy it the first night?

Amanda ignored her mother's outbursts and continued to wait for an answer to her question.

I wasn't driving, whispered Nicole.

It was only then that the Dizon party noticed another family, sitting morosely to the side, on a wooden bench.

Amanda recognized the tall boy as the senior football player who had tried to kiss her in her hospital room. Her first potential kiss, quashed by her mother.

And *now* what might her mother do to this boy?

What?! said all the Dizons at once.

He asked me out, said Nicole. And I wanted to show him the car. So, we drove to McDonald's. And then he asked if he could drive and I said no and he asked again and I said no and he asked again and I said...

And he crashed my car into a tree?! shouted Amanda's mother.

So tense was the atmosphere in the police station that only Amanda, the calmest one among them, noticed that her mother had said *my* car. Maybe that's why she was so angry, thought Amanda. Because she hoped to get the Jaguar back.

Now of course she *would* get it back. But in a form more resembling an immobile modern sculpture than a stylish SUV.

The football player's parents sulked over.

We're fully insured for the damage, said the football player's father. And we'll pay the towing and any other costs.

Oh, you'll pay all right! screamed Amanda's mother. And your son will go to jail.

Actually, Mrs. Dizon, if I can have a word with you and your husband, said the officer in charge. We called you here because your name is on the title. But we haven't charged the young man, or your daughter's friend. You see, the breathalyzer was negative for alcohol, we didn't find any drugs in their possession, his license is valid, and his record clean. Also, there were no skid marks and the impact, while great enough to total the car, doesn't indicate they were traveling at a dangerous speed.

So how do you run off the road and crash into a tree if you're not speeding or drunk or high? wondered Amanda's father.

I was changing the radio and didn't see a curve, said the football player with eyes averted.

The Parkers have promised to call their insurance agent first thing Monday morning, said the officer in charge. Teenagers make mistakes, Mr. and Mrs. Dizon, as I'm sure you and your husband probably did in your youth.

My youth is none of your god damned business! shouted Amanda's mother. I never wrecked a forty thousand dollar car. And she never should have let someone else drive it. And on the first fucking day!

Mrs. Dizon, I understand you're upset, said the officer in charge. But let's be thankful no one was injured. Mr. Parker works in the insurance business and has promised me personally to take care of all expenses. We wouldn't want one incident to ruin young Parker's future, would we? Especially considering his scholarship to play wide receiver for the Hawkeyes next year.

Oh sure, I get it, said Amanda's mother. If this were a female lacrosse player, I'm sure you'd show the same concern for *her* future.

Amanda had sidled up to the football player.

Why aren't you going to Iowa State?

They always lose to Oklahoma.

I know, right? A recruiter gave us a tour of the Cyclones' campus today—or yesterday— and it looks awesome.

Maybe, but it's in Ames. You have to decide if you want to be in a tiny city like Ames or a big city like Iowa City, said the football player perceptively.

Is Iowa City a megacity? Because I told everyone we don't have megacities in Iowa.

I dunno.

You think I should get a tour of UI? asked Amanda.

Definitely. And if you go there, I'll be a year ahead. So, you'll know someone. I'll get you football tickets.

Really?

Amanda! shouted Amanda's mother. Why are you talking to him? Get away from there.

And you! shouted Amanda's mother to Nicole. Don't ever come to my house or talk to my daughter again.

Just one more thing before you go, said the officer in charge. We would much appreciate it if the night crew and I could get a photo with your daughter for our Facebook page.

5

When Amanda got home, she decided to sleep on the couch, too tired to hobble upstairs. She slept till noon and then ventured trepidatiously into the kitchen, fearing her mother's wrath.

But Mrs. Dizon was in a nurturing mood. She had kept breakfast on a hot tray and the rest of the table was covered with notebooks, pens and other office items from a trip to Staples.

You've gotta be organized if you want to run a business, said her mother.

OK.

You know how before the school year we always buy folders and other supplies? Well, it's the same for business. Look at this appointment book.

Didn't they have Hello Kitty? Or unicorns?

No, silly. It's for professionals. When are you going to grow out of that?

I don't know. Never.

Well, maybe you can stick decals on the cover. Because what this does is help you organize your day. See, you can schedule tasks in fifteen-minute increments, and—

Wait, said Amanda. Where's the rest of the day.

Each page is a day.

But it's only from 8:00 a.m. to 8:00 p.m. And there's no Saturday or Sunday, observed Amanda, turning the pages.

So?

They obviously didn't make these for influencers. We work 24/7, Mama.

*

Amanda doodled with the silver Cross pen her mother had bought.

Can't you buy me pens with neon colored ink? asked Amanda.

Sure, next time. Listen, babe. I want to talk about Nicole. You have to understand she's not your friend. She's just using you.

That's not true!

Honey, you can't simply buy people things.

You're telling me this after having just bought me all this stuff? said Amanda, holding up the pen and appointment book as evidence.

This is different. It's for your business. And I'm your mother. What I mean is, you can't go through life paying people to like you. The world doesn't work that way.

I think it works exactly that way, said Amanda. Look at the candidates coming through here, promising subsidies for corn and soybeans so we like them. Or vote for them, which is the same thing as liking, right? So, if instead of giving Nicole a Jaguar I gave her forty thousand dollars in corn that would be cool with you? Tell me the difference, Mama?

Amanda's mother, in the pressure of the moment, could not tell her the difference.

*

There was a cautious knock on the door. Amanda's mother greeted a hipster web designer, wearing suspenders and a goatee.

Amanda's mother made room on the table and the hipster web designer opened his laptop. Amanda didn't pay attention to his name and tuned out his questions. She stood.

White Hat Ned is doing my website, said Amanda.

I'm afraid not, said her mother. You're a business now and you have to take that seriously.

I am taking it seriously. I was serious enough to accept a check for ten thousand dollars, which you then tore up.

I know Ned is your friend.

Boyfriend too, said Amanda proudly.

Be that as it may. You can't go around trying to please people.

Good, because I'm not gonna please you. Sorry, Mista Hipsta. Your services are not required.

*

I saved your ass, said Amanda later that day.

She and White Hat Ned were in her room, working on her website.

You owe me, said Amanda.

You mean, like in return I need to set up your home office and make you a website for free? asked White Hat Ned.

Sorry. I guess I'm the one that owes you. I'll find out what my mom was going to pay the hipster and I'll pay you instead. Is that fair?

I don't want your money.

What do you want then?

White Hat Ned looked at her, and Amanda remembered that he wasn't just an eminently useful computer geek but also a young man with a young man's needs.

No!!! exclaimed Amanda.

Maybe, said Amanda upon further consideration.

*

But they didn't have much time for kissing, such are the demands of website creation. And the door was wide open, per Mrs. Dizon's instructions.

She hates you enough already, said Amanda. If she finds me undressed it could really get ugly. Besides, I'm not ready for that.

I know. But you'll tell me when you are?

I'll send you a text, said Amanda with a smile.

But why does your mom hate me? asked White Hat Ned. I treat your parents with respect.

I dunno. Maybe she's not ready for me to have a boyfriend. She's always telling me to grow up, but when I do, she hates that even more!

*

Later that day a reporter and photographer from the *Sentinel* came to the house to interview Amanda for Tuesday morning's edition.

The local press had been begging the Dizons for interviews since Amanda fell down the well, and her parents felt a newspaper interview at their home, with them included, would be both convenient and safe.

But the Features writer, another hipster—two hipsters in their house in one day!—began the interview as if he were a London tabloid journo, asking about reports that the family had staged the tragedy for attention.

Amanda's parents were sitting on either side of her on the sofa and leaned in closer, as if the outrageous allegation required physically protecting her.

That's an outrageous allegation! shouted her mother. Who is

claiming such a thing? I haven't heard anyone asserting that.

You're not reading my comments, said Amanda to her mother, unperturbed. People believe all kinds of wacky things. But White Hat Ned says it's just the Russians trying to make trouble.

I'm ending this interview now, said Amanda's mother. Get out of my house!

Wait, said Amanda's father. Carole, you can't deal with conspiracy theories by getting defensive. It just makes their believers believe them even more.

I don't care what some idiots believe, said Amanda's mother. Get out of my house!

The reporter merely twirled his handlebar mustache.

I like conspiracy theories, said Amanda. I've seen crop circles with my own eyes. And there's a unicorn skeleton in the basement of the Smithsonian, but nobody's allowed to see it. But we really did land on the moon, right?

I wasn't trying to imply you guys staged the fall, said the reporter uneasily. I only wanted a response to rumors that have been circulating.

And my parents think I jumped, said Amanda. Which to me is worse than a conspiracy theory.

We never believed you jumped! exclaimed Amanda's mother, alarmed, worried this interview would traumatize her daughter more than the actual fall had.

Dad said 'jump' that one time.

Is it true that you received counseling in the past? asked the Features writer for the *Sentinel*.

Briefly, when she was ten, said Amanda's father. But that's only because she was in our classes in fourth grade and we pressured her to overachieve.

So, you aren't suicidal now? asked the Features writer for the *Sentinel*.

No.

Ahh! That's a trick question, honey, said Amanda's mother. It implies you were suicidal before. Tell him you were never suicidal.

But Amanda was more interested in conspiracy theories.

The people who think this was a hoax have never been in the bottom a well, said Amanda with indisputable logic. If you are someone who *has* been in the bottom of a well with skanky water in it, with two broken ankles, then I'll be glad to talk to you. Otherwise, shut up. I mean, if I wanted to stage this, I would have brought snacks, and hand sanitizer. I could have gotten a flesh-eating bacteria down there.

Amanda looked at her hands with sudden concern.

*

Monday Amanda took her lunch tray to the popular girls' table and sat next to the most unpopular-feeling girl in all of Iowa.

The other cheerleaders, glam girls, and non-geeky honor students showered Amanda with attention, while Nicole shyly picked at her salad.

They had never given Amanda attention before, but now they treated her like the celebrity she was:

Can you follow me on YouTube?

Can I friend you on Snap?

Can we hang sometime?

Can I interview you for my blog?

Do you need a financial advisor? My dad asked me to ask.

Sure, sure, sure, sure don't think so.

Your face looks better, said Amanda to Nicole.

I found a great YouTuber on how to cover up bruises, said Nicole. What are you doing here? Your mom said not to talk to me.

I don't think she was serious.

I think she was very serious.

I'm going to our table, if you wanna join, said Amanda.

Amanda stood up with her tray and looked at the popular girls. Bye, y'all.

*

Amanda sat across from Amy and Nipuni at their usual table. Nicole crept in behind.

But if Nicole expected her Diversity Crew friends to cheer her up, she was mistaken.

Amy displayed a picture of the totaled Jaguar on her phone.

Oh my God, cried Amanda.

Where'd you get that?! exclaimed Nicole, grabbing the phone from Amy's hand.

The *Sentinel* website. 'Expensive Joyride for Area Teens,' read Amy, taking her phone back.

I hope he catches a football better than he drives, remarked Nipuni.

And the two girls exploded with laughter.

Nicole exploded in tears and ran off.

Amanda rose to follow, but Amy grabbed her arm.

Let her go, said Amy. She wrecked your car. Why aren't you angry with her?

It wasn't my car, said Amanda.

That was a mistake, said Nipuni. You see that, right? We told you all along.

You did?

You didn't hear us asking you to buy us cars, did you? Nipuni asked, taking a bite of her apple.

We didn't ask you for anything, echoed Amy. We're your true friends. You can see that, right? You can see the difference?

You didn't ask for the Chromebook Ned gave me. You just took it, pointed out Amanda.

She picked up her egg salad sandwich, but her appetite was gone.

We want to talk about something else, said Amy.

We have a proposal, said Nipuni.

A proposal?

We realized you're gonna need a lot of help as your career ramps up, said Amy.

Yes, Amanda agreed. I've got a lawyer now. And White Hat Ned is making a website. And my mom bought me an appointment book, but it's not 24/7, so I don't know how I'm gonna use that.

But you're going to need even more help, said Nipuni.

We watched a bunch of YouTube videos about influencers, said Amy, eating her fruit salad. It's a lot harder than you think.

But I think it's very hard.

A lot of them hire publicists. Not the random influencers, but the star influencers with millions of followers, who can afford it. Because publicists are very expensive.

What does a publicist do?

She gets you interviews and stuff, said Nipuni, taking another bite of her apple.

I had an interview yesterday with the *Sentinel*. So, I think I'm good without a publicist, said Amanda.

But they also help with spin, added Amy. It's not just about getting you an interview here or there. It's about managing your press coverage and your image.

Mmmmm.

And a publicist can be a go-between, said Amy. That way you don't have to deal directly with all the requests for your time. Who arranged the interview with the *Sentinel*?

My mom.

And did it go all right?

She tried to kick him out, but he wouldn't go.

So, you want your mom to be your publicist? asked Amy shrewdly.

Point taken, said Amanda. How much does a publicist cost?

A lot, said Nipuni. Thousands a month.

But I'm proposing to do this for you, said Amy.

We, clarified Nipuni.

And you'll also need a personal assistant for clerical help. Printing things, making copies, opening mail, both email and regular mail. How many emails do you think star influencers get every day?

I'm already getting hundreds, said Amanda.

Yes, and that's probably going to get worse. If you read email yourself you won't have time for anything else. And once you start getting sponsors, you're going to be getting lots of packages. One

influencer says she spends an hour a day just breaking down boxes and throwing them away.

Gosh!

So Nipuni can do the clerical work. And I can be your publicist,
said Amy, stabbing a mandarin orange with her fork.

That's not what we talked about! exclaimed Nipuni. I want to be a
publicist too.

Deal, said Amanda, holding out her hand for them to shake.

Umm, said Amy. We want to do it as a job.

We want to be paid, said Nipuni.

She traded an anxious glance with Amy, wondering if she had
gone too far.

OK, said Amanda with a smile, her hand still extended.

Nipuni shook it gratefully.

Wait, said Amy. Don't you want to know how much we want?

How much do you want?

Five hundred dollars a month, said Nipuni with renewed confidence.

Each, added Amy.

Sure, said Amanda. But you're gonna have to wait till I get my LLC
checks.

No problem, said Amy, devouring her mandarin orange.

*

What's going on? White Hat Ned asked, sitting beside Amanda. He
had seen the girls shaking hands.

Nothing, said Nipuni.

Nothing, said Amy.

They offered to work for me as a personal assistant and a publicist, said Amanda.

Oh, that's great, said White Hat Ned. I'm sure you can use the help.

For five hundred dollars a month, said Amanda.

Five hundred dollars? inquired White Hat Ned.

Each, clarified Amanda.

You're going to pay them?

Real publicists cost thousands a month. And I don't know what it costs to have someone read hundreds of emails a day and break down boxes. So I think it's a good deal for me. And I'm sure Puni and Amy can use the money. So win-win, said Amanda excitedly, holding out her fist for White Hat Ned to bump.

But before White Hat Ned could bump—and I'm not saying he would have done so, even if Amanda left her fist over his tray for a thousand years—Martin Decker sat down on the other side of Amanda, without a tray, and bumped her first instead.

Hi girls, said Martin Decker. Hi Ned. I just saw Nicole bawling her eyes out. Boy trouble again?

You mean you don't know? asked Amy. She showed him the *Sentinel* photo.

Where the fuck did she get a jag? wondered Martin.

Aman— started Nipuni.

Her father, said Amy quickly. It's her father's. Leased. Brand new. She's grounded for like a century.

Shit! exclaimed Martin.

He scrolled through the story. So Nicole's going out with that wide receiver jerk now?

Why is he a jerk? asked Amanda, still regretting that unconsummated kiss.

Because he pressured Nicole to drive her car, said Amy. Obviously. And who knows what else he pressured her into?

I'll kill him! shouted Martin, with an anger that surprised them all.

What's it to you? asked Amy.

Ha! said Martin, reading the rest of the story. It says he lost control of the car while trying to change the radio.

That's what he said at the police station, confirmed Amanda.

I'll bet that's what he said, remarked Martin. And what did Nicole say?

6

The following morning Amanda's mother found her daughter staring at the invitation to the New Year's Influencer Festival at Turks and Caicos. Amanda had affixed it to the refrigerator with a rainbow magnet.

So, can I go? asked Amanda when she noticed her mother.

I looked at their site and did some checking, said Amanda's mother. It seems on the up-and-up. I suppose we can go, if your dad doesn't object.

I told you I'm not going with you. I can't go with you.

Then with whom?

I don't know. But I need to RSVP. The deadline is September 30. I don't need to put in my guest's name. So, can I RSVP, and if I find a responsible adult can I go?

Knock yourself out, said her mother, assuming her daughter would not be able to find a suitable chaperone and would, in the end, consent to taking her.

And where's the newspaper? asked Amanda.

Her parents belonged to that nearly extinct species that still got daily delivery of a physical newspaper.

I don't know, lied her mother. Maybe it's late today.

You know today's the day my interview is out?

Is it? asked her mother. Oh, look at the time. I have to get going. Do you want me to make you an egg before I leave?

*

Martin Decker sauntered over to Amanda while she was rummaging in her locker before first bell. He was wearing black jeans and a white Banana Republic t-shirt. Amanda noticed a Polynesian tattoo on his right bicep. His braces gleamed and his blue eyes seemed to hold in their vision no one else but her.

Good morning, said Martin Decker.

Good morning, said Amanda.

I guess you're very busy these days.

Very!!!

How long has it been since you fell in the well? A year?

Seems like it. Two weeks yesterday.

Was this a conversation? Amanda could still count on one hand the conversations she had had with dream teen boys not named White Hat Ned.

If you can find time for me, I'd like to take you out Friday, said Martin Decker.

OK.

Great. Pick you up around eight?

Wait!!!

Amanda was flustered. Did he see her blush? She was so pumped, on the one hand, that he had asked her out, while on the other hand she was so impressed by his effortless style—why couldn't she talk to people like that?—that she had answered in the affirmative without letting the ramifications circulate through her cerebral cortex—the higher functioning part of the brain.

Are you asking me out on a date? asked Amanda.

While she wanted Martin Decker to say yes because that would flatter her minimal vanity, she wanted him to say no because that would give her a kind of legal reason to see him without violating her relationship with White Hat Ned.

Martin Decker said yes.

Oh.

Amanda gazed into her locker, as if the solution to this dilemma lay somewhere between her folded sweater and her textbooks.

But you know I have a boyfriend? said Amanda at last.

I know.

So you want me to break up with him?

Amanda could feel her heart racing. She couldn't break up with White Hat Ned. Not only because she still liked him and still wanted to see him—and needed that website finished if we want to admit that our heroine had a bit of a scheming side, just a bit.

But, in addition to those reasons, she didn't know how to break up with someone. She'd never had a boyfriend before to break up with. When was she supposed to do it? What was she supposed to say? What if he slapped her or, worse, cried?

Martin Decker said no.

But I don't want to break up with him— started Amanda. Wait, did you say no?

I'm polyamorous, said Martin Decker.

Amanda stared. Really? You're a Mormon?

Look it up, said Martin Decker.

He gave her a wink and sauntered away.

*

White Hat Ned walked up a moment later.

Was that Marty? asked White Hat Ned.

White Hat Ned was dressed in wrinkled jeans and a St. Louis Cardinals sweatshirt a size too large. He didn't have gleaming braces, though his teeth could have used them. Cute as he was, his clout wasn't amplified by proximity in space or time to Martin Decker.

He sat at our table yesterday. And now he's talking to you today. What does he want? asked White Hat Ned.

Ohhhhhhhhhh, I dunno.

*

White Hat Ned kept a close eye on her after American History class and made sure to accompany her into the cafeteria. He was relieved not to see Martin Decker at their table. Amy and Nipuni greeted Amanda with distressed expressions.

What is it? asked Amanda, opening her lunchbox.

She hasn't seen, whispered Nipuni to Amy.

Go ahead and eat, said Amy. We don't want to spoil your lunch.

Amanda grabbed Nipuni's phone and saw the electronic edition of the Iowa *Sentinel*:

Suicidal Iowan Chooses Life and Gains a Following

I can't believe this, said Amanda, reading the story. I'm not suicidal. Never been.

Nipuni grabbed her phone back. You don't need to read this. Actors don't read their reviews. It's like with trolls. You'll drive yourself nuts if you read all this stuff.

But this isn't some crazy kid in a basement, said Amanda. This is a respected newspaper.

Only people in nursing homes read the *Sentinel*, said Nipuni, trying to cheer her up. The only reason we're reading it is because we knew your interview was in it today.

What do I do? asked Amanda.

Go on the offensive, suggested Amy. Do another interview. Today. But TV. All the stations are after you. Your mom is probably hanging up on them. I'm your publicist—

We're your publicists, corrected Nipuni.

Let me call one of the stations and set something up for after school. Maybe they can shoot it here. I'll lay some ground rules, and if they try to ambush you, we'll never give them any access in the future. Sound good?

OK, said Amanda.

*

She found Nicole with the popular girls. Or perhaps from now on we should say the *other* popular girls, because no one in Harding High, or perhaps all of Iowa, was more popular than Amanda Dizon. And, having passed the two-week mark—which was like two hundred weeks in social media time—with her followers still climbing at twenty-four million, it seemed her popularity was not about to wane any time soon.

Indeed, if anything, the sensationalistic and erroneous *Sentinel* interview would only gain her more followers among the mental health community.

You ran off crying yesterday, said Amanda to her friend. I didn't see you again.

Your mom will be pissed if she finds you with me.

How is that going to happen here? She's in the elementary school.

Any of these hundreds of kids can snap a pic of us and post it, said Nicole with obvious logic.

But Amanda scoffed. Don't worry. She's still trying to figure out where the Home button is.

Amanda took a minute to eat her tuna salad sandwich, because she was starving. One of the benefits, perhaps the only benefit, she now realized, of being unpopular, was that you always had time to eat your lunch.

Why didn't you tell me Martin Decker was a Mormon? asked Amanda.

Nicole looked at her friend in shock. Because he's not! What gave you that idea?

He said he doesn't care if I have a boyfriend. He asked me out for Friday and when I said I have a boyfriend he said that was cool.

Mormons work the other way round, explained Nicole. Men can have more than one wife, but women have to stay loyal. And anyway, I think they changed that rule.

Oh, said Amanda. So, what is he? He said amorous something.

He's a player. That's what he is. That's why I dumped him.

I wanted to ask you, said Amanda. Is it safe to go on a date with him? My mom thinks every guy but my dad is #MeToo.

Yeah, he's OK in that way, said Nicole, thinking. But still, you don't have experience. It's better if you're not alone with him. We could go on a double date, but your mom would kill me.

You have a new boyfriend? asked Amanda, assuming the relationship with the wide receiver was finito.

No, but I can always snap my fingers and get a date, said Nicole with the kind of confidence Amanda didn't think she would ever have, even if she got fifty million followers.

I'll tell you what, said Nicole, thinking. Tell him you want to go to the movies. I'll follow you in with my date and keep an eye on things.

*

Amy and Nipuni got permission to hold the interview in their English class. They thought a classroom would remind everyone

Amanda was a normal girl. She wasn't in therapy. Nor had she let social media stardom turn her head.

Also, it was convenient.

The reporter agreed and wasted no time setting up with her cameraman. She decided that she and Amanda would sit at desks next to each other, like classmates, and the cameraman would use a shotgun microphone rather than her holding one, to give a more natural impression.

My name is Lisa Wilson, said the reporter, who was Iowa born-and-bred.

I've watched you a lot, said Amanda. Fortunately, when we only got five channels on our TV, your station was one of them.

I know we're not *Just Us Girls*, said the Iowa born-and-bred reporter with unnecessary modesty. But I hope you're excited to do this interview.

Mmmmm.

The *Sentinel* story was awful. I wish you had come to us first. I want to assure you I won't be asking those kinds of questions. Are you ready?

Mmmmm.

The Iowa Born-and-Bred Reporter: I'm very excited to sit down with a young lady who needs no introduction to our viewers. In fact, she's already gained an international following on social media. But this all started with a horrific accident. And it was an accident?

Amanda: Yes. Definitely.

The Iowa Born-and-Bred Reporter: You didn't jump. You weren't assaulted. We can put all those rumors to rest once and for all?

Amanda: I hope so.

The Iowa Born-and-Bred Reporter: And you're OK? Except for your ankle, which is still obviously healing? You're not having nightmares about the incident? You don't have PTSD?

Amanda: What's that?

The Iowa Born-and-Bred Reporter: Post-traumatic stress disorder.

Amanda: I feel good.

The Iowa Born-and-Bred Reporter: Now that we have that out of the way, I'd like to talk about how this experience has changed you.

Amanda:

The Iowa Born-and-Bred Reporter: How has it changed you?

Amanda: I'm popular now. I wasn't before. And I have a...

She was about to say *boyfriend*. But seeing that she has consented to a date with Martin Becker, and that she couldn't recall the word *polyamorous*, she decided to say nothing about her love life.

Amanda: And I have a college fund now. And a lawyer. And I'm a corporation. But I'm still the same person I was before all this happened.

The Iowa Born-and-Bred Reporter: Rainbows and unicorns and Honey Pops and Luna your cat?

Amanda: How did you know?

The Iowa Born-and-Bred Reporter: We all know a lot about you. But what we don't know are your future plans. Will you continue to live here, or move to the big city?

Amanda: You mean Des Moines?

The Iowa Born-and-Bred Reporter: I mean Chicago, L.A., New York. Will you pursue a career in acting, modeling, fashion?

Amanda: Me?!

The Iowa Born-and-Bred Reporter: The world is your oyster.

Amanda: I don't know what that means.

The Iowa Born-and-Bred Reporter: It means you can do anything you want. Be anything you want. What do you want, Amanda?

Amanda:

The Iowa Born-and-Bred Reporter: Amanda?

Amanda: I guess what I want is...not to disappoint anyone.

The Iowa Born-and-Bred Reporter: What makes you think you disappoint people?

Amanda: Because they tell me. My parents, my teachers. 'Amanda, we're disappointed in you.' 'Amanda, you can do better.' But what if I can't?

*

No more fucking interviews! screamed her mom after Amanda and her parents watched the six o'clock news from the comfort of their living room.

Why are you yelling? asked Amanda. I thought it was a great interview. I'm getting used to them. I wasn't nervous at all, like I was on *Just Us Girls*. And Lisa was so nice. She wants to do a follow-up next month.

I'm declaring a moratorium on press coverage, said her mother. What were you thinking, saying that about your father and me?

Yes, Amanda, said her father, upset as well but not as demonstrative.

Saying what? asked Amanda.

That we're disappointed in you.

You shouldn't have said that, said her father.

So wait, said Amanda. So you're disappointed in me now for saying you say you're disappointed in me?

There was a moment of confused silence as they all tried to get their heads around this.

How do you think that makes us look? said her mother, evading the question. Your father and I always loved you.

I didn't say you didn't love me.

That's what you imply when you claim we're disappointed. We love you unconditionally.

That's not how it feels.

We accept you as you are.

Yeah, right.

7

But the Dizons' fear that their image as loving, supportive parents would be tarnished within the community was soon proved to be unfounded. The interview was a great success, with fellow Iowans appreciating, above all, that Amanda did not consider herself too important to talk to the local media.

Their fellow teachers, students, friends and neighbors, shopkeepers and restauranteurs all said what great parents they were to have raised such a courageous, humble, stable, practical daughter. You must be very proud of her, said all these people.

We are, said Amanda's mother, beaming with joy.

We are, said Amanda's father, smiling with rational exuberance.

No one implied things had ever been different, even though Amanda had stated as much, clear as a bell, for all of Iowa to her.

And in time the Dizons themselves would come to believe they had always been proud of her, had always believed their quiet, unassuming daughter would succeed in ways they could not imagine.

*

Amanda was scrolling through her phone nervously at the dinner table Friday night. But she wasn't nervous about her posts, or her followers—now at 26.5 million—or trolls and flame wars that had nothing to do with her but which nevertheless found purchase on her platform like barnacles on an oil tanker. No, she was worried because it was 7:00 p.m. and in an hour Martin Decker was going to pull into her driveway. She was worried because she hadn't told her parents.

Honey, no devices at the table, said her mother in a gentle tone.

Her mother realized, of course, that the power dynamics in the household were shifting—perhaps permanently—to its youngest member. Giving orders to a teenager was a precarious act under the best of circumstances. But what do you do when that teenager seems poised to out-earn you by a factor of ten? And has the public on her side?

That was the dilemma Amanda's mother was wrestling with over corn soufflé and roast free-range chicken on a warm autumn night at the end of September. Hence the gentle voice and smile.

But Amanda complied without arguing. She wasn't paying attention to the phone anyway but inventing a lie.

It would be dark by eight and her parents wouldn't see the car in the driveway, but just hear the horn. Amanda could run out before they had a chance to get a look. Or better, she could go out early and wait at the curb.

This would have been easy if Nicole hadn't been banned. In that case Nicole could pick her up and she could meet Martin Decker at the cinema. But of course even the sound of a Ford F-150 engine could spell doom for our sweet heroine.

So she imagined telling her parents Ned was coming. Yes, a date. Even geeks go to movies. Especially movies. They were going to see that new science fiction film, something something number six.

But what if Amanda's mother asked Ned about it later? After all, Ned came to the house all the time, and he would certainly be coming tomorrow to work on the website and check that the home office was functioning smoothly and to get in some quick kisses and maybe even...

But that's a bridge Amanda could cross tomorrow. Why worry now? After all, Martin Decker might stand her up, or hate her company. Don't at least fifty percent of first dates never result in a second date? In that case Ned would never have to know.

Or she could say it was Amy and Nipuni picking her up. She hadn't coordinated this with them, though, and what if, after she left, one of them couldn't reach her cell because she was in the theater and had to turn it off, and Amy—or Nipuni—called the Dizons' landline?

Damn landlines!

Amanda didn't know how people lived in the Age of Landlines, when a call meant for you could be picked up by a parent or sibling, when absolutely anyone in a family could answer your call. That must have been so scary.

A sharp knock on the front door sent Amanda flying. Her plate crashed to the floor, scattering her corn soufflé in all directions.

Martin Decker had not only come early—way early—but was chivalrous enough to get out of his car and risk having to speak with his date's parents.

Damn chivalry!

Her father reached the door before she could. And there stood...

The leasing agent!!!

May I come in?

Amanda's terror transferred to her parents like an exorcized demon. She sank back in her chair and wiped her brow with her napkin.

Now it was the Dizons turn to be fearful. Contracts, lawsuits, handcuffs. The totaled Jaguar.

I hope I'm not bothering you. Oh, you're eating...

Please join us, said Amanda's mother, as if a serving of corn soufflé might stave off debtors' prison.

It's a lovely evening, said the leasing agent. I don't know about you, but autumn is my favorite season.

Yes, yes, agreed the Dizons.

Would you like some free-range chicken? asked Amanda's mother. Or perhaps corn soufflé?

No thanks, said the leasing agent. I have a date later.

Me too! Amanda almost shouted.

Oh really? said Amanda's mother with a bit too much surprise, forgetting that some people over the age of thirty had a social life.

I feel sorry for the guy if he's picking you up, joked Amanda's father. Unless he's driving a Bentley, it must be pretty hard to impress a Jaguar dealer.

Oh, I'm not like that.

No, not at all. Of course, not, said Amanda's parents all at once.

We could tell you were down-to-earth when we met you, said Amanda's mother.

Unpretentious, added Amanda's father.

Forgiving, added Amanda's mother.

So, said the leasing agent at last. About the E-PACE.

Amanda, feeling bored by non-digital adult talk, had turned her eyes back down to her phone.

About what? asked Amanda's mother.

The car, said the leasing agent.

Oh, the car! laughed Amanda's parents all at once.

Was it possible the leasing agent didn't know? She hadn't pulled out any contracts, or lawsuits, or handcuffs.

Is there a...problem? asked Amanda's father, gripping the edge of his chair.

No, everything's good.

A shocked silence overtook the table.

Are you sure I can't get you a coffee? Or tea? asked Amanda's mother, offering a hot beverage when what she really wanted to do was kiss this angel on the cheeks.

No, thanks. I just stopped by as a kind of courtesy call. Mr. Parker, as you probably know, works in insurance. So he even has gap coverage. Good thing for young Parker. Do you know he's a football player?

I think we heard something to that effect, murmured Amanda's father.

Going to the Hawkeyes. At least we hope. You know Ohio State always comes in at the last minute and poaches our best talent.

Yes, yes, said the Dizons.

I saw his first game. You know the dealership is a sponsor.

No, we didn't know that, said the Dizons.

My uncle scouts for the Bears and says he's the real deal.

The real deal? echoed the Dizons.

Thank God for airbags, said the leasing agent.

Yes, thank God.

Lucky he wasn't in a BMW. Or a Porsche. Ha ha ha!

Ha ha ha, said Amanda's mother and father.

They'd still be searching for body parts.

Good old British engineering, said Amanda's father.

Anyway, said the leasing agent. Everything's settled. Right as rain.

And she snapped her fingers to accentuate her point.

Of course, I'm sure our credit rating is ruined, said Amanda's mother.

Noooo, realized Amanda's father, who was an economist, after all. It's not ruined.

Bingo, said the leasing agent. I decided to check this afternoon and your score actually went up.

How is that possible? asked Amanda's mother.

Because the car has been paid off early by the insurance, and it's not our insurance, so no hit to us, said Amanda's father.

Bingo again.

Whew! That's a relief, said Amanda's mother.

I saw the way you looked at the E-PACE in the showroom, Mrs. Dizon.

Call me Carole, please.

And it occurred to me today, why don't we put you behind the wheel? Maybe you were the person meant for this spectacular vehicle all along?

What are you saying? asked Amanda's mother with a lump in her throat.

I mean, maybe you want to take the black one this time?

*

Amanda's mother and father were washing the dishes after dinner. Amanda was supposed to clean up the shattered plate and corn soufflé but she was still sitting at the table, scrolling on her phone.

So, what do you think? asked Amanda's mother, washing.

What do I think about what? asked Amanda's father, drying.

About the Jaguar.

I think it's great. We dodged a bullet.

That's not what I mean, silly. I was wondering, how much is college, really? In-state tuition is approximately ten thousand dollars. And the recruiter said she might get a free ride.

I want to go to UI with Young Parker, said Amanda, overhearing.

Her mother ignored this last part.

I'm sure Iowa would be a similar situation, said Amanda's mother. My point is, do we really need over three-hundred thousand dollars for a college fund? She's not going to Yale medical school.

Maybe I won't go to college at all, said Amanda.

Maybe she won't go to college at all, echoed her mother. Of course, you'll go to college, said her mother after a moment.

She passed a dish to Amanda's father. But that's neither here nor there, said Amanda's mother to Amanda's father. My point is we don't need such a sum for the college fund. And, in any case, we already budgeted for the auto lease.

What about me? asked Amanda's father. My Honda has over a hundred thousand miles.

You can have the Camry, said Amanda's mother.

*

The doorbell rang.

Amanda screamed, her phone flying from her hand and sliding across the table, fortunately landing on a chair and not on the tiled floor which had minutes ago shattered a ceramic plate.

For once the phone was second priority. She leapt to her feet and dashed to the door. Over the last two-and-a-half weeks she had become quite dexterous with the cast and could walk and hop without the crutches, though she wasn't supposed to.

Still, she couldn't outrun her father, who had run the four hundred meter relay in high school.

The lawyer no longer stood on ceremony and walked right in as soon as Mr. Dizon opened the door.

Do you mind if we sit in the living room? asked the lawyer, looking even more rumpled than usual today, his tie in his jacket pocket and his wrinkled white shirt untucked.

It's been a long day, said the lawyer, sitting on the recliner and opening his briefcase on his lap.

The Dizons huddled around him as though he were Santa Claus. Well, perhaps he was. Because he pulled out a surprise as magical as any Christmas gift ever lugged in a red sack down a chimney: a contract.

Babylon, said the very rumpled lawyer with practiced under-statement.

Amanda jumped up—her ankle be damned.

They're going to pay me ten thousand?

Oh, I think a lot more than that.

He had printed copies of the contract for each of them, so they could gasp in unison.

…A sum of two hundred thousand dollars ($200,000.00)

What does she have to do for this? asked Amanda's mother, her skeptical, protective instincts coming to the fore.

Does it matter?! exclaimed Amanda.

And in that moment, all assembled agreed that it did not.

*

This was not charity like the MakeItRain account, but real income, earnings that would go into an LLC account, appear on bank statements, be scrutinized by their accountant, taxed by the government, federal, state, and county, and set into motion a social security ledger in her name that would determine her future benefits—assuming that noble safety net remained solvent when she reached my considerable age.

But let us not despair over the fate of social security, or global warming, or plastics in our oceans, or a zombie apocalypse. Today was a magical day in the history of the Archer and Dizon families. One of us, finally, had made real money.

*

They were so shocked and absorbed by Amanda's sudden rise through the tax brackets, shooting from being a dependent to owing the top bracket of 37%, that they did not hear the horn honk in the driveway.

Amanda was signing the contract when she heard her mother scream.

There was Martin Decker, standing in the foyer.

The door was open, said Martin Decker. Am I interrupting something? I thought we were on for eight?

It was 8:15, and Amanda was filled with conflicting feelings. She was, of course, still shocked about the contract. She was pleased Martin Decker had not stood her up and that he was, indeed, a witness to this proud moment. She was also deeply embarrassed that not only her parents, but also her lawyer were present at what should have been a private, even a furtive moment. And she was worried her mother would throw him out, as she had become in the habit of doing with the various stakeholders in her daughter's life.

All these conflicting feelings passed through Amanda's frontal cortex. She decided to act on pride.

I'm gonna be rich! I just got a contract from—

Shhh! said her lawyer and parents.

You aren't at liberty to disclose the terms of the deal, said the lawyer. But I can say Babylon is gonna sponsor me, can't I? asked Amanda.

It seems like you just did, said the lawyer.

Who is Babylon? asked Martin Decker.

More importantly, who are you, young man? asked Amanda's mother.

Marty Decker. Didn't your daughter tell you we had a date tonight?

Not really a date, just hanging out, said Amanda. We're just gonna see a movie, Mama.

That sounds like the definition of a date, said her mother.

The lawyer directed his client to sign and initial one more page, then gathered all the pages, rapped them on the table, and put them in his briefcase.

I know that name, said Amanda's father. You were in my class. You were smoking cigarettes when you were nine!

Yeah, but I quit when I was ten.

You're not taking my daughter anywhere. Get out of my house, said Amanda's mother.

Mama, you can't talk to my friends like that!

Actually, I can.

You always bugged me to have a social life and now that I do you chase everyone away! I'm going and that's final, said Amanda, getting to her feet and grabbing her crutches.

Young man, are you aware my daughter already has a boyfriend? said Amanda's mother. Did she tell you that?

I think the whole world knows, said Martin Decker. But it's just a starter boyfriend. I'm cool with that.

He's amor—started Amanda. Pol... What are you again?

But Martin Decker realized declaring his polyamorousness before his date's parents, and her lawyer, was not in his best interest at this time, and he remained silent on the matter.

You can go if you have a chaperone, offered Amanda's mother.

I already have—started Amanda, but realized she would hardly improve the situation by naming her banned best friend.

I'm glad to volunteer my services as chaperone, said the lawyer, thinking that despite it having been a long day, this was an opportunity not only to take in a movie, but also to safeguard his most lucrative client.

This is ridiculous, said Amanda's father to Amanda's mother. She's sixteen, that's old enough to date. And it's too young to be serious with one boy. But you guys go to the movie and come home. No drugs, alcohol—or cigarettes. And drive the speed limit.

Yes, Mr. Dizon, said Martin Decker, practiced in the art of placating parents.

And don't change the radio! added Amanda's mother, recalling the fate of the Jaguar.

*

Martin Decker drove his father's beat-up Silverado, but that didn't seem to embarrass him the way Nicole was embarrassed to drive her father's Ford F-150. Amanda admired his natural confidence.

He didn't try to hold her hand or kiss her in the car, which made her feel more relaxed, but also a little disappointed, because in fact she wanted him to kiss her and hold her hand.

She did think about Ned, and that made her feel uneasy. But society sent so many conflicting messages about relationships these days that the only rules she knew for certain was that no meant no and that it's wrong to have sex with someone when they're passed out, and those two things didn't seem like lines either of them would cross tonight.

Besides, her head was filled with the Babylon deal and everything else that was happening in her life. She felt she was just floating along, like she was watching a movie of her own life.

*

She expected to see Nicole in the theater lobby, but she wasn't there, and she didn't answer Amanda's texts.

Martin Decker offered to buy the tickets if Amanda paid for the popcorn and sodas. Amanda happily agreed, not understanding the business model of movie theaters. But then she could have treated the entire theater to concessions after her Babylon deal.

She was about to text Nicole again during the previews, despite the instructions to turn off phones, but at that moment her friend arrived, alone, and sat on the other side of Martin Decker.

Hey, said Martin Decker, surprised. What are you doing here?

Where's your date? asked Amanda.

Stuff came up, said Nicole evasively, reaching into Martin's popcorn.

Guess what? said Amanda. I'm a sponsor for Babylon Skincare!

They high fived, drawing shusses from those sitting behind.

Chill, it's just previews! shouted Nicole back.

I'm dying to tell you how much they're paying me, but I'm not allowed, said Amanda.

This is just the beginning, said Nicole. You're going to get more sponsorships, I'm sure. But don't post anything about it tonight. They probably have a morals clause.

What's a morals clause?

Also, we don't want Ned to find out before the website's finished, hahaha!

She took Martin Decker's Sprite and drank from the bottle. Hey! exclaimed Martin Decker.

You want to sit next to me? asked Amanda, patting the empty chair beside her.

I'm good, said Nicole, taking another handful of her ex's popcorn.

*

The movie started and Martin Decker took Amanda's hand.

Amanda held it tight and didn't let go. She was in heaven. She'd never been on a movie date before and here she was with the most desirable boy in class, and he was holding her hand.

A few minutes later she noticed he was also holding Nicole's hand. That was weird. Is this what polyamorousness was? Holding two girls' hands at the movies? She could hardly be jealous, though, considering that she had a boyfriend. And she noted that when he drank or ate his popcorn, he took his hand from Nicole and not from her. What about Nicole? Hadn't she dumped him? What a friend she was, making this sacrifice to protect Amanda's virtue.

*

Afterward, in the darkness of the parking lot, Martin Decker made his move.

Amanda threw her arms around him and let him French kiss her. She was in heaven.

OK, that's enough, lover boy, said Nicole, pulling them apart like a referee at a prize fight.

She took Amanda's arm. Let's go, said Nicole.

But I'm taking her home, said Martin Decker.

Your night is over, said Nicole. Thanks for the popcorn.

Actually, I bought the popcorn, said Amanda.

He didn't even pay for the popcorn? asked Nicole incredulously.

He bought the tickets.

Mandy, you're so naive! Next time make him buy the concessions.

Next time? wondered Amanda, daring not to dream about a next time. But considering her popularity, why shouldn't there be a next time, and a time after that?

It's a wonder you've kept your virginity this long, said Nicole.

I don't think anyone wanted it before, said Amanda.

*

Amanda lay in bed far into the night, unable to sleep. She posted about the sponsorship:

Inked a deal today for a sponsorship with a great store—stay tuned!!!

In truth, her thoughts were on the details she could not post: the kiss, and that two with all the zeros after it.

She finally fell asleep just before dawn, her light still on, chatting with the world, the phone gripped firmly in her hand.

8

Our cell phone Sleeping Beauty was awakened by a kiss.

Martin! mumbled Amanda.

But, fortunately, her voice was slurred and therefore incomprehensible. Because the prince in her bedroom was White Hat Ned.

Hello my Sleeping Beauty! said White Hat Ned.

Argh, let me sleep! What time is it?

It's noon, said White Hat Ned, amused. Do you always fall asleep fully clothed with your phone in your hand?

It's the new-look me, said Amanda, trying to rouse herself. Did you climb a ladder and sneak through the window?

Your mother let me in. I guess she's warming to me.

Or using you to—

Using me to what?

Amanda suspected her mother considered Ned the lesser of two evils and let him climb the stairs unsupervised as a way of nipping in the bud any romance with Martin Decker.

Can a girl have some privacy? said Amanda instead.

I don't think privacy's in your contract, said White Hat Ned. Your mom told me about Babylon. Not the details, but I'm sure this will be great for us.

For us?

Look, I got you a present. Give me your phone.

He replaced her case, the one of Mt. Rushmore she had inherited from the candidate.

I'm surprised you kept this old thing, said Ned.

I guess I had other priorities, said Amanda, still groggy.

White Hat Ned held out her phone with the back of the new case toward her. Emblazoned on the plastic was a cropped photo of the two of them together.

Perhaps a year ago, or even a month ago Amanda would have melted at the sight, would have thought herself unworthy of such a gift. This was the sort of thing that happened to girls like Nicole—not only to have a boyfriend, but to have a boyfriend who wasn't ashamed of you, who wasn't with you only because no one else was available, or only for the promise of sex. A boyfriend who wanted the whole world to know his relationship status.

But Amanda had learned—or was learning—there was another status called polyamorous, and she had the hottest boy in class buying her movie tickets—if not popcorn.

Can a girl have some privacy? she repeated. Please.

I'll wait on the stairs, said White Hat Ned, more adept at deciphering JavaScript than the mood of a teenage girl.

*

They went downstairs for breakfast—or lunch. Amanda found her parents busy transforming the rarely used dining room into a home office. *Their* home office. They had bought a printer, a video camera and a professional tripod.

Is this for me? asked Amanda excitedly, picking up the video camera.

Everything is to share, said her father, unpacking the printer.

Like the Jaguar?

Who said anything about a Jaguar? asked her father.

A Jaguar? echoed White Hat Ned. You mean another one?

For me this time, said Amanda's mother, dusting off the dining room table.

For us, said Amanda's father.

Me too! said Amanda, slipping off the iPhone case while White Hat Ned wasn't looking, and before her parents could see it.

Sorry, you can't drive without a license, said her mother.

Well, sign me up then. I've been begging to take the test.

You've been afraid to take the test, corrected her mother. Same with the PSAT.

Sign me up for that too! said Amanda. I want to go to Iowa.

You mean Iowa State? said her father, setting the printer on the table.

No. UI. Where Gramps went, said Amanda, using me as a cover when her real reason was Young Parker.

Look at you, giving orders! said her mother. What do we look like, your assistants?

You look exactly like my assistants. You're spending my money, aren't you?

We're spending the LLC's money, said her father. These are tax-deductible business expenses. But if you want us to take them back...

No, no, no, it's cool, said Amanda. Buy more if you want. I'm tired of your being frugal all my life. Who says money can't buy happiness?

People with money say that, said her father, the economist. They say that so people without money won't start a revolution and cut off their heads.

He printed a test page.

If you need any help setting up... offered White Hat Ned.

Speaking of money... said Amanda's father.

And he handed her a flat piece of plastic. A credit card.

Amanda911, LLC.

Gosh!!! exclaimed Amanda.

And these are called checks, said her father, handing her a booklet. I know your generation doesn't use them, but they might come in handy on occasion. Do you want me to show you how to write one?

That's OK, said Amanda. I can YouTube it.

It's your money, said her father, the economist. But we're still your parents. We're trusting you to be responsible. Don't let your friends take advantage of you. You need to consult with us before any large purchases.

What's a large purchase? asked Amanda, her head spinning.

Don't worry, Mr. and Mrs. Dizon, I'll keep an eye on her, said White Hat Ned. And I hope you don't think I'll take advantage of her.

Not in that way, thought both of Amanda's parents at once.

Of course not, Ned, said Amanda's mother. I don't know what we all would do without you. In fact, do you know anything about home security systems? The internet of things, or whatever?

That's a great idea, said White Hat Ned. You're going to be getting a lot more visitors now that Amanda's the richest teen in Iowa.

Can I get aligners? asked Amanda, flashing her crooked teeth. I've wanted them for so long, but you always claimed poverty. You can hardly say that now.

I think your teeth are fine, said White Hat Ned, flashing his own crooked teeth. Don't become fake.

Maybe I was born fake and I'm just trying to become real, said Amanda. I also want a tattoo.

You don't want to alienate your base, said White Hat Ned, secretly worrying that he was the one who would be alienated.

I get comments on PingPong every day about tattoos, said Amanda. People ask: 'Do you have tattoos?' 'Why not?' 'Don't people in Iowa have tattoos?' 'Is it against your religion?' 'What about a cross tattoo?' 'What about a *Jesus Loves Me* tattoo?' I took a poll. Eighty-one percent want me to get a tattoo. And ninety percent want me to livestream it.

How can more people want you to video getting a tattoo than want you to get a tattoo in the first place? asked her father, a stranger to the irrationality of social media polls.

We'll discuss it, said her mother evasively.

Amanda gave her a big hug.

Where are Amy and Puni? asked Amanda, texting. Now that they're on the payroll they should be here.

What payroll? asked her father, the economist.

Just be careful not to change too much, warned her mother, still thinking about the aligners and the tattoo.

I'm not changing at all, said Amanda. It's everything else that's changing. And it's about time!

*

After helping Amanda and her parents all day, White Hat Ned asked to take her to the movies.

Go with Amy and Puni, suggested Amanda, thinking this polyamorous thing was a great way for exhausted influencers to get out of social obligations.

But White Hat Ned insisted, and he had been so helpful that she couldn't say no.

Naturally, he wanted to see the science fiction movie something something six, and she couldn't very well say she'd seen it last night with Martin Decker.

He paid for the tickets *and* the popcorn, even knowing she had a platinum card in her Hello Kitty purse.

But when he held her hand and didn't let go, she thought of Martin Decker. And when he kissed her, she thought of Young Parker and their unconsummated kiss.

She fell asleep even before the movie began and dreamt of all the other dreamy boys in Iowa and in the world, and how her polyamorous status would allow her to reverse a lifetime of loneliness and neglect, to hold their hands, all of them, and kiss them, and...

Again, she fell asleep near dawn, still dressed, holding her phone. And again, she was awakened by Ned. But this time she was careful to hide the caseless phone from his gaze.

She heard voices and went downstairs without showering or changing clothes, just running some toothpaste across her soon-to-be-aligned teeth.

Amy and Nipuni were in conversation with her parents in the Operations Room. The two MacBooks were running, as well as Ned's PC, and the Chromebook White Hat Ned had gifted Amanda, but which Amy had commandeered. The printer was churning out something and the video camera sat on the tripod, ready for action.

Wow, this looks like the Pentagon, said Amanda.

There were newly purchased electronics as well—security cameras, which Ned began to unpack and install.

Amanda found eggs in a skillet on the stove and poured herself a bowl of Honey Pops as well.

She stood eating in the Operations Room because the kitchen table was covered with equipment and printouts of instructions and emails.

Nipuni and Amy were explaining to Amanda's parents about the three email accounts. And Amanda's mother was telling them how to screen them, and then to forward the important ones to her, not to Amanda.

What about emails from my friends? asked Amanda. I don't want you snooping.

I read that kids now don't email, they text, said Amanda's mother.

Amanda actually couldn't recall the last time she had gotten an email from someone under seventy—that being me. I emailed her occasionally as a gesture to the digital age, thinking I was communing with her world. Little did I know.

I also don't agree with your being her publicists, said Amanda's mother to Amy and Nipuni. You don't have any experience in that area. Leave that to me.

Oh, right Mom. You did a great job with the *Sentinel!* And they aced the TV reporter.

They can advise, OK? said her mother. But all media decisions go through me.

Sure, sure, agreed Amanda, realizing that what her mother meant by media was traditional media, and that her friends could handle digital inquiries from bloggers and other influencers without her mother ever knowing.

And I think five hundred dollars each is too steep, said Amanda's mother. We'll pay you twenty dollars an hour with a cap of twenty hours per month.

Both Amy and Nipuni pulled up the calculators on their phones, to the horror of tiger moms everywhere, giving the lie to Chinese and Indian math superiority.

We'll pay? asked Amanda. I thought this was *my* money?

It is dear, said her mother. Which is why I was going to ask your permission to renovate the garage. It may even be tax deductible if you do a video series on the construction. But if you don't agree, your father and I can take the money from our retirement accounts.

Why do you want to rebuild the garage? wondered Amanda. It's been like that forever.

We didn't have a Jaguar before, said her mother. Winter will be here soon and we can't leave it out in the elements.

Sure, sure. Can I get a cat castle to put in the garage? I'll show you the one I want on Pinterest. It's long and tall but not wide, so you can still get the car in, or two cars even.

Of course, agreed her mother, thinking she was getting off light.

*

After showering and changing clothes, the kids all went to the mall.

Amanda led Amy and Nipuni into Victoria's Secret, knowing White Hat Ned would not follow.

She showed them the iPhone case.

Amy and Nipuni gasped.

What do you think? asked Amanda.

For Gen Z this is like an engagement ring, said Nipuni.

What I thought, said Amanda.

So embarrassing! said Amy, secretly wishing she had a boyfriend who would embarrass her.

I mean, Ned's OK, for a geek, said Nipuni, who was beginning to develop a crush on him herself and hoped to be the rebound girl when Amanda moved on.

In a fit of jealousy masquerading as girl power—not so different from Nicole's behavior at the theater—Nipuni grabbed the case and buried it deep in a trash bin.

*

While White Hat Ned was visiting GameStop, Amanda went with her friends to a girly shop and purchased a unicorn case. But she couldn't put it on, could she, with White Hat Ned emerging from the video game store? She kept it in the bag.

What's that? asked White Hat Ned, looking at the bag.

Oh, nothing.

He's gonna find out sometime, whispered Nipuni in her ear.

What am I going to do? whispered Amanda. I don't want to hurt his feelings. I should have given it back, at least.

No, because then he could use it.

And the three girls stopped in their tracks, it having dawned on them that he could have made two copies—one for his own phone.

His phone was hanging in the back pocket of his jeans.

Amanda let him walk ahead a step and then grabbed it just enough to see the back of the case.

Hey! cried White Hat Ned.

Amanda was relieved to see it was a plain gunmetal case and pushed it back down.

Who's the horny one now? asked White Hat Ned, once again completely misreading his girlfriend.

*

With her primary objective accomplished, Amanda could walk the mall in peace. Well, inner peace. Because she attracted a posse of classmates, schoolmates and general hangers-on that more closely resembled Napoleon's march from Elba than a quiet Sunday out with friends.

She bought earrings for a girl who was either one grade above or one grade below, and a sports jersey for the brother of the girl who sat next to her in Science class.

You can't do this, said her girlfriends and boyfriend, trying to shoo the others away.

I'm having a good time, said Amanda, loving the attention and appreciation.

And, after all, the younger brother of her Science classmate was so cute. And the girl who asked for the earrings was so polite.

It was food court on the house, all the empty tables crowded in an instant by this spontaneous party. Pizzas and burgers and sodas and shakes flowed like ethanol.

Whether these kids were taking advantage of her or not I'll leave to you to decide. But they raised their voices to her in song and documented the event for a multitude of social media platforms.

You're so gullible, moaned Amy, biting into her vegetarian pizza. These people aren't your friends.

Maybe, maybe not, said Amanda philosophically. But I'm happy, and I'm glad to make them happy. Anyway, it's tax deductible, I think. Whatever that means.

It was the best $835.40 she had ever spent.

*

The following morning, the third week anniversary of her fall into the well, she was called into the principal's office before first bell.

The only other time she had been summoned to the principal's office had been for leaving school grounds during lunch, for which she got a warning. So, despite her newfound fame and fortune, her limbic brain reverted to the instinctive terror of that glass pane with the stencilled words: *Principal's Office.*

But rather than having to endure an agonizing wait in the assistant's office, as is customary, she was whisked in to see the principal, a serious-minded man of color who had served in the special forces.

And instead of handing her a detention slip for some unwitting infraction, he shook her perspiring hand.

I've been wanting to meet you, young lady, said the serious-minded principal. I apologize for not inviting you sooner.

Invited? thought Amanda.

Yes, sir, said Amanda aloud, confused but relieved.

Have a seat...

The serious-minded principal did not sit behind his imposing desk, but rather in the chair next to Amanda. He left his office door open because it was no longer considered a good idea by enlightened society—and legal counsel—for men in positions of power to lock themselves in rooms with young, powerless women, or girls—or boys. Come to think of it, whoever thought that was a good idea?

Amanda, for her part, was not used to dealing with Black people in positions of authority. Her natural inclination to please was further heightened by a fear of saying something offensive, not just about race, but also about the military. She couldn't help noticing a picture on his desk of him in uniform, and a medal in a case. Her parents were pacifists, against all the wars. She had to be careful here.

It's my goal to get to know all of my students, said the serious-minded principal. But because I just transferred here last year, I haven't gotten around to meeting everyone.

Amanda decided it was better not to remind him of the warning he had given her for leaving school grounds.

How is Harding High treating you, Amanda?

Great, sir.

The serious-minded principal flashed a smile, but only for an instant. You don't have to call me *sir.* We're not in the Army.

But the photo in uniform, the medal in the case, made Amanda think they were in the Army, at least in this office.

Has your American History teacher talked to you? It seems you're at risk of failing. You're not turning in your homework, and you missed a paper due.

Amanda tried to remember. Yes, Mr. Cargill had talked to her, but had she been listening? Yes, there were always tests and papers in class, in all classes. It was so confusing.

If you'd like we could arrange tutors to help you, especially during this busy time for you.

You can do that?

We don't want to you start the year on the wrong foot.

No, sir.

But I didn't invite you just to talk about your grades. I also want to make sure you are happy here. I know there are private schools reaching out to you.

There are?

Obviously, we can't compete with a twenty thousand dollar a year academy with brand new textbooks and a twelve-to-one student-teacher ratio. But I believe a public education, like the military, can impart experiences that one just doesn't find in elitist institutions. Especially if you want to go into politics.

Politics?

I want you to know, Amanda, anything you want or need, anything we can give you here at Harding High, my door is always open. Now tell me, Amanda, are there any causes you are interested in?

Amanda was about to answer unicorns, but she knew imaginary animals—allegedly imaginary—did not rise to the level of the kind of causes the principal was alluding to.

Cats, said Amanda at last, fixing on an animal whose existence no one could dispute. World hunger. Climate change.

Her eyes landed on the medal again. Our troops, added Amanda. Of course.

Because if there are any causes that are close to your heart, I'm sure we at Harding High can get behind that, said the serious-minded principal.

Cool.

Actually, a cause of mine, which I'm sure you know from my

announcements, is youth smoking, especially vaping.

Actually, Amanda had not been paying attention to his announcements. Before falling into the well, she had kept her head down in school, neither wanting to draw attention nor pay attention, hoping she could sleepwalk until graduation, and then...and then... well probably sleepwalk through the rest of her ordinary, fearful life as well.

You've never smoked, have you, Amanda?

I'm afraid of fire, sir.

Well, it's tempting enough for a normal teenager. But for models and celebrities it's even more of a temptation. To relax, to lose weight, because your peers are doing it. You have to be strong, young lady. You have to set an example.

Yes, sir.

I was wondering if you'd like to read the morning announcement, said the serious-minded principal. You can say hello or whatever you want to the school, then read this PSA about the dangers of vaping.

He handed her a one-paragraph script.

Sure.

As we all know, our sweet heroine had appeared on national television, and given print and TV interviews. Yet putting her mouth to the microphone on the assistant's desk and speaking to her entire school was oddly exhilarating.

The serious-minded principal showed her how to press the microphone on and off.

What do I say? asked Amanda nervously.

A simple greeting, whatever you like. Then read the message.

Amanda thought for a moment.
Hey everyone, this is Amanda Dizon. I hope you guys had a great

weekend. It was great seeing some of you at the mall yesterday. That was such a great time, right?

I just want to take this opportunity to remind you of the hazards of vaping. E-cigarettes contain nicotine, which you all know is highly addictive, as well as other dangerous chemicals. Don't give in to peer pressure. I haven't.

She pressed off.

The serious-minded principal nodded gratefully and clasped her on the shoulder.

Amanda saluted and limped away, as if walking on air.

*

She scanned hurriedly through posts before American History class began, forgetting White Hat Ned was her neighbor and could see her new phone case.

So that's what you bought at the mall! exclaimed White Hat Ned, his disappointment and sense of betrayal evident in his voice to a radius of three desks.

Isn't it cute? said Amanda, holding it up. The horn points out. I can use it to stab molesters.

Where's the case I gave you?

Ah...my mom confiscated it.

Of course, realized Ned. I'm sorry. A bridge too far.

Yeah. Whatever that means.

It means she's back to not liking me. She probably thinks I'm one of those Iowan boys who wants to marry at seventeen and have eight kids.

It's legal to get married at seventeen? wondered Amanda, who had never thought about such things, the idea of marriage and children being as abstract to her as the postmodern paintings she had seen on a visit to the Art Institute of Chicago.

Mr. Cargill entered the classroom and more immediate concerns rose to her attention.

Is there a paper due today? whispered Amanda to her now-appeased boyfriend.

It was due Friday. Don't tell me... But of course, how can you have time for schoolwork? You barely have time to shower. I'll be glad to help you.

Thanks so much, said Amanda, taking his hand.

And this time she didn't think of Martin Decker or Young Parker or any of the other dream boys in Iowa and beyond.

*

Nicole was eating with Amy and Nipuni, being filled in on Sunday's events. But Amanda had other priorities and drew her away for a private discussion.

The insurance paid off the car, I want you to know, said Amanda.

That's a relief.

I also think I should tell you we're getting another one. The black one.

Really?! exclaimed Nicole, before realizing that it couldn't possibly be for her.

My mom wants it. But I'll be able to drive it too once I get my license.

I'll help you pass, offered Nicole.

I don't think that's a good idea.

At least I can help with the written test, offered Nicole, wanting to be useful in some way.

I also want to know if you can help with some of my schoolwork? I'm falling behind.

Sure, bestie. Anything you want. I'm grounded for school nights and have an 11:00 p.m. curfew on weekends, so I have time on my hands.

I also wanted to thank you again for coming Friday. I think you saved my virtue.

Probably, said Nicole. Marty's not a third date kinda guy.

So, you had...um...sex with him?

Amanda assumed Nicole was not a virgin, but Nicole saved erotic confessions for her popular friends and Amanda had always been too shy to ask.

In fact, Amanda didn't talk about sex with anyone. Amy and Nipuni were virgins as well, from sexually conservative households. And the only time Amanda's mother had talked about sex was to give her a book on puberty when she was eleven, and of course when she tried to give her the #MeToo printouts.

Otherwise, the extent of Amanda's sexual education was a few explicit young adult novels she had read for English class, Netflix series, and the occasional Google search that erroneously returned a porn site.

Yeah, I had sex with him, answered Nicole, leaning across the table and whispering. But like I told you, he's possessive. That's why I dumped him.

He told me he was...

But again, Amanda could not recall the word polyamorous.

Anyway, you're not going to have sex with him, stated Nicole. You had your date.

But what if he asks me out again?

Say no.

But what if I want to say yes?

Nicole looked at her friend in alarm. Why would you want to do that? I just told you he's not a third date guy. That means you need to put out on date number two.

What if I want to? asked Amanda, not bothering to whisper.

Shhhh!

Nicole stepped around the table to sit beside Amanda, as the principal had. But unlike the principal, Nicole didn't have to worry about sexual harassment charges, so she sat with their hips touching and put a hand on her friend's knee.

You can't, said Nicole, as if her point required no elaboration.

But you did.

You're not me, whispered Nicole. Has your mom even put you on the pill?

She gave me something for anxiety. Oh, you mean birth control pills.

Ahhhh! exclaimed Nicole. You're not ready for sex, OK? You're not me.

Amanda sipped her fruit drink through the small straw in the box.

And what about Ned? asked Nicole, trying another tack. He'll be so jealous. Maybe he'll kill himself. Do you want his suicide on your conscience?

I could have him too, said Amanda with, what to her, seemed shatterproof rationality.

Nicole dug her nails into Amanda's jeans so hard her friend cried out.

Are you crazy! exclaimed Nicole, before catching her breath and lowering her voice again to a whisper. What are you talking about? You want to be a slut?

That's a patriarchal word, said Amanda.

She could not for the life of her remember *polyamorous,* yet, somehow, she was able to recall this phrase shouted by her mother at an acquaintance who had used the term at a dinner party years ago.

What about feminism? asked Amanda. Are we modern women or not? What did Susan B. Anthony and Martin Luther King fight for if we can't go out with two boys at once?

Nicole just stared, thankful that none of their schoolmates were recording this. Or so she hoped.

Or more, said Amanda defiantly.

What about your business? said Nicole, trying a third tack. You want to lose everything we've worked so hard to achieve?

We?

You know how football coaches warn their players to stay away from chicks? It messes up their game. Chicks are a distraction. Well, it's the same for you. Boys are a threat to your influencer career.

Amanda slurped up the last drops of her juice, considering her friend's advice carefully.

Maybe...

No sex before you're eighteen. Promise.

Maybe...

Promise. Say it!

OK, said Amanda, beginning to feel intimidated, but also warmed by her friend's solicitude. I promise.

Remember you're bound by a morals clause! added Nicole, for emphasis.

10

Two months later, the last Wednesday in November, Amanda's grandmother died. Her mother's mother. My ex-wife.

This did not come as a surprise. Her grandmother had been debilitated for many years with COPD. But it came as a shock, as the deaths of parents and grandparents always do, even as we expect them.

Amanda and her mother felt guilty for having been so preoccupied with Amanda911, LLC these past months. They hadn't visited her as much as they felt they should have.

Fortunately, funeral arrangements had been made years before. A simple graveside memorial would be held beside her deceased partner at their community Unitarian church, which had accepted them when others hadn't.

What complicated things was my presence. I had given Carole my hostel's name and phone number after arriving in Ho Chi Minh City, as I normally do when traveling. She called me to announce my ex's passing, probably with a sense of duty or merely as a courtesy. I could sense her surprise when I said I was coming. She said that I didn't have to; that she would understand. I said that I did have to and I would email my flight number after I bought my ticket.

It's a sorrowful thing when the last of your grandparents dies. Because, if you're lucky, you have four of them, and four to a young child is a universe. Granted, they are old when you are still beginning your life, but they are always there, even at a distance, until one day you realize all of them are gone.

Amanda hadn't known her father's parents well, and they both died before she was ten. When Carole told me her mother had passed away, my instinctive thought was sadness that Amanda no longer had grandparents.

Then I remembered I was still alive. Sweating like a pig in the open-air bars of Saigon, but alive. Maybe not a grandfather. Maybe time to be one.

*

My relationship with Amanda was far from ideal, but not complicated. We had nothing in common and nothing to say to each other. I considered her a disappointment. She thought of me as a failed father and an absent grandfather, but was too kindhearted to reciprocate my disappointment.

My relationship with Carole was even further from ideal, and very complicated. I hadn't been a terrible father, but I hadn't been a good one either. And when I divorced her mother, Carole took her mother's side, as children of divorce often take the side of one parent over the other. I went off to travel the world and stretch my savings in places where the dollar went furthest, while Carole's mother stayed in Iowa and developed an illness that required increasing care. So the choice for my daughter was an easy one if, indeed, her preference had not been decided long before.

*

I must have looked a wreck, drunk and sleep-deprived, as I emerged into the terminal at Des Moines International Airport.

Carole fell into my arms and sobbed. An observer might have deduced she loved rather than hated me, but I think it was just the grief, exploding.

Her husband then gave me a hug and a firm handshake and said how good it was to see me again, alas under these circumstances, but he hoped I was doing well and they had made the spare bedroom up for me with my old bed...

I didn't hear the rest.

I was staring at Amanda.

Or rather I was staring at a unicorn phone case with a human face behind it. Because my granddaughter was videoing or livestreaming or taking pictures or whatever teens and influencers with thirty million followers do with their phones.

She swept one arm around me and tried to take a selfie with the other, but I took her phone, unicorn and all, and stashed it in my blazer pocket.

I framed her smooth, glowing face in my large, rugged hands. No more splotchy skin. Lip gloss. Eyeliner that made her trusting green eyes pop like the jade souvenirs I'd seen in Southeast Asia. Shimmering hair, the first time I'd ever seen it styled, with vermilion highlights.

She wasn't wearing jeans a size too large, or overalls, or a rainbow t-shirt with stains, but was color-coordinated, perhaps by a professional dresser at one of her sponsors. Skinny jeans, a lilac knit sweater, floral Vans, a white Swatch, a pewter *Amanda911* pendant.

But she, or her parents, or her sponsors, hadn't gone too far. No one would have mistaken her for a movie star or a model. She was still Amanda, but a better version. At least to look at. Her intellect, her aspirations, that remained to be seen.

You have braces now!

They're aligners. I want to get a tattoo. Do you have tattoos?

I took off my blazer and rolled up my sleeve to show her *Amor Fati* inscribed in script. It's from Nietzsche, I said. It means love your fate.

Oh, whatever, said Amanda. I want to get one of my cat, Luna. She's a black cat.

Black cats are good luck in Japan.

I'm glad you came. Your room is next to mine.

She hugged me tight, this time with both arms, and cried but not from grief, from love.

*

My family has come up in the world! I said, buckling into the front seat of the Jaguar.

The best car I ever owned was a Fiero that broke down every hundred yards, I told them.

I don't know why I said my family. It didn't feel like my family, if it ever had. Perhaps it was pride that they were doing so well. When I first learned of Amanda's success I figured, as did most, that it would blow over in a week. When it did not, I worried the sudden excess would tear her apart, would tear the family apart. It warmed my soul to discover the opposite had occurred. It had brought us together.

At home I collapsed on the sofa. Carole asked if I wanted something to drink.

Rum and Coke.

She brought me orange juice.

I distributed the gifts I had bought while in transit at the Hong Kong International Airport. Duty-free European perfume and cologne for the parents, a Hong Kong Disneyland tote for the daughter.

But then I saw the Operations Room and all the boxes piled around the table, so that one could only walk through the room sideways. Clothes and hats and shoes and, naturally, totesß. Sent from sponsors to post and share, or from other companies hoping for a free review.

I'm sorry, I said ruefully, marveling at all the handbags and totes. I should have brought you something else.

But I love it. I love everything you give me, said Amanda sweetly, giving me a kiss.

The magnitude of the transformation in my granddaughter's life only hit me at that moment.

I understood, in an abstract, if not in a personal way, that some talented or persistent or fortunate people earned great deals of money based on the fruits of their self-expression. So the Jaguar did not surprise me. Nor did the television interviews, or the millions of followers.

But to see this pile of stuff, much of it quite expensive, piled like detritus from the sinking of the Titanic in my former dining room, blew my mind. She wasn't just going out into the world. The world was pouring into her. The whole world.

*

Where's my phone? said Amanda in a panic, thinking she had left it at baggage claim.

She was relieved when I handed it back to her.

But it was more than relief I perceived. Of course it was. I was reminded that all life's pleasures have a cost. All this free stuff piled in the dining room had a cost.

And that cost was the look in Amanda's eyes when she realized her phone was not still at baggage claim. It was a look I had seen too often in my life. In heroin addicts in my college days when they shot up. In meth addicts in the Philippines when they lit up. In gambling addicts at the casinos in Macau when the roulette ball stopped in their groove. And the look in my own bloodshot eyes, reflected in a barroom mirror in Bangkok or Berlin, when I found enough baht or euros for one more drink.

*

Can I smoke?

Of course not, said Carole.

I went out back and lit up. She followed me.

It was very dark. After the lights of Asian megacities, I was surprised not only by the thousands of stars, but that they failed to illuminate anything on the ground.

Don't you want a coat? said Carole. Do you even have a coat? You can wear one of Robert's.

The brisk Iowan air feels invigorating after the polluted heat of Asia, I said.

I looked up and saw the light on in Amanda's room.

I thought you quit smoking? You're setting a bad example, said Carole.

I am a bad example. I quit intermittently. At least I don't smoke those ridiculous e-cigarettes. Worse than tobacco, I tell you. Anyway, your daughter is busy elsewhere. You think after my coming all this way she could spend another fifteen minutes with us.

You know how teenagers are.

She's not just a teenager. She's a celebrity. She's a fucking influencer. You'll lose her soon enough, if you haven't lost her already.

Why was I being negative? In the car I had marveled how Amanda's fame had brought us together. Maybe it was the jet lag. Maybe it was being alone with my daughter.

I walked to the garage. I hadn't notice it when we parked.

This is an improvement, I said, pulling on the light.

Luna scattered from her cat castle, a labyrinth of boxes and ledges along the wall.

Although the old garage had a romantic sensibility, a kind of shattered tree effect, I said.

I turned off the light and started walking in the grass, stepping carefully because the darkness was so deep.

I heard Carole's footsteps behind me.

It was easier to talk to her when I couldn't see her.

I'm sorry about your mother.

I know you are.

She was the one who left me, you know.

And you left everyone. You were never present to begin with.

You don't understand what it is to be a writer.

You say that like it's a disability.

You can be a great husband, father, grandfather. Or you can be a great writer. I tried to be a great writer.

Be careful, the well.

The round stone shape only came into my vision at the last moment. I caressed the cold ridges of the rocks.

I thought putting a wooden cover over it was sufficient, I explained. But safety protocols weren't so advanced in my day. We didn't have seat belts, and we didn't fill in moribund wells. I figured if I wasn't tempted to jump in, no one else would be.

She didn't jump. You know that?

She doesn't have the imagination to jump, I said.

*

Amanda's door was open and I stepped inside.

She was sitting at her desk, typing on her keyboard faster than I could ever type.

Gramps, let me show you your room. I helped Mom get it ready, said Amanda, leading me into the spare bedroom. Everything's clean and there are towels, and a pitcher of water, and a space heater if you get too cold.

I don't trust these things, I said. Afraid I'm gonna burn down the house.

I brought up books from the basement so you'll feel like you're in a library, said Amanda, pointing to a row of bookshelves. My old walnut bookshelves.

I couldn't find your book. But I did find your typewriter, said Amanda, pointing to my pale green Hermes manual. Maybe sometime you can show me how it works?

You mean you don't know how a typewriter works? It's not a slide rule.

Are you writing a book now?

I've been writing books for forty-five years, I told her. I finished one.

11

But before I would sleep off my jet lag for fifteen hours, before the graveside memorial that would go horribly awry, let me catch you up on the last two months.

Amanda's mother went online to check the LLC credit card balance and was shocked to see that it exceeded a thousand dollars. It turns out Amanda had purchased a few more things since the food court orgy at the mall.

Carole immediately confiscated the card and gave Amanda a lecture about budgets.

But it's tax deductible, said Amanda.

Her mother explained that tax deductible expenses were not free, but amounted to a discount, usually not more than forty percent.

Amanda acknowledged that possessing both an eagerness to please others and a platinum card was a volatile combination.

*

Two representatives from Babylon Skincare had a Zoom conference call with Amanda, her parents, and her lawyer, who was not rumpled at all for the remote meeting, but well ironed out in his best gray suit. They wanted to make sure Amanda understood her obligations per the contract. She didn't, but her parents, Amy and Nipuni had that covered. They also discussed Amanda's tastes, as well as Babylon's new products.

She was to expect a big box to arrive the next day. Any Babylon products she wanted would, of course, be provided free. However, she was encouraged to visit their store at the mall and take photos and videos.

Amanda tried to listen attentively, only zoning out when they read the fine print. At the end they asked if she had any questions.

Do you have a morals clause? asked Amanda.

*

Nicole tutored Amanda on the written part of the driver's license test. Amanda was flummoxed by the laws governing when to stop for school buses, and this led to more than one pencil broken in frustration.

Do I stop in the opposite direction if there is just one yellow line? asked Amanda. What if it's snowing and I can't tell the color of the lines, or if it's one or two? What about city buses that take sports teams to games? Do I have to stop for them?

Just stop for anything, said Nicole at last, equally frustrated. Any bus, or any vehicle that looks like a bus, stop.

Nicole could not help her with the driving part, as she was still banned by the Dizons. Which meant Amanda's mother coached her.

I want to drive the Jaguar, said Amanda, forced to learn on the Camry. You don't trust me.

It's not a matter of trusting you, said her mother.

We only have the Jaguar because of me. Why can't I drive it if it's not a trust issue?

Nicole said it was bad for your brand.

Oh, now when it's convenient you're quoting Nicole!

Watch the road! screamed her mother.

Needless to say, these sessions did not go well. Shouting matches and tears.

She passed the written test, missing only those questions involving buses.

She failed the driving test.

But the entire world commiserated with her.

I failed my first three tries. Don't give up!

When I see a school bus coming, I turn the corner.

And her followers, especially in foreign lands, and cities like New York and L.A., were fascinated by the particulars of the Iowa driver's test:

Which side of the road do you drive on?

Are there any curves in Iowa? If not, how do you practice turning?

Are the roads paved?

What do you do when there are cows in the road? Here in India cows are sacred you know.

Do kids drive to cornfields in the middle of nowhere to shag?

*

But the driver's test was tic-tac-toe compared with the PSAT.

Her parents wanted her to be tutored, but Amanda refused.

It's a *practice* test, hellooooo! said Amanda. If I'm gonna practice for the practice test, I might as well not even take the *actual* practice test!

Nicole scheduled to take the PSAT at the same time.

Look, said Nicole in the classroom, before the proctor arrived. It's multiple choice, and it just goes up to *e*. That's five possibilities. So, we'll have a code one through five, one being *a*, two being *b*, get it? You sit behind me and I'll give hand signals.

You want me to cheat on a practice test? wondered Amanda. No!!!

I'm just trying to help.

How is that helping? Besides getting caught, which might violate my morals clause, this is a practice test to test my knowledge. But if I cheat, then I'm only practicing cheating. And unless I can cheat on the actual SAT, it's no help at all.

I see your point, conceded Nicole.

You're just making me more nervous, said Amanda, taking the prescription bottle her mother had given her in New York and swallowing one of the white tablets.

Give me one, said Nicole.

You suffer from anxiety too?

What are you talking about? asked Nicole, taking the bottle and popping two in her mouth. They're Tic Tacs.

Amanda was aghast her friend had just put two of them in her mouth.

Spit those out! They're my mom's anxiety meds.

Look, said Nicole, showing her the bottle. Your mom took one of her prescriptions, emptied the bottle, ripped the label off and put in Tic Tacs. You're so naive!

Nicole put one of the Tic Tacs in Amanda's mouth.

Suck on it.

Amanda sucked on it.

Oh my God! exclaimed Amanda. And I was worried I'd get addicted!

*

The practice SAT was only a practice in disillusionment. Not only was Amanda not calmed by the fake medicine, but the realization that her mother had tricked her made concentrating on the test impossible. For the first twenty minutes all she could think of was all the times she had swallowed a Tic Tac with a full glass of water, thinking it was an addictive pharmaceutical.

When she glanced up at the clock after answering the first three questions, half an hour had gone by. She stared at the long columns on the answer sheet, burst into tears, and fled from the classroom.

Don't despair, Amanda. It's just a practice test.

I'll tutor you for free if you follow my blog.

A good breakfast is critical.

If you don't know the answer, take an educated guess.

Why does a mega star like you need the SAT?

I can't believe your terminal likability, said Nicole at lunch the next day. I get a micro zit and everyone shuns me. You screw up and gain a million followers!

*

The fact that Amanda was still trending upward after nine weeks in the spotlight was not lost on corporate America. Her lawyer, who had hired a full-time assistant and bought two new suits, inked several more sponsorship deals.

Amanda was on her way to becoming a millionaire.

*

She was almost sad to see the cast come off. Pretty much everything good that had happened in her life, happened while she was wearing the cast.

I suppose you want to keep it, for the autographs, said the orthopedist, trying to cut between the names.

Actually, Amanda had received several requests to auction it for charity, as well as numerous unsavory cash offers from middle-aged men.

But she decided to give it to Harding High, after the principal made a personal request.

There was a simple ceremony, featuring the no longer serious-minded but now ebullient principal placing the cast in the trophy case, between a finalist for boys tennis and a 3rd place in girls volleyball. They posed together for the school paper, but of course it was Amanda's PingPong account that had inspired the installation. For the next week the now ebullient principal would be the most Liked principal in the world.

*

With the help of Team Amanda, she squeaked by first quarter. Not that it was a pretty sight, her report card. Not a single *A*, and *D*'s in American History and English.

Before showing the report card to her parents, she placed a frantic call to Mr. Cole.

What do I do? asked Amanda. People want to know about my grades. Is this like varsity football, where I have to maintain a certain grade point average or I can't play?

Don't worry, said her lawyer. Basically, unless you run a meth lab or violate PingPong's *Terms of Service*, you're good to go.

Amanda sank down on her bed in relief. Most kids are worried to tell their parents. But she had reached such a pinnacle in her life that she no longer cared what they thought of her academic achievement.

Still, she sucked on a Tic Tac from her mother's old prescription bottle to calm her nerves. Just because.

*

Nicole had been wrong about Martin not being a three-date guy. About girls having to go all the way on date two or get ghosted. Either that, or Martin made an exception for our sweet heroine.

Because by the time I flew into town they'd gone out five times, and he hadn't so much as tried to grope her. French kisses, and nothing more.

He might as well have been White Hat Ned.

I don't understand it, said Nicole one day over BLT's at lunch. What's his game?

Why do you think so poorly of everyone?

Because people are rotten, said Nicole. Everyone has an angle, except you. The question is, what's Marty's game? He hasn't asked you to buy anything?

I took your advice and reversed who buys the movie tickets and who buys the concessions, and he's gone along with that, said Amanda. He even said sure when I ordered a grand Starbucks peppermint mocha instead of a small Coke.

Hmmm, muttered Nicole. And he hasn't asked for anything else? Something big?

Like a luxury automobile? wondered Amanda.

Ouch. That's below the belt, moaned Nicole. What about social media? Maybe he wants to be an influencer too?

Nope.

The girls spent a minute in silent contemplation.

Maybe he's trying to get back at you for dumping him, said Amanda at last.

Nicole frowned.

That's not fair to you, said Nicole. I'm sorry. Forget what I said. He likes you. He just never noticed you before. None of us did. Not even me.

*

And what about White Hat Ned, you might wonder?

Amanda tried to keep her relationship with Martin Decker—it wasn't really a relationship, was it?—off social media. And Martin, for his part, didn't post anything himself. He also agreed not to sit at Amanda's table at lunch or hang at her locker.

So, what was his game?

It's easy to stereotype people. But just because Martin Decker was crush-worthy and popular, and a player and not a third date kind of guy, doesn't mean he couldn't be a gentleman with the right woman.

When I interviewed him for this book, he admitted he never approached Amanda before she fell in the well because he didn't think she was pretty, she wasn't popular, she was extremely shy and, except for Nicole, they didn't share any friends or activities in common. In other words, why should he approach her?

And as you'll remember, it was Amanda who approached him when she requested the kiss at the hospital cafeteria.

She was a good kisser—something he couldn't have known before. And after she started dressing better and taking care of herself, Martin Decker realized she wasn't bad looking. Not a Nicole. She'd never be a Nicole. But not someone he'd be embarrassed to be seen with on a Friday night.

She was now the most popular girl in Iowa.

But what impressed Martin Decker more than anything was that Amanda was easy to be with. She was the first girl he'd ever dated who wasn't possessive. Everyone was wondering what he wanted from *her,* but no one was considering the situation from his perspective. They didn't think that, being popular himself, girls always wanted something from *him.*

Amanda was the first girl he had ever encountered who was sans drama, who accepted that he saw others, who didn't pry or start rumors. On the contrary, she didn't use him to boost her own clout. She was the first girl who didn't care what he drove or wore, who didn't try to improve him. She was the first girl who let him choose the movies, every time, who didn't bog him down in negotiations for everything—except paying for the concessions, and he suspected she would have caved even there had he pressed the matter.

She didn't care if he held her hand or didn't hold her hand, or even if he held his ex's hand during double dates gone amiss—yes,

Nicole showed up again with some lame excuse about her date having a cold and took the seat next to Martin and held his hand and ate his popcorn and drank his Sprite from the bottle without even wiping it first.

And because he was free to see other girls, he felt no need to pressure Amanda for sex. He could go out on a Friday night and have a good time the whole time. And no after texts.

White Hat Ned, on the other hand, wanted a lot. No one asked what his game was because people assumed geeks naturally want to wire up networks and install operating systems. People assume geeks are just as happy to set up a home office for a girl with leprosy as for the most popular girl in the school; that they would be so focused on debugging that they wouldn't even notice the difference.

And even when White Hat Ned's love for Amanda had become evident, kids didn't say: 'Oh, that's his game!' 'He's just another player.' Rather they felt sorry for him because Amanda seemed embarrassed by his attentions. He wore his heart on his sleeve, but her Facebook status still read *single*. People thought of him as friend-zoned, with minimal benefits, even though she consented to call him her *boyfriend*. And Amy and Nipuni knew he wasn't even on the payroll.

*

It was after Amanda's third of fourth date with Martin Decker that a geek friend of White Hat Ned's sent him a picture of Amanda and Martin Decker holding hands at the concession stand.

The next morning White Hat Ned burst into her room. Fortunately, she was already awake, showered and dressed, sitting at her computer. And fortunately, not livestreaming, because had the green light been on, the whole world would have been witness to a scene so vapid and unseemly I hesitate to even document it here.

But I will.

White Hat Ned: Are you seeing Martin Decker?

Amanda:

White Hat Ned: Are you seeing him?

Amanda: Define seeing.

White Hat Ned: You were spotted at the movies last night.

Amanda: Yes, sometimes we go to the movies.

White Hat Ned: You mean there have been other times!!!

Amanda:

White Hat Ned: You've been having an affair behind my back?

Amanda: Affair? What are we, forty years old? And it's not behind your back. I told you I was polyamorous.

[Yes, she had finally nailed it!]

White Hat Ned: Does your mom know?

Amanda: You're gonna tattle on me? What, are we four years old? Tell her yourself if you want. She'll be glad. She's worried we're too close. And she hated you until you installed the security system.

White Hat Ned: Mandy, you need to choose. Him or me.

Amanda: You've been watching too much *Game of Thrones*. Take a seat. Chill.

White Hat Ned: Have you... With him... Are you still a...

Amanda: You're starting to get on my nerves!

White Hat Ned: Promise me you won't...

Amanda: Why are people always asking me to promise them things? Listen, I promise not to do anything with him that I don't do with you.

White Hat Ned:

Amanda: Can you take a look at this YouTube? It keeps buffering.

12

The funeral was a quiet affair held on a cold and gray day for a few family members and friends, and thirty-five million people in the PingPong universe.

Well, it was planned as a quiet affair. It started out as a quiet affair, before dissolving into an international acid bath of punditry over the hang-ups of old people like myself—the Luddite class—or conversely the dangers of internet addiction, the toxic voyeurism of social media, the treadmill of the star influencer.

Amanda had never been to a funeral before. Her wardrobe contained every color in the rainbow, except black. Well, because black wasn't in the rainbow. And her mother only had a single black dress, and that only because many years ago she has browsed a *Cosmopolitan* magazine while waiting at the checkout line at the supermarket. She never read *Cosmo*, considering it beneath her intellectually. But as there was no *American Scholar* at the Aldi, it was either browse the *Cosmo* or watch the price check drama unfolding at the register. The *Cosmo* article she read stated that every woman must own at least one black dress.

So she bought one. And never wore it until her mother died.

She didn't think to buy her daughter a black dress, as Amanda was still a girl and the Dizons were frugal.

So the night before the funeral they went through all the unsolicited clothes stored in the second guest bedroom.

They didn't find any black dresses, but there was a pair of black jeans that fit, and black heels. Amanda had never worn heels before and practiced awkwardly in the hallway. I voiced my fear that spraining an ankle after recovering from a broken ankle was a steep price to pay for obeying societal convention, and her parents agreed. On further reconnaissance we found a pair a black

Vans and everyone was happy.

For the rest we found a black sweater and a navy parka.

For my part I was always ready for a funeral, black being pretty much everything I wore, even in the smoldering heat of Southeast Asia. All I needed was a coat, and every Iowan has plenty of those.

But our efforts to dress Amanda appropriately were all wasted, as we discovered upon entering the small stone Unitarian church. The minister was wearing green, and my ex's cohort of lesbian friends were dressed in everything from biker pants to a stained Nirvana t-shirt.

The minister, a rosy-cheeked woman not long out of divinity school, pulled us aside to ask if any of us would like to speak at the service.

I raised my hand.

I failed to compose a eulogy, I admitted. You must understand, I suffer chronic writer's block. Nevertheless...

But Carole shot me a scornful look and I didn't press the matter.

What about you? asked the minister of Amanda.

I didn't write anything either, said Amanda. Was I supposed to?

That's all right, said the minister. You can speak from the heart.

I'd prefer to eulogize my mother alone, said Carole, fearful not only of what I might say, but casting a glance at the woman in biker pants, her support of the LGBTQ community apparently not extending to graveside speeches memorializing her mother.

Can I be a pallbearer, though? asked Amanda in a timid voice.

The minister looked at her parents and me.

You'll have to put down your phone, I said.

I need two hands? asked Amanda.

She looked around the spartanly furnished church, expecting to see the casket.

Where's the coffin? I've never seen a dead person.

The minister took Amanda's hand, the hand that wasn't holding her phone.

We don't do open casket, said the minister.

Whew! said Amanda. I wish someone had told me that before. I was so afraid.

There's nothing to be afraid of, princess, I told her, taking her hand after the minister let go.

Gramps, have you been drinking?

Shhhh.

*

We filed out of the church somberly.

Amanda hurried over to the hearse and started taking pictures with her phone.

Stop that! I yelled.

Now the minister took *my* hand, as if I were the child here, ignorant of Unitarian funeral customs.

Perhaps it's her way of expressing her grief, said the minister.

It's a fucking insult, I whispered under my breath. What about *my* grief?

*

Robert drove behind the hearse, leading the procession of lesbian friends, straight friends, and an adult family of cousins I couldn't recall ever meeting, though they swore they were at our wedding.

I sat in the back seat with Amanda. I wanted to hold her hand, but she was scrolling on her phone. I wanted to throw it out the window, but instead I merely looked out the window at the harvested fields.

*

Don't make a scene, whispered Carole as the casket was removed from the hearse.

Talk to your daughter, not to me. All she makes are scenes.

I was referring to video scenes, but at that mournful moment my wit was lost on my daughter.

After minimal instruction from the minister, we lined up and grasped our handles, the four of us plus one of the cousins and—yes—the woman in the Nirvana shirt.

I stood beside Amanda, at the end, and we whispered in the lowest of voices as we walked over the cold ground.

Amanda: It's not as heavy as I thought.

Sutherland: Have you ever carried something with five other people?

Amanda: True. But I bet she didn't weigh much.

Sutherland: More than you, I bet.

Amanda: I'm not anorexic.

Sutherland: I didn't say you were.

Amanda: I eat cereal and ice cream and drink soda and coladas.

Sutherland: You could be bulimic.

Amanda: What's that?

Sutherland: You really don't know what bulimic is? That's reassuring. It's when you deliberately throw up after eating.

Amanda: Oh yeah. Princess Diana. But I could never do that.

Sutherland: Promise me you never will.

Amanda: I promise. You must have really loved Grandma. I mean, you came back all the way from Cambodia.

Sutherland: Vietnam.

Amanda: Whatever. Mom says you didn't love Grandma.

Sutherland: And you believe everything your mom tells you?

Amanda: Of course not.

Sutherland: Well, then...

*

We set the coffin down and gathered around as two workers lowered it into the grave, using a rope underneath, which they pulled up after.

So that's how they do it, said Amanda. I never even thought about it.

Dearest family members and friends... began the rosy-cheeked minister without delay, sensing that no one wanted to stand long out in this cold.

Or perhaps she was just uncomfortable that a unicorn was pointed in her direction, capturing her every nervous tic for teens in Hyderabad and Brisbane. For Amanda was livestreaming my ex-wife's funeral.

Blah blah blah. Blah blah blah blah blah blah blah blah blah blah blah blah blah blah blah blah blah blah blah blah blah blah blah blah Corinthians.

Was I the only one offended by Amanda's behavior?

Put that thing away! I said under my breath.

I should admit I'd had three or four rum and Cokes that morning, having bought several bottles at duty-free and stashed them in my carry-on.

Let her be, said Carole.

Blah blah blah blah blah blah blah blah blah blah blah blah blah blah blah blah blah blah blah blah blah blah blah blah blah blah blah blah blah blah blah blah blah blah blah blah blah blah blah blah blah blah blah blah blah blah blah blah Amen.

Carole trembled throughout her eulogy. I don't know whether it was the cold or her grief or nervousness at being caught on camera for her daughter's thirty-five million PingPong followers.

Blah blah blah blah blah blah blah blah blah blah blah blah blah blah blah blah blah blah blah blah blah blah blah blah blah blah blah blah blah blah blah blah blah blah blah blah blah blah blah blah blah blah difficult marriage.

blah blah blah blah blah blah blah blah blah blah blah blah blah blah blah blah blah blah blah blah blah blah blah blah blah blah blah blah blah blah blah blah blah blah blah blah blah blah blah blah blah blah blah blah blah blah blah blah blah blah blah blah blah blah best mother in the world.

Blah blah blah blah blah blah blah blah blah blah blah blah blah blah blah blah blah blah blah blah blah blah long suffering...blah blah blah.

After she finished, I took Carole's hand and tried to comfort her.

That was very poignant, I said. Actually, I hadn't listened. It was too much having to hear what a saint her mother had been, when I knew better. But why had I come then? What was I expecting?

Anyway, I could always listen to the speech on PingPong or YouTube or my daughter's website if I changed my mind. Good to know nothing is lost in the vlog-o-sphere.

Hey, hey! I shouted.

Carole had tossed some earth into the grave, and I had too.

Now Amanda stepped up, and I assumed she would do the same.

Instead, she pointed the phone down.

Hey, hey! I shouted.

They want to see, said Amanda, not even looking up, as if her followers had requested a view of the weathervane on the church.

I tried to wrestle the phone away from her, as I had at the airport.

Maybe it was my cold fingers, or the rum and Cokes, or that blasted unicorn horn case, but the phone slipped away.

It landed with a thud, settling on the unicorn horn on the mahogany coffin, streaming still.

Oh my God! cried Amanda.

And she continued to air record, as if the phone were still in her hand, feeling its oblong shape, the way an amputee feels a phantom limb.

With gasps from all—perhaps even from the departed herself, who can say?—we peered into the grave, where a late model iPhone recorded us like a messenger from God.

PART THREE

In the Darkness

1

I don't believe even the progressive theologians of the Unitarian Church have a doctrine regarding cell phones falling into graves. Maybe I'd find hundreds of examples if I Googled:

What do I do if my phone falls into an open grave?

Surely Amanda couldn't have been the first. But I'd say she was most certainly the first to lose her phone while it was still streaming, being viewed by countless millions.

Actually, of course, the millions were counted. The millions of views, the millions of Likes, the millions, even, of Shares.

Amanda gained four million new followers. The gravesite video, in various edited forms, made the news from Ulster to Ulaanbaatar and was discussed by everyone from *Just Us Girls*, who commiserated with Amanda's loss, to the British tabloids, which accused her of staging the event. (Whether that staging came to include my ex's death itself depended on the degree of conspiracy theory mania of the individual tabloid.)

After the phone fell onto the casket we stared into the open grave, wondering what to do. I secretly hoped we might leave it there, though that would certainly preclude my ex from resting in peace, at least until the battery ran out.

Amanda started crying when she realized she was holding a phantom phone, fearing immediate punishment from both the living and the dead, as well as the loss of her primary connection to the world.

Who knows what would have happened had enough time elapsed? Perhaps the workers who had lowered the casket would have been summoned to try to retrieve the phone with a shovel without being too disrespectful.

Perhaps someone would have called 911. Perhaps the minister, her tolerance reaching an end, would have blinded the phone by throwing earth over it.

But before any of these options could be attempted, the woman in the Nirvana t-shirt jumped in, as if she were stepping off a high curb, collected the phone in one hand, and waved her other arm for volunteers to pull her up.

*

Amanda couldn't sleep that night, fearing the phone was haunted. She had backed away when the woman in the Nirvana t-shirt tried to hand it to her, relenting only after it was doused with antibacterial lotion.

Even then she held it with her father's handkerchief, and cleaned it several more times at home, like Lady Macbeth trying to wash the blood of King Duncan off her hands.

She saw my light was on and came into my room.

Gramps, I have a problem.

She set her phone on my bed, protected by the handkerchief.

I'm glad to see you finally admit your internet addiction.

What? No. I'm afraid it's haunted. Should I just buy a new one?

Why don't you take a poll?

I was being sarcastic, but she thanked me for my genius idea and kissed me goodnight.

Her respondents overwhelmingly concurred that the phone wasn't haunted. Many suggested prayers, or spells, just in case. Some, not incorrectly, noted that the phone probably contracted more bacteria from her kitchen counter than from the gravesite.

*

The following night Carole convened a family meeting at the safe space that was the back room at the Olive Garden.

I had to ask permission to order a rum and Coke and was denied. One glass of white wine was the best I could negotiate.

Amanda no longer had to ask permission to order virgin coladas, but that was about the extent of her extravagance. Indeed, since the sponsorship money started to roll in, she hadn't spent much on herself at all. She had more clothes, shoes, jewelry and makeup than she knew what to do with. Even the pewter *Amanda911* pendant had been the idea of the marketing gurus at Babylon Skincare.

Her tastes in fashion were moderate in any case, and she wasn't adventurous when it came to eating, preferring lasagna to lobster, cheeseburgers to sushi.

She had no desire to travel the world, to live in a mansion, or a glamorous city. Not even to impress others. Hadn't she already impressed enough people?

For most of us, money makes us want to chase happiness. For Amanda, the sudden influx of money made her realize how close to happiness she had been all along.

Can we agree at the outset of this conference that this is a safe space and no one will say anything that may be construed as offensive to others? said Carole, sipping on her vodka martini.

You mean you're leaving the table? I quipped.

You're not helping, Sutherland.

Why do you always call Gramps *Sutherland?* asked Amanda.

This is not the direction I want the conversation to go, said her mother.

Because your mother and I are pals. BFFs, I said.

A lot of people from our generation call their parents by their first name, said Amanda's father, trying to be diplomatic.

She didn't call her mother by her first name, I remarked quietly.

OK, enough, said Carole. You're not going to hijack the conversation. Don't make everything about you. And I know about the booze in your carry-on.

Who says booze anymore? Even people my age don't say booze.

You searched his room? asked Amanda. Do you search my room too?

Amanda suddenly felt guilty, although the most incriminating item in her possession were Tic Tacs in a prescription bottle.

Yes, if I suspect someone is keeping contraband in my house, said her mother.

No one says contraband either, I told her.

I smiled at Amanda.

She's just getting back at me, fifty-five years later, for finding a bong in her room.

You smoked weed, Mom? asked Amanda.

Everyone smoked. You knew we smoked. Not anymore.

Hashish. Peyote buttons. Dexedrine, I whispered loud enough for even the waitress to hear.

Would you like another Dexedrine—I mean martini? asked the waitress, as flustered as the rest of us.

Carole shot her a leave-in-two-seconds-or-no-tip look.

I hope you're not recording this? asked Amanda's father.

Amanda said no, but her mother made her turn off the phone and place it on the table for safe measure.

What happened at Grandma's funeral was a sign, said Amanda's mother in a soft voice, stroking her daughter's hair. Your father and I should have recognized your addiction sooner, but we were so caught up in your success...

Addiction? cried Amanda.

I have to give credit to your grandfather for seeing what the rest of us failed to see...

You think I'm addicted to my phone, Gramps?

Since you fell in the well what is the longest time you've been without a phone, not counting the times I took it away? interrupted Amanda's mother.

When I sleep, of course.

But you sleep with your phone.

Everyone under fifty sleeps with their phone, Mom.

Do you turn it off?

I put it on mute.

That's not turning it off! I can't recall the last time I saw you without the phone in your hand.

I'm not playing Angry Birds, Mom. This is my job. I'm working. You don't do an intervention for someone who works all the time. The family of that star doctor at the Mayo Clinic doesn't take him to Olive Garden and say: 'You have an addiction. Stop saving so many lives.'

Amanda looked at her father. Dad, do you think I have an addiction?

Amanda's father suddenly remembered their last trip to the Olive Garden, when he had alleged that she might have jumped into the well, which ended with her crying in the restroom.

His earlier courage to confront his daughter as a parental unit dissipated.

I... I...

Gramps, do you think I'm addicted?

I most certainly do. Although I was not informed this was to be an intervention. I don't want you to feel betrayed.

What do you know about it?! screamed Amanda.

Actually, I'm an expert in addiction. I have one Ph.D. in English Literature and another in Addiction.

I was joking, but inwardly I felt quite distraught. Yesterday at the funeral was the first time I had ever been angry with Amanda, and now was the first time I saw her regard me with anything but fondness.

At least I'm not a drunk... shouted Amanda, tears starting to flow. In her haste to flee she knocked over her virgin colada and ran to the restroom, followed by her mother.

Amanda had a problem that required a family solution, but Carole had not made things easy by ambushing her.

The only back room in the Olive Garden that turned out to be a safe space was the ladies' room.

*

Thanks to my daughter's snooping, my carry-on was lighter by three bottles of rum. Or two, considering that I had already finished one bottle. But I would soon be at a duty-free again.

Amanda knocked on my open door.

I want to say sorry for calling you a drunk at the Olive Garden.

No harm done. I probably should apologize for grabbing your phone at the funeral.

She stepped into the room.

What are you doing? asked Amanda.

Packing.

You're not going?

I am.

Why? You just got here. Do you have another family in the Philippines, or Cambodia?

You're my family.

I stood to my full height and she came over and threw her arms around me.

Don't go.

It's not my house.

This was never not your house.

You're really leaving? asked Carole, peeking in. What's your hurry? You have a poker game waiting in Macau?

I don't want to overstay my welcome...

What welcome? You were never invited.

Carole smiled, probably the first time she had smiled at me in twenty years.

Look Sutherland, I know we don't have the best relationship. But Amanda needs you. She just lost a grandparent. Don't make her say goodbye to you too.

I pushed Amanda to arm's length so I could see her eyes.

You really want me to stay, princess?

Mmmmmm.

You know I might take your phone away again. I might smash it next time.

I can always buy another one. I'm rich now.

Actually, Robert and I were talking, said Carole. And he agrees with me. And I'm sure Amanda would be delighted if you stayed here. At least through the winter. See how it goes. If you follow our rules.

You mean your rules.

We also want to help you financially. We know you don't have much savings left. Admit it, you're living on fumes. And what kind of income do you have? Teaching English for ten dollars an hour?

You know I'm too proud to take charity.

We're not talking about charity. You can join Team Amanda.

Nonsense. What would I do?

You can help me in English, said Amanda. I got a *D*.

You got a *D* in English? With your pedigree?

What's a pedigree?

We were thinking you could help with content. Write blogs... suggested Carole.

Ghostwrite for my granddaughter?

I don't know. Or maybe write her biography.

She's sixteen. She doesn't have a biography!

Hey! interrupted Amanda with sudden excitement, turning to her mother. I know who I want to take me to the Influencer Festival!

No...no... said her mother.

It's my decision, said Amanda.

It's his decision too. And he'll never agree.

They both looked at me.

Amanda took my hand. Have you ever been to Turks and something?

Turks and Caicos, said Carole.

No, but I hear it has some of the best beaches in the Caribbean.

Then come. I've been invited to a three-day festival for influencers around New Year's. All expenses paid. But Mom won't let me go without an adult.

Why doesn't she go with you then?

You really need to ask?

And your dad?

Helloooo! He's my dad.

And I'm your grandfather. How is that different?

You're cool. You're not gonna embarrass me.

But I despise influencers. I think it's a superficial con game. Worse than network television.

You don't even have a phone, said Amanda. How can you hate something you don't even know about?

Amanda did not realize how pointed that argument was to me. Because how many people criticize a book they haven't read? My daughter and my book, for instance.

I'll go, I said.

Really? said Carole with an undisguised expression of shock.

I'll even get a phone, so I can supervise her properly.

On one condition, said Carole. You promise not to drink.

I promise.

2

We had about a month before the trip, which gave us sufficient time to either thoroughly prepare or blow everything up.

Job one was getting Amanda's passport. Not a problem, but her parents hadn't even sent in the application, so I volunteered to help with that.

For my part, I had to buy and learn how to use a phone and sign up for social media accounts. I was proud to become Amanda's 37,596,522th follower.

Or was I?

At the time I had been asked to chaperone her I agreed out of a sense of familial duty. But as the countdown began, and I began my own research into the influencer phenomenon, I acquired an ulterior motive.

I thought I might write an article.

My proposed title was "Superficial Superficiality."

My thesis was that we always had superficiality in art, culture, commerce. Advertising was superficial in that it used artists and writers, and later filmmakers, to sell products. A movie was superficial if it followed the same formula as a thousand movies before it. Greeting cards were superficial in that givers used mass-produced sentiments instead of expressing their own feelings directly to the recipient.

But traditional superficiality still had a basis in some kind of ability or expertise. Andy Warhol began his career drawing shoes for sales catalogs. But he was a real artist. Pulp films were made by people trained in filmmaking. Greeting cards were written by writers and poets, however insipid. They had some training or ability in what they did. They did something.

But what did Paris Hilton do? Or the Kardashians? Certainly, there are influencers who have a particular talent, such as profession-al chefs or musicians. But what about those who open packages, or play video games, or try on clothes, or simply document their lives, like my granddaughter?

That's a new level of superficiality, which the world has never known until now—super superficiality.

So, I wrote to the *New Yorker* magazine proposing to write a pro-file of influencer culture during the festival.

They replied faster than expected:

Dear Sutherland Archer,

We thought you died twenty years ago?

Yours,

The *New Yorker*

*

Maybe I would try *Vanity Fair.*

But as the days passed, I decided to set the project aside. After all, this would be the first quality time I would spend with my princess. Besides which it carried a certain adult responsibility. I couldn't be scampering around interviewing and observing oth-ers when my job was supervising her. And wouldn't I be exploit-ing her for my own literary needs? Particularly if the results were negative, as they most certainly would be. Hadn't I done that once before, with her mother?

I had.

*

I got to meet Nicole, Amy, Nipuni and White Hat Ned. Yes, Nicole had regained house privileges, although there was no formal announcement. One day Carole came home to see the Ford F-150 parked on the curb. When the girls came downstairs for snacks and Nicole awkwardly asked: 'How's it going, Mrs. Dizon?' Amanda's mother simply nodded and that small gesture served as absolution.

The household possessed three cars, but it had been years since I drove, and my license was expired. Just as well, since many of my trips were to Vincent's Bar and Grill. I couldn't bring alcohol onto the premises, but that didn't mean I was condemned to sobriety for the entire winter.

The four kids supplemented Uber in ferrying me across the frigid landscape, and this gave me a chance to get to know them, as well as through their social media. Nicole always drove with both hands on the wheel. I felt bad she had made such a costly mistake.

And I felt bad that my granddaughter had stolen her dream. Nicole was smart but undisciplined. She wanted to be an influencer, but as I would later learn many influencers are introverts, with lots of time on their hands. Nicole's popularity in the real world got in the way of her digital career. Even her best friend's stardom couldn't get her a thousand followers on PingPong.

I became her 950th follower. Not even enough social media clout to wrangle a free sundae at Dairy Queen.

*

Amy was a natural entrepreneur but hadn't found anything to sell until Amanda's accident. She and Nipuni had been best friends since primary school, insulated even within the Diversity Crew. When Amanda found herself mistakenly relegated to their group, they took her on because she was a white girl who accepted them unreservedly. And she was easy to manipulate.

Unfortunately, there wasn't anything worth manipulating her for. She didn't have money, she wasn't a great student, and she didn't have any other friends, except Nicole, who kept her own social circles separate.

Amanda was just someone to hang out with, until she became so much more.

I became Amy's 1,247th PingPong follower, most of whom were Asian girls she'd never met.

Puni's parents didn't allow her to have a PingPong account. But she did answer questions about Bollywood films on Quora. I followed her there.

*

White Hat Ned was a behind-the-scenes guy and didn't talk much during our drives, unless I asked tech questions, in which case he was very forthcoming. He was the only one of the four who asked about my book, but since it wasn't science fiction he expressed no desire to read it.

He then told me he wrote some fan fiction himself, if I wanted to give him feedback. He didn't have a PingPong account, being a behind-the-scenes guy, so I followed his fan fiction—a new world to me—and left a supportive comment.

*

As for Amanda's addiction, she agreed to embargo her phone at 10:00 p.m. on weekdays, and not use it during family meals, or funerals.

She still used the computer in her room long after her stated bedtime, as I could observe from the blue light emanating from beneath her door. But this was darkness enough, I supposed.

*

I can't say I was particularly useful during this time, but I did help Amanda with her schoolwork, and I don't think it's presumptuous to say my efforts bumped her up from a *D* to a *B* in English.

I refused to write her papers for her, which meant it took me five times as long to help her do it herself.

I don't know why you can't just dictate to me, said Amanda.

Because that's cheating.

Everyone else does it.

That doesn't make it right.

I think it does. If everyone agrees to do the same thing of course it's right.

In her rainbow unicorn brain, she had just undone the hard work of Kant's categorical imperative. But I said nothing.

I looked for your book, said Amanda. But it's not on Kindle.

It was published when the Amazon was just a river and a jungle.

Our library used to have it, but doesn't anymore.

How do you know. Did you read it?

I tried to when I was thirteen, but it was too hard.

At least you tried, I said, encouraged by her effort.

I asked Mom, but she doesn't have it. Why is that? I mean, they have a gazillion books, but not yours? What's up with that?

A clerical oversight, I suppose.

So I had to order it from an Amazon reseller. It cost me two hundred bucks! Ha.

You shouldn't have done that.

I'm gonna take it on the trip.

This time I'll be here to explain it to you, I said.

I'd rather figure it out myself and have you write my school paper, said Amanda.

*

The media and marketing people were off for Christmas week but, as you know by now, an influencer is never off. And all trips are business trips, even when they're to white sand beaches in the Caribbean.

And that means an influencer's team is not off either, especially when there is an Influencer Festival to prepare for.

This would signify many firsts for Amanda. First time out of the country. First time in a place where English was not the main language—though most of the influencers would be from the U.S. First time traveling with me any place farther than the Baskin-Robbins. First time sleeping in a hut—apparently the organizers equated music festivals with communal toilets. First time packing ten swimsuits. Yes, ten! As per her sponsors.

I'm surprised you approve of this, I whispered to Carole, as my granddaughter modeled the swimsuits.

She was paring the selection down from twenty to ten, in front of her parents, me, Amy and Nipuni.

Her father voted exclusively for the one-pieces.

Carole had sent White Hat Ned on some meaningless errand.

I thought you would object to the objectification of sixteen-year-old girls, I said. Especially your daughter at an event where the lights of recording devices will be forever green.

It's good for other girls to see a real body like hers, said Amanda's mother. The profusion of models creates unrealistic expectations.

She's as thin as a model, though, I pointed out.

Amanda, did you hear what Gramps said? He thinks you look like a bikini model!

Really? asked Amanda, who never would have had the courage to model swimsuits a few months ago. Indeed, last summer she had worn a one-piece and camisole to the pool.

We're all counting on you to scare the boys away, said Amanda's father to me.

I'm worried about the men, I replied, realizing my little princess had grown into a young woman.

Anyway, it's in her contract, said Carole, ending the debate.

*

Did I mention people sent her trees? In the weeks before Christmas trucks arrived almost daily bearing trees, some real, some requiring assembly. Some fully decorated with their company's ornaments. The ones from her sponsors we took, and photographed. There were two in my room alone. The others we gave away.

I realized it was an unusual Christmas, in that instead of shopping for decorations and gifts, as the rest of the world did, everything came to us; and in the spirit of Christmas, we gifted most of it.

Carole made the wise decision not to do family gifts this year. But Christmas Eve she invited Amanda's class over to plunder the second bedroom of its clothes and accessories, and drink hot chocolate provided by a beverage sponsor.

*

Carole and Robert also had a party for their friends, children invited. It's easy to forget that Amanda's parents had lives of their own. Friends of their own. Insipid people. Typical provincials. County government employees and schoolteachers. The kind of people who gave me a *B-* on a paper worthy of publication in the *Paris Review*. But still, they had friends, and lives of their own, however much those lives increasingly orbited their daughter.

*

Amy, Nipuni and White Hat Ned came for lunch on Christmas Day, before going home to their families. Long enough to help Amanda record a Christmas greeting to her followers.

She had asked me to write it, but after three hours all I had was:

Falling down a well was both the best and worst thing that ever happened to me.

So we tore that up and Carole wrote an insipid poem inspired by a lifetime of greeting cards, but which had the benefit of not suffering from terminal writer's block.

*

Before we knew it the 29th arrived, a windy, dreary day. A great day to go south.

It seemed half of Iowa saw us off at the Des Moines International Airport. A sea of cell phones recorded us at business class check-in, as did the local TV stations. Amanda politely gave everyone interviews and we might have missed the flight had Carole not shooed them away.

This is your job, Sutherland! shouted Carole as she gave the boot to another reporter. Are you sure I can trust you with this assignment?

All my life I've been trying to attract press, not repel them, I answered meekly in my own defense.

*

Have you ever flown business class? asked Amanda as we took our seats in the first row.

Many years ago, when it was easy to get upgrades.

I could fly like this even without going anywhere, said Amanda. They make you feel so special.

It's about time people made you feel special.

You always made me feel special, Gramps.

How can you say that? I was never here.

The flight attendant lightly touched Amanda's arm.

Would you like something to drink, ma'am?

Two virgin coladas.

Two?

Well, I thought it would be easier for you to bring me two instead of drinking one and asking for a refill. I know you're very busy.

The flight attendant beamed. This was probably the first time anyone in business class had cared about her workflow.

And you, sir?

Sounds like a good strategy. Two rum and Cokes.

She went to fill our order.

Gramps! You promised Mom not to drink.

I promised not to drink at the festival.

Amanda considered this for a moment.

No, I think Mom meant for the whole trip. And this is the start of the trip.

Who is the policeman of whom here? I wondered.

3

We changed planes in Atlanta for the flight to Providenciales. Amanda ordered two more virgin coladas, but I argued that she needed to expand her horizons. The teenage years were years for experimentation.

I persuaded her to try margaritas instead. I ordered a virgin strawberry margarita for her and a real one for myself.

Gramps, you're drinking too much.

Actually, this is what we call a step down. I'm stepping down from rum to tequila. Then for dinner maybe just a beer, and perhaps a glass of wine before bed.

I'll report you to Mom!

You're gonna narc on me?

This better be a joke, Gramps. If I see you drink at the festival I'm going to scream. Remember, we have to be role models.

We?!

*

We were greeted at the tropical Providenciales Airport by a festival associate holding an *Amanda911* sign, who gave us each a welcome basket that contained, among sponsored products, a new phone.

This was a necessity, as our U.S. phones were locked and wouldn't work here. The new phones were pre-loaded with all the major social media apps, as well as the festival app.

Logging into this app was optional, but allowed influencers and their guests to geo-locate one another on a resort map and private message. This would help in my efforts to supervise my granddaughter but, as with all things digital, I worried about our privacy.

Answer me something, I asked both Amanda and the festival associate as we waited at baggage claim. He was a local man in his early twenties, dressed in the blue and yellow festival logo colors. Why don't you worry about all the data you give to corporations to archive and sell? For governments to collect? In my day we worried that the FBI might have a file on us. And by file, I mean a manila folder with a few pieces of paper and perhaps a photo or two. But your generation donates your innermost thoughts, your daily image, your whereabouts, your political views, your relationships not only to the FBI, but to everyone.

I refuse to take naked pics, said my granddaughter.

That's your answer? You don't take nude photos. That's your Maginot Line against the assault of data collection?

Yeah, duh.

I think people in Russia or China worry about that, said the festival associate in a British accent. But for us the main problem, I think, is exes. You know, your ex steals your Facebook account. That happens a lot. People are always creating new accounts, or secret accounts.

But the corporations have the data, I argued.

I don't think we worry about that so much. My country may be underwater in a few years. We could have nuclear war. We can't worry about everything.

My bags, shouted Amanda.

We were allowed two checked bags each, but I only needed a carry-on, so Amanda used the four suitcases. I realized my granddaughter was a diva, like an opera singer of old who travelled with trunks containing enough outfits to dress half the women at the hotel.

*

The Influencer Festival was the brainchild of Emerson Frost, a Silicon Valley billionaire who thought Burning Man contained the wrong-colored sand and not nearly enough water. The 150 influencers and their guests were comped their trip, and the models, celebrity chefs and musicians were paid. He sold sponsorships and documentary rights, but the festival wasn't meant to make a profit. Rather he used it as a tax-deductible party and a way to promote his cloud data company.

He had built thatched-roof huts; communal showers and toilets; an amphitheater; a windowless e-sports auditorium equipped with rows of consoles and big screens; an indoor disco with a bar; three restaurants in white tents, with bars of their own; a swimming pool with bar service; and a dedicated cell tower. All behind a secluded white sand beach.

And there was a dock long enough to moor his yacht, and other pleasure boats. And a helipad.

Wow! said Amanda as we were driven through the gate. This is like a camp for rich people.

Our hut's only nod to modernity was a single outlet with a surge protector. But there was no electric light, not even a lock on the door. There were two twin beds made from bamboo. The only other furnishings were a full-length mirror—almost as essential to influencers as electricity—two rattan tables, and lots of clothes hangers in a closet that was almost as large as the living space.

Being used to hostels, this was actually luxurious to me. And for Amanda, if you included the closet, it was larger than her room.

Cool, said Amanda. Which bed do you want?

I wondered how the more pampered influencers among us would greet their lodging. I imagined them feeling along the walls for the light switch, having neglected to read the resort description in detail. Peering into the closet for a toilet and shower. Calling an associate on their new cell phone to ask if these were the servants' quarters.

I imagined some of them pleading for a berth on Emerson's yacht. Or anyone's yacht. I imagined some of them threatening to blast Emerson on social media if they weren't transferred to a luxury hotel.

But I underestimated the deviousness of the influencer class. Sure, these were powerful people, who needed to be pleased. But none of them was a billionaire. And they calculated power the way their apps counted Likes and Follows.

So when Emerson Frost emerged from his yacht in his trademark white suit and panama hat and greeted everyone by name and asked if they found their accommodations to their liking—'Because,' he said, 'if you prefer, I could put you up at one of the hotels,' (and he said *hotels* as if describing a species of vermin)—the influencers gave responses along the lines of:

No, no, no, it's wonderful, the outdoors.

or

It reminds me of my best childhood memories at Camp Little Bighorn.

or

I always wanted to rough it, like the Antarctic explorers.

or

My followers love minimalism.

or

I'm allergic to air-conditioning.

In truth, I think Amanda and I were the only ones who were happy with the accommodations.

*

It was paradise, after all. Especially after the rain and sleet and snow and bitter wind and gray skies of Iowa. Even Boracay, in the

Philippines, rated one of the best beaches in the world, was stifling at the time I was there, low season, monsoon season. The breezes were cooler here, the air unpolluted by swarming trikes and motorcycles. If only the princess I was meant to keep from harm wasn't policing me in turn, I could have had a fantastic time.

*

I went to the nearest men's room to shower and change into shorts and sandals. When I came back Amanda still hadn't unpacked, but was sitting on her bed Skyping with mission control. Amanda's parents, the three amigas, and White Hat Ned waved to me.

I know there are going to be a lot of drugs, said Amanda's mother. With all the models and rappers. Don't let her take anything, Sutherland! No parties.

This is *all* a party, Mom!

Don't worry, I have everything under control, I said.

And don't you drink, Sutherland. Remember your promise. You're on duty.

Amanda started to speak, but I squeezed her arm.

Gotta go mingle. We'll check in tonight, I said.

I told Amanda to freshen up and change, while I unpacked her four suitcases. I found my book at the bottom of one, the copy she had just bought on Amazon for two hundred dollars. The first and only edition. Except for a tear on the dust jacket, it looked as though it had never been read.

I set it on her pillow.

We walked around the grounds to get the lay of the land. A reggae band was playing at the amphitheater.

What do you want to do? asked Amanda as we circled the beachside pool.

I want to drink. What do you want to do?

She threw off her Vans and ran to the beach and into the water.

I trailed her wearily to the water's edge.

Don't go out too far. That's good. That's enough.

Could she swim? I didn't know. All our preparation and I hadn't ascertained this most critical piece of information.

Amanda!

She walked or swam or floated further out. It was hard to tell in the glare. I'd left my sunglasses in the room.

I looked at the pier to my right, where Emerson Frost's yacht was moored, along with two others. I looked for other swimmers. There were a few, but none as far out as she. Were there sharks in Turks and Caicos? There must be.

I took off my sandals and ran in. The water was warm and clear, but not hot like Boracay.

Did they have riptides here? Another question I forgot to ask.

I swam fifty yards out, to where I could no longer touch bottom. The waves weren't strong, but again, the question was, was she a good swimmer? Did they have sharks or riptides?

Amanda!

She swam back, past me, and I followed.

She ran up the beach, obviously agitated.

Are you all right? I asked, running to catch up with her, looking for blood or missing flesh.

I can't believe I left my phone in the room!!!

*

Dinner was buffet style, prepared by influencer chefs. Not television chefs. Not cookbook chefs. Not Michelin star chefs. But enthusiasts who had leveraged some level of training and experience into a mass following, which led to their own restaurants, cookbook deals, and television appearances.

There was no reservation system, so we explored each of the three restaurants to see what Amanda preferred, she being the unadventurous eater.

She settled on Texas barbecue, which was exotic enough to her, as her parents only took her out for ribs once or twice a year.

We sat at an empty round table and she slathered on the influencer chef's signature barbecue sauce.

This isn't the best food for exhibitionists, I realized, dabbing barbecue sauce from her cheek. Too much collateral damage.

Why should I care? I'm not a model.

I looked around. I didn't see any models. They were probably at the sushi restaurant. I saw lots of young, raggedy-looking men I took to be e-gamers.

I went to the bar and got two virgin coladas for Amanda and a Coke for myself.

When she saw my glass, she put her hand over the top.

Your promise?!

It's just Coke, princess. You want to try it?

You bet.

She took a sip and was visibly surprised not to taste alcohol. Not that she was exactly sure what alcohol tasted like.

Sorry.

About halfway through our dinner I finished my soda and went to get a real rum and Coke. Of course, she wouldn't have the nerve to challenge me again. I was free and clear for the rest of the trip.

In time our table filled up with a group of e-gamers, all male, two with their fathers because they were fourteen and sixteen.

You're the girl in the well, said the sixteen-year-old, a Chinese American immigrant wearing a Joker t-shirt.

I am.

Do you play Fortnite?

No.

Do you play WoW?

What's that?

World of Warcraft.

No.

What about LoL? League of Legends.

No.

Minecraft? Farmville? Angry Birds?

Nope.

What video games *do* you play?

I got to level six of Candy Crush, but then gave up.

Oh.

I noticed the other gamers were either on their phones or laptops, busy gaming or texting while they ate.

In the awkward silence that ensued I tried to make conversation with the boy's father. But they had emigrated from Szechuan and the father didn't speak English. I only knew a few words in Chinese, and after that we were back to square one.

Who's your favorite Joker? asked the sixteen-year-old e-gamer.

You mean there's more than one? asked Amanda.

There's Jack Nicholson, Heath Ledger, and Joaquin Phoenix.

You're forgetting Cesar Romero from the real *Batman*, I interjected, glad to use the little popular culture I knew to good effect.

Dude, your dad knows his Batman! said the sixteen-year-old e-gamer to Amanda.

He's not my dad, he's my granddad.

Oh, are you an orphan?

No, but it's not cool to come with your—and then Amanda saw the sixteen-year-old e-gamer's father staring at her, and saved us all embarrassment by leaving the thought unfinished.

Who's your favorite superhero? asked the sixteen-year-old e-gamer, gamely not giving up on probably the only approach-able female at this event for someone his age.

Elsa.

Elsa's a princess, not a superhero.

Why can't she be both?

Black Panther is a king, so maybe. But what about her powers?

She has superhero powers.

Her powers only cause trouble. She doesn't use them to save people.

She saves Anna.

Anna saves her.

So, this is what our civilization has come to, I thought. Our best and brightest arguing over whether a Disney character is or is not a superhero.

The e-gamer was saved by the bell, or ringtone.

I have to go practice with my team, said the sixteen-year-old e-gamer. I'm playing in a Shards of Lancaster tournament tonight if you want to come watch.

Sure.

Great. I just PM'ed you on the festival app.

Thanks.

You have barbecue sauce on your chin.

*

Our white-clad host strode into the tent, to the flash of many phones, and made the rounds of the tables.

When he stopped at ours, he shook Amanda's hand and kissed her cheek—hopefully now free of barbecue sauce—and said the tragedy of her fall into the well had captivated the nation, if not the world. If she needed an anxiety coach, he could hook her up.

I'm great, really.

And you are her father? Her manager? I hope not her sugar daddy! said Emerson Frost to me with a capped-tooth smile.

I'm the one who needs a sugar daddy, I said.

Gramps is a writer.

Really? Well, we're all writers these days, aren't we?

He shook my hand vigorously and paused long enough for Amanda to take a photo before moving on to the remaining e-gamers at our table.

*

We went to hang out at the pool.

Plenty of models here, and no e-gamers. Too bright for e-games, I thought. And the water might short their laptops.

I noticed that no one wore name tags or gave their name when greeting us, or asked ours. For that matter, there had been no registration upon arrival, no printed materials, no schedule or orientation.

It was all on the app.

If you wanted to know the bio of the chef whose food you were eating, you only had to click on his avatar. Same for the influencers at your table. By aiming my phone at a model lying in a chaise I was given her name and nationality—Juliana Nacimiento, Brazil—her website, her Twitter account, her YouTube account, whatever other accounts she wished to list, and the option to private message her.

I decided to PM her, as an experiment. Jumping into the deep end, so to say, with my social media water wings.

A minute later she sent back an emoji that blew kisses.

Hot dog! Maybe my cynicism regarding millennials was premature? Maybe social media wasn't as horrific as I thought.

She looked up and waved.

I nudged Amanda, and we walked over. But with so much information revealed already on the app, what was there to say?

You're so sweet, said the Brazilian model to me in a lovely Portuguese accent.

Me?

For chaperoning your granddaughter.

Naturally, she had already accessed this information through my profile on the festival app.

I sat down on the chaise beside hers and motioned for Amanda to do the same.

But you don't have any accounts on your profile, said the Brazilian model, glancing back at her phone.

This whole social media world is new to me.

He has Facebook and PingPong, said Amanda.

I just didn't list them on my profile, I explained.

But you must, said the Brazilian model, as if I had failed to bring my passport to the island.

She was wearing a canary yellow bikini and designer sunglasses that probably cost more than my entire wardrobe. She had shimmering brown skin, but no tattoos, just a diamond stud in her naval.

If you don't have a platform you don't exist, said the Brazilian model, with an expression of scholarly seriousness.

*

The app announced a sunset cruise. So after a nap back in the room, we changed into seaworthy attire, sprayed on mosquito repellent, and walked back to the beach, where a flotilla of watercraft were ferrying influencers from the dock.

I was leading Amanda to a small sailboat about to load, when I felt a tug on my arm.

You're with me, said our white-clad host, smiling at both me and Amanda.

A woman who looked like a model was hooked to his other arm, and we walked thus connected to the end of the pier, where his Oceanco mega-yacht, the *Qumulus*, was waiting with sunglassed security guards to help us on board.

Oh my God! gasped Amanda, looking at all the teak and chrome and gold. Techno music pulsed from recessed speakers. Myriad photos of our host with non-digital celebrities and heads of states gleamed from within gold frames. Leather furniture, hot tubs, white-tied servers circulating with hors d'oeuvres and champagne.

Champagne! I exclaimed.

I took two glasses and put one in Amanda's hand.

This isn't the rot they sell at the corner grocery for Midwestern New Year's parties.

You want me to drink it?

I want you to experience and appreciate the good things in life, I said. And while I certainly deplore most of what passes for culture among these superficial snobs, Cristal is not one of those things.

You don't get a chance like this every day, I added. Me, I never have.

And I raised my glass.

She took a sip and made a face.

Gramps!

But it's New Year's.

It's not New Year's. It's the 29th, pointed out Amanda. Maybe you can have one glass on New Year's Eve. Maybe.

OK, but at least take a selfie, I suggested. You can caption it:

Just for show.

She snapped a photo as the boat lurched into the water. I used the sudden motion to get lost among the influencers long enough to down both glasses and return them to a server's tray.

I found her under the arm of a rapper. Dark bare chest, shiny medallions around his neck, tattoos of weapons, prison bars, dollar signs. Mista Sista. The headliner. Oh no.

I grabbed her away and led her to the railing to behold the sunset.

She pressed the video button and said:

To all my friends and family and followers, just look at this amazing sunset on Turks and Coco! And look at this boat, this amazing yacht owned by Mr. Frost. I've never seen so many celebrities in my life! And the marble floors and gold and silver... Nicole, I wish you were here. You would love it so. But you would probably crash the boat on a rock, hahaha. And here's my Gramps, say 'Hi,' Gramps. Oh, what's wrong? Oh, shit. And I was worried I would get seasick! Are you OK? At least I can tell my parents you didn't throw up from drinking too much. I've kept my eagle eye on you.

*

Neither of us wanted dinner. Amanda had gorged herself on ribs at our late lunch, and I was on a diet of ginger ale. Besides, the Shards of Lancaster tournament was about to begin.

The gaming center was the only air-conditioned building on the grounds. It was dimly lit, with three rows of consoles for the gamers, and twenty rows of seats for the spectators. It hadn't yet begun and we found our player—sorry, I never looked up his name on the festival app.

He took off his headphones to ask Amanda what she had been doing. Amanda told him about the yacht and wished him luck. He pointed out his teammates, then pointed to his father in the second row, who had saved us seats. Then he put his headphones back on and entered the medieval realm of Lancaster.

I wonder if Ned plays this game, I said, as we took our seats.

I meant it as a hypothetical question, just a point of curiosity. But there are no hypothetical questions in the digital age.

No, he doesn't, said Amanda a minute later, having texted him.

With nothing more than a notification on the festival app, the tournament began. We could follow the action on the three big screens behind the players, a video for each of the three teams.

Though I didn't know the name of our guy, he was in the blue row, so I deduced he was on the blue screen, but which avatar I couldn't say.

The game took place on hilly terrain in what was probably some Japanese programmer's notion of Scotland. We saw the three squads battle each other with longbows, swords, axes, maces and magic spells. We could hear the clanking of armor but not the voices of the combatants talking to each other. At one point a dragon appeared and scorched a village.

Our e-gamer's father stared in what was either rapt appreciation or a jet lagged trance.

We left after twenty minutes.

*

Ready to turn in, princess?

Yes. I want to catch the sunrise. And we got up early today.

Back in our hut she looked at my novel on her bed.

She fingered the pages but was too tired to read.

I tried to read it at the library, when they had it, said Amanda. But it was too hard. Why do you write such long sentences with so many commas and dashes?

It's called style, I said.

Why doesn't Mom ever talk about it? Why don't we have a copy?

I lay down on my bed, glad at this moment the cabin didn't have lights. There was only the moonlight and the blue haze from Amanda's phone, charging. Some things are easier to say when you can't see the person you're saying them to.

It's my fault, I confessed.

Oh, said Amanda.

You see, in my novel there's a little girl. And she gets kidnapped and killed.

That's terrible. But so?

You mom thinks she's that girl.

Why?

I don't know. Maybe because I called her Carol.

But why would you call her Carol?

No other name would do. I took the e off at least.

But was your character like Mom?

Yes, very much.

But why would you make her like Mom?

Are you taking her side?

I don't know. Did you have to kill her off?

There would be no story otherwise. You see, it's about a small town's collective guilt and grief. I didn't want to base the girl on your mom. But I've always had terrible writer's block. And then it came to me, the book. Like nothing I'd written before. But only if the character was like...well...your mom was as a young girl.

Oh.

Your mom should have understood. For God's sake, she studied English Literature. It's how a lot of books get written. Fiction taken from life. But fiction nevertheless. Your mom couldn't see that.

Amanda was silent for a minute.

If you ever want to write a character based on me and kill her off, I won't be mad.

Thanks, princess. But I would never do that. I learned my lesson.

4

The last thing I wanted to see was the sunrise, but I couldn't very well let my granddaughter loose among the influencers. So I roused myself and followed her to the beach, feeling hungover.

I needn't have worried. These influencers were a partying lot and nearly all were passed out in their huts, dreaming, no doubt, of followers falling from the sky.

There were lots of people about, festival staff quietly bringing the day's food, taking out trash, cleaning the pool.

The beach was ours.

I sat down on the sand while Amanda took photos of the breaking dawn.

Wow, said Amanda. I've never seen a sunrise like this. Have you?

Usually before sleep, not after.

The water is warm, even this early, said Amanda, testing the surf.

When she was finished we noticed a couple not far off, taking video. The festival app told us they were travel bloggers from Chicago.

I sauntered over to ask about their travels.

They were a couple in their late twenties or early thirties, very pale I thought for travel bloggers, or vloggers, since their platform was YouTube. He was wearing a brown fedora and she a yellow sun hat.

Grace Bay is rated one of the top beaches in the world, said the husband, standing beside his wife, who was holding the video camera at the end of a selfie stick. But while the sand is white and the water clear, it's not one of the best beaches we've visited, is it Karen?

I think it's too narrow, said Karen.

You better hope our host doesn't see this, I said when they stopped filming. He might kick you off.

Our followers appreciate that we're discerning, said the husband. If they want sugarcoated travel bureau videos there are plenty of vloggers that do that.

How many countries have you visited? I asked.

Six, said Karen, almost proudly.

Six! I exclaimed, having seen on the festival app that they had over half a million subscribers. What makes you experts on beaches, or on anything? I've been to forty-six countries, and countless beaches, and all of them, including this one, have been perfectly wide enough.

Are you a travel vlogger too? asked Karen.

He's a novelist, said Amanda.

Oh, really, said Karen. Have you written anything we've heard of?

*

All my life that's been a conversation killer, I told Amanda as we helped ourselves to the breakfast buffet.

You shouldn't insult people, said Amanda.

They deserve it. They're insipid.

Whatever that means.

It means uninteresting, bland, lacking character. If this breakfast sausage had no taste it would be insipid. People who have nothing to say are insipid. People who talk too much, with no meaning behind their words, are insipid. Travel vloggers who have only been to six countries are insipid.

Am I insipid?

Oh look, they have a pancake station!

*

I resolved to atone for insulting the travel vloggers by socializing with another influencer in a non-judgmental manner.

The restaurant was nearly empty, but there was one man, bearded, wearing a black Nike shirt, sitting alone, his plate filled with fruit.

My festival app told me he was a wellness guru with three million followers and a new book. Of course.

But never mind. I led Amanda to his table and politely asked if we could join him.

You're more than welcome to join me, said the wellness guru, rising to greet us. He frowned at our pancake-covered plates, oozing with maple syrup and whipped cream.

But not with those trays.

You're the girl in the well, said the wellness guru. And this is your—

Grandfather, said Amanda, pre-empting him.

You should be arrested for abuse, said the wellness guru, looking up at me. You do know sugar is a drug? You might as well be handing your granddaughter a needle filled with heroin.

May I? asked the wellness guru, laying one hand on Amanda's tray and one hand on mine.

He certainly may not, I thought. But after my contretemps with the travel vloggers, I held my tongue.

Amanda's face revealed an expression of pure horror as he dumped our wondrous, untasted pancakes into a trash can.

He then went to the buffet and returned with a small plate of fruit, a bowl of unsweetened oatmeal and a cup of green tea for each of us.

Now doesn't this look much better? said the wellness guru, motioning Amanda and me to sit on either side of him.

*

Thanks a lot, Gramps, said Amanda as we walked back to our hut. I've never had pancakes from a pancake station before. And now I still haven't. Just don't talk to anyone else, OK?

But a cameraman was approaching carrying a shoulder-mounted video camera. A woman wearing a white pants suit and holding a cordless microphone accompanied him. She told us they were making the official documentary of the festival and did I have a minute to talk to them.

I said not a word but pointed to Amanda.

Amanda: I'm gonna be in the documentary?

Documentary Woman: That depends on what you have to say.

Amanda: I don't have much to say. I'm probably the least interesting person here.

The documentary woman looked at her phone to see Amanda's profile.

Documentary Woman: You're the girl who fell in the well?

Amanda: Mmmmmm.

Documentary Woman: You must be pretty interesting, to have so many followers.

Amanda: I think people just want to know about Iowa. They really have no idea.

Documentary Woman: Now that you're being invited to places like Turks and Caicos, do you think you'll still want to live in Iowa?

Amanda: That's where my parents and friends are. And my cat. Oh God, I hope Mom remembered to feed Luna.

Documentary Woman: Is this your first time meeting other influencers?

Amanda: Yes, ma'am. Is this going to be on Netflix or what?

Documentary Woman: What do you think of the influencer community?

Amanda: It's great. Except when they throw your breakfast away. Isn't that like a crime?

Documentary Woman: Do you think you might find romance here?

Amanda: Whoa! Not with Gramps tailing me everywhere. Sorry, Gramps. That's not how I meant it. I mean, I wasn't even thinking about it.

Documentary Woman: I bet there will be lots of hookups here before the New Year dawns, with all the beautiful, famous and rich people invited to this special event.

Sutherland: Are you chronicling the festival or making a porno? Let's go, Amanda.

Amanda: But I'm not a model or musician, so I don't think anyone will want to hook up with me, whatever that means to you. In Iowa it means going to the Dairy Queen. Besides, I don't think my boyfriend would be cool with that. Or Marty. Or the wide receiver. And anyway, I'm only sixteen, and practically everyone here is an adult, which makes hooking up with me a crime, unless the laws are different in Turks and Coco. Do you know? And the only boy my age I've seen at the festival is more interested in killing dragons than bedding me. Can I say that, bedding? I got that from a Netflix historical romance show.

Sutherland: We're done.

Documentary Woman: You mean you have more than one boyfriend back home?

Amanda: No, I only have White Hat Ned. But I see other guys. I'm polyamorous.

Documentary Woman: I didn't know Iowa was a hotbed of sexual liberation.

Sutherland: Stop talking, Amanda.

Amanda: When is your film gonna be finished? Better to leave out that last part. People think it means Mormon. And it's not like I'm doing anything anyway. I have a morals clause.

Sutherland: Stop filming now or I'm going to throw your camera into the sea!

Documentary Woman: Just one last question, Amanda. What's been the best part of the Influencer Festival for you so far?

Amanda: I'd like to say the pancake station. But I'll never know.

*

You have to be very careful what you say, I told Amanda as we walked along the path to our hut. Please don't say anything about sex or polyamory.

That's a shame, said Amanda. It took me so long to learn that word.

People don't understand it, as you pointed out. Thinking you're a Mormon is the least of your problems. People associate polyamory with concupiscence.

Gramps! English pleeeeease.

Isn't there a dictionary on that phone of yours? I meant that people will assume you are promiscuous.

Hellooooo. Don't know that word either.

They'll think you sleep with everyone.

But I don't sleep with anyone.

The public doesn't know that.

I don't care. I don't care. If it doesn't violate the morals clause, I don't care what people think.

But I care. And I'm sure that your parents care. And if you send the wrong signals here, in this digital Gomorrah, you're going to need pepper spray to fight off the attention.

Yeah, right. With all the models and glam bloggers. Like anyone's going to look at me.

The filmmakers looked at you. She can interview anyone and she chose you.

Just because we crossed her path. And I'm sure she'll talk to everyone else. I won't be in the film, you'll see.

*

All three restaurants served the same buffet for lunch.

We peeked in cautiously, scanning for the wellness guru.

Seeing the coast was clear, we took our place in the buffet line.

I noticed the other diners' eyes upon us. I assumed they were staring at Amanda, who was wearing cutoffs and a tight salmon shirt from one of her sponsors.

I heard snickering. As I arrived at the prime rib station, I realized they were looking at me.

Ha, Gramps, look!

Amanda held up her phone, which showed a GIF of me throwing up on the yacht.

You're famous! said Amanda.

You little—

Hey, it wasn't me. I told White Hat Ned to edit you out. But I'm not the only one with a camera.

Fuck, I said under my breath, as the carver piled my plate with prime rib.

I scanned the restaurant, where diners were looking from their phone to me, and snickering. One asshole even put a finger in his throat and roared with laughter.

What's the biggie, Gramps? You always say you don't care what people think. In fact, when I told you I didn't care if people know I'm polyamorous, I got that from you.

Well, I lied.

Why can't they have 24-hour breakfast here, like at the Waffle House? Do you think they'll have the pancake station tomorrow?

Anyway, continued Amanda. The thing about digital is we have short attention spans. And new things are always hitting. So by dinner everyone will be on to something else.

Promise?

I promise. And if not, maybe this is what you needed all your life—attention. Just like me. Maybe you'll get a book deal out of it, haha.

*

I gathered courage and led Amanda to a table where only two places remained.

The snickering subsided and one of our table mates was polite enough to ask how I was feeling.

You'll find out soon enough, I said, pointing with my knife to the stack of medium-rare prime rib.

What's he doing? I then whispered to the middle-aged Asian woman beside me. I nodded at a young man across, who was filming while he ate, describing his food.

He's a taster, said the middle-aged Asian woman. He makes videos tasting different kinds of food, usually by theme. This video is about the festival food, but usually it's different pastas, or chocolates, or biscuits.

A whole video on tasting biscuits?

I'd love to get your take on the prime rib, said the taster, overhearing us.

Not on your life, I wanted to say. But instead I smiled like we were camp buddies.

I'm a vegan, said the taster. So, I have to outsource meat and cheese dishes.

Why the hell did you become a taster? I wanted to say. I thought it was like having visited only six countries and calling yourself a travel vlogger. Did any of these people actually have experience in the areas they were blogging and vlogging and podcasting about?

But instead of pursuing this line of inquiry, which I'm sure would only lead to raised voices, micro aggressions and perhaps macro aggressions, I asked the middle-aged Asian woman what she did, being too lazy to look at her profile on my phone.

I unbox sex toys.

Of course you do.

Beside her was an Asian man I took to be either her husband or a very convincing robot she had recently unboxed.

The taster seemed to have a spouse as well, or partner, or whatever.

The other two table mates sat to Amanda's left.

What do you gentlemen do? I asked.

I have a podcast on conspiracy theories, said the man next to Amanda. He was the first obese person I'd seen here, except for some of the staff. He was bald and wore dark plastic glasses.

Are there any new conspiracies I should know about?

The Russians landed a man on Venus in 1968, said the man with dark glasses. Of course, he didn't land. He burned up in the atmosphere. The Soviets covered it up, embarrassed by the fiasco. And the U.S. kept it under wraps because we were racing to get to the moon, and that would have been anticlimactic if people knew the Russians had already been to Venus.

So you accept that the moon landing happened, and that the earth is round?

I only deal in real conspiracies. Sadly, some people will believe anything.

And what about you? I asked the man sitting next to him, probably in his sixties, wearing wire-rimmed glasses and a bow tie.

I chronicle my cats' lives on Instagram.

You have cats? asked Amanda, suddenly interested.

Unfortunately, I couldn't bring them. Quarantine restrictions, you know.

I have a cat, said Amanda. How many do you have?

Fifteen.

Fifteen!!!

A man with fifteen cats. How refreshing, I said. I thought only lonely old women kept more than two cats. Good for you for breaking that stereotype!

*

Rather than giving me energy for the hot afternoon, lunch depleted me. If I had been in a lunatic asylum I would have expected more sanity.

Let's take a nap.

I'm sixteen. I don't take naps!

Then you can watch me take one. Or better, read my book.

There's a fashion show at the pool, said Amanda, looking at her phone. Bikini models. You're too tired for that?

I was not.

*

A rum and Coke from the poolside bar was just what the doctor ordered. In this world of narcissists, amateurs and lunatics, sobriety was hazardous to my health.

The chaises had been replaced by rows of chairs, and a catwalk extended across the diameter of the pool.

The rapper with the prison bar tattoos served as MC, the first time I'd heard anyone make announcements since our arrival. He introduced the models and read what they were wearing from index cards, stumbling over the descriptions, perhaps because they didn't rhyme or have the word *bitch* in them.

Have you ever been to a fashion show, Gramps?

Does the Banana Bar in Amsterdam count?

I haven't either. Do you think I should learn to wear heels?

She said this because all the models were walking in stilettos, despite the fact that they were already as tall as basketball players and wearing only bikinis.

Considering that you fell down a well while wearing flat shoes, I'd hate to think what harm you might cause yourself in heels.

Nicole has five pairs. I think she'd wear them to school if she could. Oh look, there's Juliana!

Don't wave—we don't want her tumbling into the pool.

But Juliana saw us and gave a smile. And afterward she came over to pose for selfies.

Why don't you walk across before the crew takes the catwalk down? suggested Juliana. I'll post the video to my YouTube, and you can share.

Am I allowed?

The show's over. Why not?

I'm not a model. I'll look silly.

That's the point. Be silly!

Take your drink, I said. I'll go get refills.

Amanda took off her shoes and placed her foot on the catwalk as if it were a diving board. Most of the spectators had left, but untold millions from all corners of the globe were peeking in.

And the rapper was still here.

Can you announce her? asked the Brazilian model.

What do I say? wondered the rapper with the prison bar tattoos.

Just anything. Our final model of the day, the fabulous Amanda Dizon from the heartland of America. Distressed shorts by BambE. Salmon cotton top by Harris Brothers.

He turned his microphone back on.

Now let's kick it with Amanda, eyes like a panda, finest bitch in all the Turks, givin' all the guys the works, walking out where danger lurks. Shorts by BambE. Salmon cotton top by Harris Brothers.

Amanda set her drink on the catwalk and laughed at the impromptu rap. It sounded like love poetry to her.

She started walking as if the catwalk were a balance beam. Halfway across she stretched out her arms, as if she were losing her balance, and then staggered and fell into the deep end of the pool.

Before I could reach the water, the rapper had jumped in to pull her out. Not that she needed saving.

Hahaha, she laughed, emerging from the pool in the arms of the rapper. Hahaha! Was that silly enough?

*

Back in Mission Control, White Hat Ned happened to have been watching the fashion show. Imagine that. Just happened to be watching supermodels in bikinis on the festival livestream.

After it ended, he reached for a slice of pizza, but the livestream remained on.

He heard the rapper say Amanda's name. He looked back just in time to see what I've just described. Although in his mind it was much less like an impromptu bucket list video and more like a pair of lovers frolicking.

Holy shit! gasped White Hat Ned.

He never finished his pizza.

*

Rain drops pattered on the swimming pool as workers disassembled the catwalk.

Juliana and the rapper had gone. Amanda and I were sitting on the edge of the pool, finishing our drinks.

And one of us was checking her phone.

I'm not doing anything scandalous, said Amanda to our jealous knight in a white hat back in Mission Control, in a voice call for once rather than texting.

No, I'm not going to edit it out, said Amanda, with authority. Helloooo. He's famous. If he shares it, I'm gonna get more sponsors for sure.

I can't cheat on you. There's nothing to cheat.

*

Why are boys so jealous? asked Amanda after tapping off.

Not just boys, I pointed out.

Were you like that at his age?

I was never his age.

Of course, you were always cool. He's just insecure. And I thought *I* was insecure. Wouldn't we all be happier if we just let everybody do what they want?

A wise sentiment, princess. Care for another refill?

*

In a matter of minutes the sky had gone from blue to gray. A gusting wind was shaking the palm trees. The festival app warned of a severe storm tonight and posted a link to local satellite weather.

Did we pack umbrellas? asked Amanda as we watched the pattern of raindrops on the swimming pool.

We don't need umbrellas. We're in nature.

I rose, but walked toward the beach, not our hut.

Where are you going? asked Amanda, putting on her shoes and following.

One of my favorite things to do is walk on the beach in the rain, I told her.

But we might catch cold.

You don't catch cold from the cold, or the rain. That's a myth. And anyway, the temperature is still hot, and it's hardly raining.

I'd be happier with an umbrella, said Amanda. How far are we going?

We were the only ones on the beach, except for workers ferrying supplies, and the wellness guru holding an exercise class.

We walked in the opposite direction.

They're taking the boats out in the rain? asked Amanda, looking at the pier.

They're anchoring them in deeper water in preparation for the storm, I explained.

Oh. Do they think it might be a hurricane?

I doubt it. Hurricane season was months ago. It's probably just a storm, like at home, the only difference being instead of waking up to three feet of snow, we'll wake up to sunshine and a few palm leaves on the ground.

I always thought it would be cool to be one of those TV reporters in a hurricane trying to stay on their feet while the wind blows, said Amanda.

This is the first time I've heard you speak about a career!

Oh, I don't want to be a reporter. I just want to stand in a hurricane and try to hold on to my umbrella and microphone.

It was very pleasant walking in the light rain, on the soft sand, drink in hand, with perhaps the person in this world I loved more than any other.

So, what *do* you want to do with your life? I asked her.

I dunno.

Have you ever had a job?

Not a regular job. I helped my parents in the field before they lost the farm.

I take it you don't want to be a farmer?

Not unless it's cannabis. Just joking! Besides, people say weed is very hard to grow.

You want an easy job?

Hey—wait. I have a job now. And it's not easy. It's every day, every hour. You just don't take it seriously, do you?

No, I don't.

It's not a job you need to go to college for, like my parents. Or Mr. Cole. It's not traditional, like a farmer. But it's still a job. And it's 24/7, which makes it harder in some ways.

What if it doesn't last? Influencers are a new phenomenon. What would you want to do if influencing went the way of the chimney sweep?

What's a chimney sweep?

My point exactly.

Amanda thought for a moment.

I wouldn't mind working at Dairy Queen.

Dairy Queen?

Ice cream every day. And it's cold in summer. I wouldn't want to work in the summer heat, like a lifeguard. Not that I can swim good enough to be a lifeguard anyway.

So that's the extent of your ambition? Working at a Dairy Queen?

Why not? It's pretty simple. It's not like working at Olive Garden and carrying those heavy trays. Plus, everyone's smiling. Did you ever see a depressed customer at a Dairy Queen? No one's gonna shoot up a place that sells ice cream, hahaha.

We walked for a few minutes in silence. I was thinking of my research, consisting of reading her posts, watching her interviews, talking to her friends.

You know... I said.

Can we turn around now?

In a bit. Walking is healthy. And you don't get enough exercise.

Now you sound like the jerk who threw away our pancakes.

You know, I was thinking about your posts and interviews. Did you ever say how you fell down the well?

It was an accident. I said that a million times. I didn't jump. I wasn't thrown in there by aliens. I wasn't pushed by a stalker. Like I would have a stalker!

But how did you have an accident? What were you doing at the well? You never said, did you?

I dunno.

People either formed their own conclusions, or didn't care enough to press you for details.

Mmmmm.

But I care. I feel partly responsible.

But you haven't lived there for years. You said yourself people didn't used to fill up wells. Anyway, I don't blame you. I don't blame anyone. It was just an accident. Shit happens. And look at all the good things that have come from it. I don't want to think about that day.

Was the cover on? The wooden hinged cover.

Yes, but not all the way. And I pushed it off.

Why would you do that?

Amanda stopped and looked at me. The rain on her face could have been tears.

Promise you won't tell Dad.

Promise.

She started walking again.

I was getting ready for school. Mom and Dad had already left. I was in my room looking out the window. I was dressed and had my phone in my pocket. I just went to the window and looked outside, like I sometimes do, before going downstairs.

I saw Luna. I saw her jump up on the well and then fall in.

I see!

I never told anyone this. I never had to, because after I say it's an accident, they don't pressure me for details. I stay quiet or change the subject. I didn't want to make up a story, but I didn't want to tell the truth either.

And what is the truth?

When I saw Luna disappear in the well, I freaked out. I ran all the way to the well and looked inside.

Luna wasn't at the bottom, like I expected, but on a ledge a few feet down.

I called her name but she didn't come. I thought she can't get out, so I reached for her. But I couldn't reach her.

I pushed the cover off. That's why the cover was found lying next to the well after I was rescued.

I thought I'd just lower myself a bit, to the ledge, and scoop her up. But when I tried to grab her, she shrieked and jumped out. And I lost my balance and fell in.

That's terrible. Poor child. But why don't you want your father to know?

Because he hates cats. He's allergic and I had to plead with him to let me keep her. She was a stray. So what do you think he would do if he knew I fell in the well because of Luna? He'd give her away.

I don't know about that.

Well, I don't want to take the chance. Do you understand now? And fortunately, no one asked exactly how it happened, until you.

Can we turn around now?

*

We continued to network at meals. I insisted we go to the restaurant where sushi influencers were doing their thing.

Amanda was so fascinated by the way the rolls were made, and the virtuosity with which the chefs wielded their knives, that I had to pull her away.

At our table were three models—I was right about models and sushi—as well as a cryptocurrency blogger, a tech products reviewer, and a cannabis whisperer.

We were just talking about weed, said Amanda, taking micro bites of her salmon roll.

We don't call it weed said the cannabis whisperer, a thin hipster in his early thirties with a goatee and purple lenses on his frameless glasses.

Oh, sorry.

Have you ever smoked marijuana?

No, but some of my friends have. And my parents. And you for sure, Gramps. Right?

Could you pass the soy sauce please?

I'm having a cannabis tasting event in my hut tonight, if you'd like to come, said the cannabis whisperer. It's only fifty dollars and we'll be sampling eight varieties.

Can we go? Amanda asked me.

No.

But you're always saying I should try new things. Like this sushi. What's the difference?

Your morals clause, for one thing, I told her. Your parents' wrath for another.

Can I watch? asked Amanda.

No, I said.

Well, you can follow me at least, said the cannabis whisperer. I'm going to livestream it.

Cool, said Amanda.

Are there no rum whisperers? I silently wondered. Perhaps that was a void I could fill.

*

We could hear heavy metal music from the restaurant and walked to the amphitheater, where the night's music festival had begun.

This wasn't Woodstock, but scheduled from 7:00 p.m. tonight and tomorrow would be a steady stream of bands and singers, across most musical genres, including some famous names.

We took a seat in the back, but it began to pour and we ran to our hut, the dirt paths turning to mud.

We should have packed umbrellas, said Amanda, wringing her long hair. And how are we supposed to go to the bathroom in this rain? People on PingPong used to ask if our home had an outhouse. Well now I have an outhouse!

Use the closet to change, I suggested. You have enough dry outfits to survive a forty-day flood.

The wind roared through the trees and lightning flashed in the dark sky. The thunder made Amanda jump.

You're not afraid of storms, are you? I asked, taking my turn in the closet to towel off and change, although I only had two pairs of pants—one short and one long—and three t-shirts.

Duh, yeah.

You should see the storms in Southeast Asia during monsoon season. This is a mild shower in comparison.

What are we supposed to do now?

What does the app say?

'All activities cancelled until further notice' read Amanda.

Storms are a great time to read a book, I suggested, lying down on my bed with a thick novel I'd brought for the trip.

Amanda took up my book, but put it down again after a few minutes and returned to her phone.

You don't like it?

I forgot I have to post. And I should check in with Mission Control.

I heard Amanda commenting on the storm for her followers. I heard her ask her mother if she had fed Luna.

I must have dozed off, because when I looked at my watch it was 11:30 p.m. And Amanda was gone.

*

I knocked on the closet. I peeked outside and called her name. The rain was still pouring. She must have gone to the bathroom.

I returned to my book. But when she hadn't come back after ten minutes I grew concerned. I looked on the festival app for her location, but my phone wasn't working. Not being familiar with cell phones, I assumed it needed charging.

I stepped outside, where it was pitch dark, except for darting narrow lights from cell phone flashlights.

Hey! I called.

A man wearing a poncho trudged over.

Can I use your phone? I've lost my granddaughter and my battery is dead.

It's not your battery, said the man in the poncho. The electricity is out. Cell service too. Hand me your phone.

He turned my flashlight on.

See, said the man in the poncho. Your phone doesn't need charging. At least now you can see where you're going.

What do I do now? I asked.

How should I know? It's *Lord of the Flies* time. Everyone for themselves.

Where can I get a poncho?

But he had wandered off.

*

I slogged through the mud to the sushi restaurant. It was deserted, the buffet cleared.

I went to the restaurant where we ate barbecue. There were a few people at one table, loudly debating the nature of the outage.

I tell you it's a test, said a man I recognized as the conspiracy influencer. Frost has his own cell tower. You're telling me the generators *and* the tower are down? At a digital gathering? It's like *Survivor.* He's probably secretly recording us, seeing how we will react.

Have you seen Amanda? I asked them. The girl I was with at dinner? My granddaughter?

None of them had.

See, said the conspiracy influencer. We're falling apart already. If this lasts till dawn there will be deaths or suicides. Take 150 people who rely on connectivity and plunge them into darkness. I have to admit it's a clever experiment.

How anyone had the resources to create a thunderstorm, even a billionaire tech titan, was a question I decided not to ask the conspiracy influencer. I was more interested in finding Amanda before any number of bad things happened to her.

I hurried back to our hut, but she still wasn't there. I went to the women's bathroom and called her name. Then I started going past the huts, peeking in and shouting her name.

I ran to the beach, where scores of influencers were standing alone, or in pairs, or small groups, like castaways awaiting rescue.

Some paced on the pier, as though they hoped our host's yacht would return any moment to rescue them.

The lack of digital connectivity seemed to have pulled the plug on the influencers' ability to socialize. Rather than find comfort in the group, they failed to form a functional group at all.

Where are all the staff? asked an anxious, rain drenched woman after I asked her if she'd seen Amanda. Why isn't anyone helping us?

I had come here to experience their digital world, but now they were experiencing mine: a primitive night on the beach. And they found it as terrifying as I found their world superficial.

I decided to try the e-games building. And there she was, sitting on the floor with her e-gamer friend and his teammates, watching them play on their phones.

Normally a sixteen-year-old girl alone with young men on a dark and stormy night would be cause for concern. But these were e-gamers, and I suppose the only risk she faced in their company was to be slain by a dragon.

You have service! I exclaimed.

Satellite phone, said her friend without looking up. We used it to make a hotspot.

I wanted to suggest that there were more socially responsible ways to use a satellite phone during a power blackout than connecting your buddies for a midnight raid through some virtual world, but then I remembered the disconnected influencers on the beach and thought to hell with it.

I sat down against the wall, beside Amanda, and put my arm around her.

Gramps, you're soaked!

Yeah, well the guy with the poncho wouldn't tell me where I could get one. Why didn't you tell me where you were?

You were sleeping.

You had me so worried!

Why? You said storms aren't dangerous. I mean, what could happen?

This from the girl who fell down a well.

I kissed her forehead.

I thought I'd lost you again, I said.

Again?!

*

I woke up soaked to the bone, with a sore back and neck, Amanda and the e-gamers sleeping on the concrete floor around me.

My flashlight was out, and this time my phone battery really was dead. But light streamed through the cracks under the door.

I woke Amanda and we stumbled outside. Dawn had just broken and the clouds were dissipating. It was quiet except for the sound of water dripping from the trees and thatched huts.

Crew members were silently carrying food and other supplies, preparing for the day as though nothing had happened. Electric and cell service still hadn't been restored.

I was probably the only one who didn't care. And who was accustomed to cold water showers. I changed into the only dry clothes I had left—a pair of khaki shorts and a Boracay t-shirt.

In the hut we plugged our phones in so they would charge when the electricity did come back. Amanda collapsed on her bed and fell asleep.

This time I was the one who crept outside to explore.

*

There was coffee in the restaurant and I drank two cups. I wanted to bring Amanda pancakes, but the buffet hadn't been set up yet. So I went to the beach.

There were two boats at the dock, but not our host's yacht. A dozen or so influencers were individually harassing crew members.

I demand to speak to Emerson immediately!

You can't treat us this way!

Do you know who I am?!

Of course, you can drive me to the airport. I'm not staying here another minute!

Is this a reality show? Which network? I knew I'd seen that documentary filmmaker before!

I'll give you two, make that three hundred dollars if you get me a satellite phone for twenty minutes. I promised my followers an update.

*

I found a cooler filled with beer. The ice had melted but I wasn't about to complain. I took my pick of the empty deck chairs on the beach and watched the rising sun.

I heard cheering and sat up to see our absent host's yacht pull into the dock.

I followed the others, curious.

Emerson Frost stood on his yacht, looking dry and well-rested, flanked by his security detail.

I heard influencers shouting, complaining, even making threats. But when he smiled and announced that they were welcome to use the satellite phone in his private quarters they bleated like sheep and leaped aboard.

Four at a time, said our host, before disappearing back inside.

I looked at the influencers waiting in line.

Shouldn't we tell the others? I asked.

They glared at me as though we had found an oasis in the desert and I had suggested sharing our lifesaving secret with all the other tribes.

I walked back to the huts and shouted out:

Free satellite service on the *Qumulus*. First come, first served.

Influencers emerged from their quarters like rats in a flood and ran toward the beach.

Amanda was still asleep. I decided to lie down as well, shut my eyes and dream I belonged to a less ridiculous species.

5

We woke at ten. The electricity was still off. We found influencers bribing crew members to use their cars to go into town, which was rumored to have service. At the beach there was a line the length of the pier waiting to use Emerson's satellite phone.

Amanda took a place at the end of the line.

What are you doing? I asked.

I have to post. My contracts.

A few hours won't matter. Let's get breakfast, then go to the pool.

What if the electricity is down all day?

It's an act of God. That's probably in your contracts.

What if they're atheists? asked Amanda.

It's just an expression. It means you aren't accountable if an act of nature, like the storm last night, keeps you from fulfilling the contract.

Oh.

Look at all these idiots. We're in one of the loveliest, most relaxing places on the planet, but everyone's stressed out, standing in lines, fighting over generators, hijacking vehicles. They'd rather be in a digital space that doesn't exist than appreciate this real paradise.

You're right. Let's go eat. Do you think they'll have the pancake station?

I think it's probably bread and yogurt today, princess.

The electricity came back on at three and the cell service resumed shortly after. Everyone's mood immediately improved, except mine. It was nice making eye contact, eating with people who weren't scrolling on their phones, talking to my undistracted granddaughter.

At dinner everyone walked and sat with their heads bowed again, as if praying to the God of Social Media.

The six-country travel vlogger couple sat at our table, looking surprisingly happy.

I thought you would have chartered a boat to your seventh country at the first drop of rain, I said.

Never crossed our mind, said the husband, seemingly immune to my sarcasm.

We made a video for our *Roughing It* playlist, said the wife. The mud was unbelievable. I ruined two pairs of shoes!

Yes, it was just like the Battle of Stalingrad, I said.

*

The pool was glorious. And the pool bar made it more so. And in one of the cabanas, we spotted a tattoo artist, giving complimentary tattoos.

Amanda went to check him out.

I put my name down, she said breathlessly upon her return. I want *Luna* on my arm, with a picture of a cat. He says it will only take half an hour and shouldn't hurt much. And it's free. Can I do it, pleeeeeease?

No.

Well, I'm doing it anyway and you can't stop me. I didn't smoke weed because of you guys and when you were all my age you were doing that and more. It isn't fair. I'm doing this.

I was struck by her sudden assertiveness and the irrefutable logic of her argument.

Not too big, I said.

She gave me a hug. Mom's gonna kill me.

No, she's gonna kill *me!*

*

I was enlisted to take video. The tattoo artist was videoing as well, for his TV show. We lived in a world that was all stage, no audience.

Amanda proudly showed the tender tattoo of her cat to Nicole via Skype, but wore long sleeves when talking to Mission Control. She decided she would wait to post it on PingPong, in case her parents might see it there.

At night, as we sat in the fifth row of the packed amphitheater, listening to the A-list musicians and counting down to the new year, I thought again about my observation that we now live in a world that is all stage and no audience, because hardly anyone was looking at the stage.

Rather they were looking at their phones, recording the event or taking photos and captioning them for their followers. The father of the e-gamer and I seemed to be the only ones without devices in our hands. Even the crew—even security!—were taking selfies.

During a break between acts Amanda leaned toward me.

Why did you say last night that you almost lost me again? When was the first time?

New Year's Eve was a time to reflect on the year about to end. But my granddaughter's question took me back many years. To my divorce from her grandmother, long before Amanda was born. To my self-imposed exile. To my infrequent trips back to Iowa after Amanda was born. To the last time I had seen her, at the Baskin-Robbins, where we sat in silence while she ate her ice cream.

The first time was when you were born, I said. Your mom sent me an announcement, and I phoned her to say congratulations. But for reasons that probably involved too little money and too much procrastination, I didn't come back to visit until you were two.

When I left after that visit I thought I might not see you again. I was getting old, after all, and not taking the best care of myself. The next time I returned to Iowa you were six. And then you were nine. Each time I flew out I thought I had lost you. The gifts I sent were a feeble attempt to keep a connection with you.

Why do you have to leave again? said Amanda. I don't want to lose you either.

The next performer came on. It was Mista Sista, the rapper with the prison bar tattoos.

Amanda went to the area in front of the stage with a bunch of other influencers to dance.

When had she learned to dance? Somewhere between American History class and business class she had lost her inhibitions.

Speaking of inhibitions, black-tied servers were passing through the amphitheater with flutes of champagne.

I took four.

There was no clock on stage to count down to the new year. But then everyone had a clock on their phone. Someone had even coded a glowing ball on the festival app that started dropping the modest height of the screen at 11:30 p.m. and hit bottom at midnight, exploding with virtual fireworks.

There were real fireworks as well. There was applause and kissing. I received a friendly handshake from the e-gamer's father.

Emerson Frost took the stage.

Happy New Year everyone! I'm glad to see you all here, looking no worse for wear after the storm last night. I want to assure you I was just as taken off guard as the rest of you and got little sleep. It was not a test, as some of you believe. I personally selected all of you as my guests, so there was no reason to test you. The only thing tested was my cell tower, which will be getting an upgrade. And maybe I'll pave some of the walkways, and buy more generators.

There was tepid applause. He gave the microphone back to Mista Sista, and the young influencers up front began dancing again.

Mista Sista lifted several of the women up on the stage. I recognized Amanda among them.

Oh no.

I received a call from Mission Control.

Sutherland, what's going on? Are you there?

I'm here.

I'm watching the festival livestream. Is that Amanda?

It is.

Where are you?

Row five. Is that close enough?

Get her off there! And is that a tattoo?

Amanda had pulled her shirt down over her shoulders, or someone else had, revealing the cat tattoo.

Tell me it's a temporary tattoo.

Hmmmmmmm...

You're not drinking champagne, are you?

You know I hate champagne.

*

White Hat Ned was also watching the livestream in the Dizons' dining room. Though he wasn't well-acquainted with hip hop artists, he recognized the rapper as the man who had pulled Amanda out of the pool yesterday. And now he was dancing with her.

Ned looked on the festival app. Mista Sista. Platinum records, a Grammy.

His heart sank. This is always how it went for guys like him. Do all the heavy lifting and the Martys and Grammy-winners of the world charm her away. How could a geek like him compete with broad shoulders and prison bar tattoos?

He should have at least asked to be paid, like Amy and Nipuni.

He grabbed Nipuni's hand, who happened to be sitting next to him. He needed a shoulder to cry on, but this would do, especially since she didn't let go.

And then all those present at Mission Control, as well as the entire influencer universe, or at least those livestreaming the end of the festival, saw the headlining act kiss Amanda full on the lips. And Amanda not slapping him, not running away. Perhaps it had been Amanda who initiated the kiss. It would require a slow-motion replay to determine who took the initiative, but who had the stomach for that?

Certainly not Ned, who ran out the back door. He needed some air, and the air in Iowa was biting cold.

He let it sting him. He walked and paced. He might have thrown himself into the well if it hadn't been sealed up.

*

He went back inside and stormed up to Amanda's room and went on her computer. He needed to be alone, and somehow being in Amanda's room made him feel he hadn't lost her yet.

He went on his Facebook account and drafted a self-pitying PM to her:

I know you never really loved me...

Then an angry message:

How dare you kiss strangers when I'm sitting with your parents working my ass off without pay...

Then a transactional one:

I think it only fair, given all the free labor and advice I've given you, that you make me a partner...

But in the end he didn't send any of them.

He scrolled through his Facebook for several minutes, trying to distract himself, while Amanda's parents were drinking champagne—I mean sparkling wine—in Mission Control.

He saw an ad for StandWith, International, asking him to sign a petition to protest the treatment of Uyghurs by the Chinese Government.

What about the treatment of me? Who is going to sign a petition to protest Amanda's treatment of me? wondered White Hat Ned.

And then he had a devious idea.

He logged into Amanda's PingPong account, then linked to the StandWith, International page and signed the petition in her name. Another petition popped up, to support the Hong Kong protestors, and he signed that too.

He logged out and went downstairs and furtively drank two glasses of sparkling wine, which made him feel queasy. The three amigas had already left. Amanda's parents saw he was in no condition to drive home and made a bed for him on the sofa.

6

Amanda was welcomed back to school like a conquering hero. Everyone wanted to know about her celebrity encounters and personal details of whichever influencers they followed.

There were congratulatory texts from her sponsors, and inquiries from potential new ones. Mr. Cole asked if he might stop by that night.

She showed off her tattoo, and the only people displeased were dog lovers and her parents.

White Hat Ned barely acknowledged her in American History class and was absent at lunch.

Hey, there's an email from a book publisher in New York that wants you to write your story, said Amy, working through lunch period on her Chromebook, the one White Hat Ned had tried to give Amanda. Should I keep or delete?

Delete.

No, keep, said Nipuni.

OK, keep.

*

That night I was woken by a scream. Amanda!

I rushed to her room. Was she on fire? Had a serial killer climbed through the window?

No, she was sitting at her desk, her hands covering her mouth, staring at the computer screen.

Your PingPong account has been suspended for violating our *Terms of Service* regarding political content.

It must be a mistake, I said.

Of course it's a mistake! said Amanda. I never post anything political. I don't even know anything about politics to post! Do you think it has to do with my tattoo? Maybe *Luna* means *revolution* in Chinese?

I doubt it, princess. Let's go back to sleep. I'm sure it will be resolved by morning.

No! I have to fix this now.

Amanda's parents called up to see if everything was all right.

Yes, I said.

No! said Amanda.

It was 1:00 a.m.

She called Mr. Cole, who surprised everyone by saying he would be right over.

Then she called White Hat Ned.

What happened, tell me again? asked Ned in a groggy voice, feeling the sweet taste of revenge.

*

An hour later we were all gathered at Mission Control.

Mr. Cole, appearing for the first time without a suit, wearing chinos and a flannel shirt, was perusing a printout of PingPong's *Terms of Service*.

Everyone else, except White Hat Ned, of course, was reading the two petitions Amanda had allegedly signed.

I've been hacked.

Are you sure you didn't sign these by accident? asked Amanda's father. Maybe you weren't paying attention?

No, of course not.

Not that it's a bad thing. I mean, we support these causes, said her mother. We'd be proud of you if you chose to stand for the oppressed of the world. For my part I protested the takeover of Tibet. But from a business standpoint—

Mom, I've been hacked!

I'm sure it'll all blow over, said White Hat Ned, beginning to realize the seriousness of his action.

Ned, *you* have my password.

Ah...yes...

Who else? Amy and Nipuni have my email password, but not my PingPong.

I'm not sure, said White Hat Ned evasively, wanting to shine the interrogation lamp away from his eyes.

No, you're the only one, said Amanda. Not even my parents have it, right?

Right, said Amanda's parents.

So that means it was hacked from outside. Maybe Russia?

Can we appeal to PingPong? asked Amanda's father of the lawyer.

Yes, said the lawyer, having finished reading the *Terms of Service*. I'll draft an email and send it at once.

I think we should leave this to Mr. Cole and get back to sleep, said Amanda's mother. You still have school tomorrow, young lady.

But I've been hacked! repeated Amanda. And they say the first twelve hours are critical to catching the criminals.

I think that's for abductions, said the lawyer.

Shouldn't we at least change the password? Ned?

Ummm... Sure...

Well, don't just stand there. Change it.

And she gave White Hat Ned a big hug, which made him feel absolutely awful.

*

A hush greeted Amanda as she staggered into school, exhausted and unkempt.

Did your lawyer send the appeal? asked White Hat Ned nervously in American History class.

Yes.

Well, I'm sure they'll reverse their decision.

But how long? Look!

And she showed White Hat Ned apprehensive emails from her sponsors.

White Hat Ned cleared his throat.

They won't abandon you. You have contracts.

Which I've now violated. Oh, if I find those hackers! I've never been so angry at anyone in my life. I swear I could kill right now!

White Hat Ned swallowed hard and looked out the window, fearing his guilt was evident on his face.

*

At lunch it seemed the entire cafeteria was staring at their phones, at Amanda's PingPong page. Or former page.

This account has been suspended was the social media equivalent of yellow police tape. Amanda911 was now a crime scene.

Nicole grabbed Amanda's arm.

Didn't I always tell you to diversify? said Nicole.

I don't know what that means.

You need other platforms. This is what happens when you rely on only one. You do have YouTube and Instagram accounts, right? We just have to build those up.

We?

I'll help you of course. And Puni and Amy. So even if you're off PingPong for a while your followers can find you. You're still a star.

I'm an outcast. I'm in social media jail.

And you have to keep taking care of yourself. You look terrible. Here, let me brush your hair.

*

When Amanda got home she only wanted to sleep. She didn't even go upstairs, but collapsed on the sofa, her phone turned off.

Her parents were in the dining room with Mr. Cole, video conferencing with her sponsors.

Babylon wants to speak to you, said her mother.

No.

They believe it wasn't you who signed those petitions. But they want to hear it from you.

No.

*

When she woke a couple hours later the three amigas had joined them.

Where's White Hat Ned? asked Amanda.

No one knew.

Amanda turned her phone on and texted him, then called him.

Where are you? shouted Amanda.

Home.

What are you doing at home? I need you to find the hackers.

I can work from here.

No, you can't. Get over here. Pleeeeease. I need you.

OK, said White Hat Ned, feeling validated and doomed at the same time. He told his parents not to wait up for him.

*

A week passed and her account was still suspended.

I should get a tattoo on my forehead: *SUSPENDED,* said Amanda in Mission Control.

Her suspended account glared like a billboard of failure from one of the computer screens.

Can you turn that off?!

We need to see it in case it comes back on, said Nicole.

Well, I don't want to see it, said Amanda, storming upstairs.

White Hat Ned was at her desk, pretending to be searching for the hackers, although he was actually playing video games and biting his nails.

He quickly changed the screen when Amanda appeared.

She put her arms around him.

Thank you for being there for me, said Amanda. Any luck with the hackers?

Not yet.

Take a break. Let's fool around. You want a massage?

No, that's OK, said White Hat Ned, feeling any reward would be worse than punishment. I should be getting home.

*

The deliveries had slowed. Amy and Nipuni no longer had to unpack dozens of boxes every day and sort items into piles according to whether they were from sponsors or not, and whether they were clothes or shoes or cosmetics.

Mr. Cole appeared in his best suit with bad news.

PingPong has denied our appeal, said the lawyer to Team Amanda in Mission Control.

He passed around printouts of the denial.

Because it's a Chinese company, there's really not much recourse we have legally, said the lawyer. And they aren't easily swayed by public opinion.

What's the next step then? asked Amanda's father.

I've engaged a Chinese law firm in Shanghai. We need people on the inside, who know the system and have connections.

Do I have any sponsors left? asked Amanda.

I'm afraid not, said the lawyer. Most have terminated our agreements due to failure to comply. Babylon has suspended the contract pending further notice.

Suspended, suspended, I hate that word! screamed Amanda.

We have to build you up on another platform, then we can sign deals again, said the lawyer. Even with only a hundred thousand followers we can get sponsors again, and that should be child's play. I would think with a concerted effort we could get a million in a couple weeks. We need to do some press as well. Maybe we should hire a professional publicist.

No! I don't want to talk to anyone now.

But now is exactly when you need to talk, said Nicole. Maybe reach out to Mista Sista. He likes you, and a word from him and you're gold again.

Everyone shot Nicole looks of derision, except for the lawyer, who thought it was a smart idea.

I've also taken the liberty to hire a forensic computer analyst, said the lawyer. I know Ned has worked tirelessly on this—thank you, Ned. But it's time to bring in professionals. Someone will be coming tomorrow to check all of your computers here, just on the offhand chance the hacker gained access in the house.

That's impossible, said Amanda's mother.

Yeah, impossible, mumbled White Hat Ned, feeling the blood drain from his face.

*

A few minutes later White Hat Ned was in Amanda's room, trying to erase the traces of his crime. And it was a crime, wasn't it? He could go to jail, couldn't he? His future would be ruined, his only career option the FBI or CIA, who recruited their cybersecurity people from penitentiaries the way Wall Street recruited from the Ivy League.

But more than the fear of prison time was his guilt at having let Amanda and her parents down. At having given the girl he loved reason to hate him and scorn him forever.

He had gained her love and her parents' trust. He was practically a member of the family, and not in a friend-zoned sort of way, but in a future husband and son-in-law sort of way.

I would like to think White Hat Ned would have eventually come clean of his own accord. But Mr. Cole's announcement sent White Hat Ned into panic mode, so we will never know.

What are you doing? asked Amanda, throwing her arms around his neck.

Her affection felt like a noose. She wasn't his girlfriend but his executioner. Except she didn't know it yet.

White Hat Ned jumped to his feet and walked to the window. It was a cloudless day with a light dusting of snow. The filled-in well in the distance looked like a period to the story of his life. It had launched Amanda's career, but had been the instrument of his own destruction.

You're not the only one who's shy, shouted White Hat Ned in a sudden outburst that startled Amanda.

Huh?

You're not the only one who's afraid of rejection, who doesn't want to disappoint anyone. You know, I liked you since seventh grade. But I didn't know how to talk to you. To girls. It wasn't until the hospital and you got your first kiss that I felt the courage to...

Are you OK?

No! No, I'm not OK. I'm terrible. I'm a terrible person.

Hey, I don't blame you for not finding the hacker. It's not your responsibility.

You don't know how jealous I was. You threw away the iPhone case I made. You went out with Martin Decker almost every week...

Not every week.

You said I was your boyfriend, but you never changed your Facebook status. I knew I couldn't compete with these other guys. And then when I saw you with Mista Sista, in the pool, and then kissing him on New Year's...

I'm sorry if I hurt you.

No, I'm sorry. I'm so, so sorry.

Amanda froze. Where had she heard that before?

Nicole. But surely White Hat Ned hadn't crashed the black Jaguar. It was parked in the garage, not a scratch upon it. So what could it be?

Did you sleep with someone? asked Amanda. Nipuni? Because I think she likes you. Is something going on between you?

No... No!!!

Because if there is something between you, I'm certainly upset. And it is disloyal. But I guess I can't fault you guys too much considering I've decided to be poly—

There is no hacker! I'm the hacker.

Amanda took a deep breath.

I snapped. When I saw you two kissing, something in me snapped. I just wanted you not to be famous anymore.

You...

I saw the petitions on my own Facebook page and knew if you supported them on your own PingPong account you might get in trouble.

Amanda could barely speak.

You...did...this?

But I thought they would just give you a warning. Or take your account down for a day. Just a day. Or ask you to post a retraction. I never thought they would suspend you permanently.

You...

And I'm sure once Mr. Cole gets a Chinese lawyer they'll get it all taken care of.

You're not a White Hat. You're a Black Hat!

Amanda searched for something more to say. Something to express her anger and hurt. But all that came to mind was her mother's favorite phrase:

Get out of my house!

7

Mandy, what's happening? asked Amy outside Amanda's bedroom door. We just saw Ned leaving in tears.

Go away.

Hey Mandy, this is Puni.

He's all yours. Why don't you go after him? You can have little Black Hat babies for all I care!

Nicole tried the door but it was locked. She pounded on it.

What the hell? asked Nicole. So, you had a lover's quarrel. We have a business to run.

He's the hacker! He destroyed everything.

There was silence on both sides of the door.

Are you sure? asked Amy.

He confessed.

I'll kill him with my bare hands! said Nicole.

She ran down the stairs. Amy and Nipuni followed to restrain her before blood was shed.

*

Honey? Darling? I brought you supper.

It was 9:00 p.m. and Amanda's mother stood outside her bedroom door with a tray.

You have to come out sometime.

I don't, actually.

Your father and I know what happened. We talked to Ned, and to his parents.

Is he in jail?

We don't care about him. We care about you. And right now it looks like you're the one locking herself up.

I'm locking the world out.

OK. Well, I'm just going to set this tray down. You need to eat. Is there anything I can bring you, or do for you?

Feed Luna.

All right. If you promise me one thing.

What?

You won't try... You won't...

I won't kill myself, Mama. I should, but I won't.

*

Amanda sat in the darkness all weekend. Phone off, computer off, lights off, curtains closed. She only opened the door to go to the bathroom or to take the food her mother left her on a tray on the floor in the hallway.

Why don't you talk to her? Carole asked me Saturday night. Maybe she'll listen to you.

You're talking to a writer. We *like* to lock ourselves away from the world. I'm afraid I'd just encourage her.

This isn't the time for jokes.

Carole was pacing in my room while I sat on the edge of the bed.

What do you want me to say? We know where she is. She's eating. She's not missing school.

She needs to get active on YouTube.

Is that for your benefit or hers?

Carole stopped pacing and glared at me. You never understood anything about business, said my daughter.

Maybe not. But I understand what it is to be sixteen. It wasn't that long ago we were throwing around the word *addiction*. Remember? And now you want to force her back on social media? Think of this weekend as a detox.

But she could lose everything!

Not everything, I corrected.

*

Nevertheless, later that night I decided to knock on her door.

Go away, Mom!

I said nothing but tickled Luna's belly till she meowed.

Amanda opened the door and I let her cat rush inside.

I thought you should have some company, I said.

Thanks, Gramps. I guess you want to lecture me.

Have I ever lectured you?

No.

I closed the door and went back to my room, where that long novel I had brought to the festival was still waiting to be finished.

*

Late Sunday afternoon Amanda's parents and I stood in the upstairs hallway.

Carole knocked softly.

Sweetheart, are you awake?

Not hungry. Go away.

Turn on your computer or phone. Look at the news. There's a girl... An emergency...

A moment later the door cracked open and Amanda, dressed in her Disney pajamas, peered out. Her eyes were red and her hair unbrushed. It was dark in her room.

What are you talking about? asked Amanda.

I think you should come downstairs.

Amanda followed us down to the living room, where cable news was on. A college student was trapped in a cave in Indiana.

Oh my God, said Amanda.

She stared at the TV, showing rescue crews outside the cave, showing the anxious parents, showing the victim herself, wearing a mask to protect her from floating dust particles, lodged in a narrow vertical opening hundreds of feet inside the cave.

She asked to talk to you, said Amanda's mother.

What do you mean?

There's a local news truck outside. It's the woman who interviewed you at your school. The one you liked. They have a live feed to the cave.

But you don't have to, said her father.

No, of course not, said her mother.

What do you think, Gramps?

You know what I think.

Fame brings responsibility, recalled Amanda.

She started for the front door.

Wash up and dress first, said her mother.

No.

Amanda went outside barefoot, in her pajamas, as she had done once before. But this time no one was mocking her.

The reporter smiled and said it was nice to see her again, although she wished the circumstances could be different.

The reporter held up a tablet with a video feed to the girl in the cave—her name was Cathy—while the reporter's cameraman shot the scene for their own story.

Amanda could hear the sound of a jackhammer, but then it stopped. She heard the sound of a hose washing the rock, and then a vacuum removing the dust.

The tablet showed the college student's face, now without the mask. Round, with blonde matted hair. Sweat pouring from her brow.

Hey, Amanda! You're there.

Yes.

I'm one of your followers. It's terrible they suspended your account. But I'm sure you'll get it back, said the college student, managing a smile.

I guess you're wondering how I got trapped.

You don't have to tell me, said Amanda, thinking of her own secret.

I was exploring the cave with some friends and we went through this crack. But they were all skinnier, and when I tried to get back, I got stuck. And then I panicked and just made it worse and couldn't get through either way. So now they're trying to cut the rock away, but they have to be careful not to make the ceiling collapse, so I might be here overnight.

Oh my God.

The college student started to cry.

I'm panicking like crazy. I think I'm gonna have a heart attack. I asked for a tranquilizer but they said they need me to be alert.

How long have you been there?

Since morning. Every minute feels like an hour. They brought a yoga instructor and a hypnotist, but that didn't work. I wanted to talk to you.

Why?

You understand what I'm going through. You were so brave...

Actually I—

Do you think you could come here? The news team said they can fly you out. If you're not too busy, I could really use your support.

Amanda stared into the college student's blue eyes, wet with tears.

OK.

*

Amanda quickly washed and dressed and we all accompanied the reporter and cameraman to the airport, where the network had chartered a plane to take us to Indiana.

This is very good of you to do this, said Amanda's mother, holding her hand.

I don't know how I'm supposed to help. What if I'm more scared than she is?

*

Less than an hour later we were on the ground, where a van drove us to the cave. It was dark outside, but argon lights from the rescue crew lit the cave entrance like a movie set.

All the major networks were there as well, with their own lights and cameras.

The reporters thrust their microphones in front of Amanda when she stepped out from the van, but the reporter from Iowa and Amanda's parents pushed them away.

Members of the rescue crew gave us all hard hats and masks and led us into the brightly lit cave. We could hear jackhammers in the distance.

Suddenly Amanda stopped.

Wait, said Amanda. I don't know if I can do this.

Her mother took her hand.

What if there's a cave in? asked Amanda.

That's why we're working slowly, said one of the rescue team. Don't worry.

Then why did you give us hard hats?

You don't have to go on, said Amanda's mother. You can talk to her by video.

Amanda took a deep breath.

No, I'm OK.

We followed a downward curve and could feel the air grow colder. We saw the workers up ahead. They had put down the jackhammer and were carefully chipping at the rock with hammers, while someone else vacuumed up the dust.

A couple, who must have been Cathy's parents, welcomed Amanda with effusive gratitude. When they stepped aside, we could see their daughter. Or the part of their daughter wedged in the crack.

Amanda pulled her mask down and put her hands over her mouth.

Oh my God.

But the college student smiled. You're here!

Amanda stared. The college student was wedged in the cleft of rock as though she'd been frozen there. Her torso was visible and her arms and right foot were free. But her legs were trapped and her left leg not visible.

There was an IV in her arm, keeping her hydrated. A nurse stood off to the side and nodded to Amanda.

Come here, said the college student.

Amanda hesitated, as if she were witnessing some awful spell and by touching the college girl would herself be frozen to the rock.

She slowly stepped forward and clasped the college girl's outstretched hand.

Tell me how you coped in the well. It must have been terrible.

It had been terrible, and Amanda did not want to think about it. All these months her life had been running so fast she hadn't had a spare moment to think about it. But what she saw before her seemed so much worse.

It was less than an hour, really...

You broke your legs.

My ankles. Really just one.

I'm afraid they're going to have to amputate me, but they say they will not. But people lie, to keep you from freaking out. You know that film, where the climber gets trapped and cuts off his own arm?

No, said Amanda. But I'm sure they won't amputate. Maybe they can call the surgeon at Mayo Clinic who was going to fix my ankle?

The college student squeezed Amanda's hand.

Thanks so much for being here. You don't know what it means. You're an inspiration. I mean, I can't feel sorry for myself compared to what you went through. And you're younger. With broken legs. And you were alone.

I think I'm gonna faint, said Amanda.

Ha! You're just trying to cheer me up. It's working.

No, I really think I'm going to faint.

The nurse stepped in to check the IV and Amanda asked in all seriousness if she could have one herself.

The crew asked them to put their masks back on and began chipping away at the rock.

Can you stay here for a while? Talk to me? asked the college student.

The nurse handed Amanda a bottle of water and Amanda gulped it down.

What do you want to talk about? asked Amanda.

I don't know. Anything except caves and wells, I guess.

Where do you go to college?

I'm a sophomore at Indiana.

Really? The Big Ten. I'm thinking of Iowa. Or Iowa State. I don't know. I have to take the SAT first, and I can't even pass the PSAT.

It's not hard, said the college student. I can help you study.

Really?

Although I bet you have millions of people to help you.

Not anymore, said Amanda.

Don't worry. You'll get them back. They have to reinstate you.

It's a Chinese company. They can do what they want.

True. Bummer. That's terrible.

But it's not like being stuck in a cave. Or a well.

They both laughed.

I really admire your taking a political stand. That was brave.

It wasn't me. It was White Hat—I mean Black Hat Ned, my boyfriend. He got jealous and blew up my account.

I know you have to say that to get PingPong to reinstate you. But I know what you did, just like I know you were in the well a lot longer than you let on. You're too modest.

No, I'm not.

Amanda excused herself to go to the bathroom. When she returned the college student's mother hugged her again and said this was the first time her daughter had smiled or laughed during this whole ordeal.

The reporter from Iowa informed her the network had arrange a hotel.

Go ahead, said Amanda. I'm not leaving.

But it may be all night, whispered Amanda's mother. You heard what they said.

I don't care, said Amanda.

She took the college student's hand again, feeling stronger than before, no longer worried she would faint.

Hey, where's your camera? asked the college student. Why aren't you documenting this?

I left it in Iowa. I'm off the grid.

Why? Because of PingPong? Don't let that discourage you. Look at all these cameras here. All the networks are covering this. Jump back in.

I don't want attention anymore. Do you? You know how cruel people are. They'll make jokes about you. They'll tease and bully you. They'll say you got stuck because you're fat. They'll call you names. Social media is superficial. It's cruel.

Hey, they can all say what they want. You don't think I've crapped in my pants already? There's only one thing I care about and that's not dying in this fucking cave. Two things, if you count not getting my legs amputated.

You're right. Of course.

But let's not talk about unpleasant things. Tell me all about the Influencer Festival.

*

Amanda woke on the cold floor of the cave. Someone had put a pillow under her head and covered her with a wool blanket.

There was a lot of commotion around her, but no sound of jack-hammers, or chisels. No dust floating in the air.

Sounds of joy.

The college student was free. Weak and exhausted, but not too frail to hug her parents, and the rescue team. Amanda rose to greet her.

You're free. You have your legs.

They cried in each other's arms.

You're an angel, Amanda. You're a hero.

No, really...

8

When Amanda returned to school Tuesday morning, she dreaded having to encounter Black Hat Ned in American History class. But she needn't have worried. He took pains to avoid eye contact.

At lunchtime she saw him sitting at a far table with Nipuni.

Traitors, thought Amanda. Good riddance.

She sat down at Amy's table. Nicole was sitting with the popular girls, but didn't come over.

Martin Decker tapped Amy's shoulder. Can I talk with Amanda?

I'll leave you lovebirds alone, said Amy, picking up her tray.

Can I take you out Friday? asked Martin Decker.

Sure. I guess. But you didn't have to chase off Amy to ask me that.

There's something else.

You hacked my account too?

What? No. I wanted to ask...

Yeah? Go on.

Geez. I've never been nervous around girls before. I guess it's because you're a celebrity.

I just got back from a cave disaster, said Amanda. If you're gonna make fun of me I'm walking away now.

Martin Decker put a hand on her arm.

Is it OK if I see Nicole? I mean, see her too?

Amanda spilled her juice, but Martin Decker didn't bat an eye.

It took Amanda a few moments to process this. She bought time by clumsily wiping up the juice with her napkins. Her first reaction was relief that the news he wanted to tell her was not that she'd lost another thirty million followers or wasn't being asked to rush to the scene of a dreadful accident.

I know you're polyamorous, said Martin Decker. But with friends these things can be dicey. But Nicole says she's cool with it and promised me she's not jealous of you anymore.

Jealous of me?! Nicole? Since when has she been jealous of me?

Since you surpassed her nine hundred followers on PingPong. Since you stole her ex-boyfriend. Although stole isn't the right word.

Nicole?!

Amanda glanced over at the popular girls' table, but Nicole would not meet her gaze.

She agreed to take you back? asked Amanda.

Is that what she told you? I broke up with *her.*

Why would you break up with her? She's Nicole.

Because she's too possessive. She drove me crazy. She even scratched me once on my Polynesian tattoo. Look, you can still see the marks.

And he lifted his shirt sleeve to show her.

Nicole?!

But she promised to change. And since all you and I are doing is holding hands and kissing, I need... Well, I want to see other people. And Nicole is—well, I'm sure she's told you.

No. We never talk about that.

Martin Decker laughed.

Yeah, I remember. She told you the jag crashed because her date was changing the radio.

That's not what happened? asked Amanda, beginning to wonder if everything she ever thought she knew about everyone was a lie.

Do you know anyone who ever ran off the road and hit a tree because they were changing stations? asked Martin Decker.

I guess not, said Amanda. But then how did they crash?

Nicole grabbed him, said Martin Decker.

She grabbed the wheel? Why would she do that?

She grabbed *him*. Do I need to draw a picture on my napkin?

Slowly, the picture drew itself in Amanda's mind.

Ohhhhhhhh.

But how do you know? asked Amanda, suspecting Martin Decker might be toying with her.

Because she did the same thing to me when we were first dating! Fortunately, we were on a straight road at the time.

*

Amanda thought she was still in the darkness, off the grid. Her millions of followers having vanished in an instant, like a mirage. Had it been thirty-two million? Or thirty-five? She couldn't remember. She hadn't even brought her phone to school. It still lay on her bed, turned off, as was her computer. Except for the video call with Cathy in the cave, she hadn't looked at social media since locking herself in her room.

So it was a shock to her that she was still in the spotlight. That her followers hadn't vanished like a mirage but were real and searching for her in places other than PingPong. That people who didn't know about her before, knew about her now.

A caravan of media trucks was parked outside Harding High, just beyond the buses.

Oh my God.

Amanda walked to her bus—yes, she was taking the bus—because Nicole was still afraid to look at her. And Amanda didn't want to ride with Amy because that meant riding with Nipuni too, and she just wasn't ready for that. And she didn't want to ride with Martin Decker, well, just because. She simply wanted to be alone. And the best way to be alone right now was to sit on a bus with thirty other students she knew less well than the friends she thought she knew so well.

But before she reached the bus a dozen reporters surrounded her, ignoring the security staff's instructions to stay off school grounds.

Questions ricocheted off her skull like Nerf bullets, collecting in a pile at her feet that she would have to pick up and sort through eventually. But not now.

She heard:

Amanda, what did you say to the girl in the cave?

and

When did you decide to become political?

and

Do you think PingPong should be banned in the U.S.?

and

If you could vote, which candidate would you choose in the upcoming election?

and

We got a hold of a clip from a yet-to-be released documentary about the Influencer Festival in which you referred to yourself as polyamorous. Is this true, or were you joking?

and

Are you still a virgin?

and

What do you have to say to the people of Hong Kong?

and

So, what's the latest with you and Mista Sista?

and

Did you lose all your sponsors when you were banned from Ping-Pong?

and

Are you disillusioned with corporate America?

and

What other social causes do you support?

and

Are you a socialist?

and

Are you a capitalist?

and

Will you go to the White House if you are invited?

and

Will you meet with Chinese leaders if you are invited to Beijing?

and

Do you want to speak at the U.N.?

Amanda stopped before the open bus door.

Excuse me?

A reporter showed her Emerson Frost's Twitter feed, where he posted:

Young people should have a voice in our future. Amanda Dizon needs to speak at the United Nations.

Oh my God.

How does it feel to be a hero?

I'm not a hero, said Amanda faintly, trying to negotiate the steps onto the bus.

*

There were more media trucks parked on the curb outside her house. And more questions, like Nerf bullets, harmless but annoying.

At least she hoped they were harmless.

She noticed Mr. Cole's car parked in the driveway, as well as a sedan with rental car plates.

Her father came outside to rush her in.

Gathered in the living room were:

Her parents.

Myself.

Her lawyer.

A man and a woman in business attire who looked familiar.

Everyone rose upon Amanda's entrance, except me.

Hi Amanda, said the woman, extending her hand.

It's great to finally meet you in person, said the man, extending his hand.

Amanda ignored their extended hands. She saw a briefcase. Papers on the coffee table. A folder with the logo of Babylon Skincare.

Then Amanda remembered. They were the representatives she had talked to by video. They had been so friendly then. And they were friendly now.

Can I get you a glass of orange juice? asked Amanda's mother, as though she were a waitress and not a mother.

What's going on?

Our friends from Babylon flew out to discuss our latest venture, said the lawyer with a satisfied smile, fingering the most recent addition to his wardrobe: a gold pocket square.

But you suspended me, said Amanda, setting down her backpack and looking from one representative to the other.

The situation with PingPong is unfortunate, said the man, still standing, but having withdrawn his arm.

We want to make a new arrangement with you that isn't dependent on social media platforms, said the woman, taking a step closer to Amanda and looking into her eyes.

I don't understand.

You would create content exclusively for Babylon Skincare's site, said the lawyer.

And on your own website, added the woman from Babylon.

And participate in promotional events, added the man from Babylon.

It's a million dollars, whispered her mother, as if saying the figure any louder might jeopardize the deal.

Until you suspend me again, said Amanda, looking at the representatives.

It's guaranteed, said the lawyer with obvious pride at his negotiating skills.

I don't know, said Amanda. I can't deal with this now. All my life you keep me off the internet—now she was looking at her parents—then you set up Mission Control, then you tell me I'm addicted and need help, and now you want me out of the darkness, back on the grid. Not to mention all my life you acted like hippies just wanting to be farmers and schoolteachers and money's not important, and now I'm supposed to care about a million dollars, even though everyone suspended me, and I'm supposed to think I can't lose everything again, it's guaranteed—continued Amanda, now looking at her attorney—because you're such a smart lawyer, Mr. Cole, and of course you are, but we all know nothing in this life is guaranteed.

I'm going to my room.

*

That night I found Amanda sitting on the well, Luna in her lap, scrolling on her phone.

How did you know I was here? asked my granddaughter.

I followed the light, I said, meaning the blue glow of her iPhone.

Oh yeah.

I never thought I'd say I was glad to see you using your phone again.

Haha, said Amanda.

Mind if I smoke?

Of course I mind.

Pretty cold tonight.

I guess, said Amanda.

She was wearing her winter coat, unzipped, over her pajamas. She was wearing slippers without socks.

I miss the beach, I said.

Why don't you go back?

I can't afford business class.

I have a million dollars. You want me to sign on their dotted line? I'll buy you a ticket anywhere you want to go.

Without a chaperone?

True. You'll drink and smoke yourself to death without teenage supervision. What about Amy? She's not attached to anyone that I know of. She stole my Chromebook. She can steal my grandfather.

I think I promised to pass the winter here.

Yeah. Like you ever keep your promises.

She laughed, and I laughed with her.

How is the girl in the cave? I asked.

She texted me. She doesn't have to get her legs amputated.

That's good news.

She invited me to visit her at Indiana University.

First the football player at Iowa, now the girl in the cave. You don't have to go to college. You can just visit other students. A lot cheaper that way.

And I don't have to study.

Luna scampered off after a mouse or squirrel.

You probably don't remember the last time I saw you. You were nine. I took you to Baskin-Robbins.

I remember. You bought me bubble gum ice cream. It was my favorite because it looked like a rainbow. I can't stand it now. My flavor is mint chocolate chip. But you didn't get anything. I guess they don't serve rum and Cokes at Baskin-Robbins, hahaha.

You should eat more ice cream, said Amanda. Less rum. Less tobacco. More mint chocolate chip.

We didn't say a word to each other that day, I said. I thought you were insipid. Now look at you.

I'm still insipid, said Amanda. I still don't have anything to say. Everyone else speaks for me.

That's why you have to be the author of your own story. But even then, people will fill in the blanks. It's human nature.

I don't want to be a hero. I'm not.

Only true heroes say that, I pointed out.

Don't confuse me. I didn't save that girl in the cave.

Is that what she says?

I don't even know who the Uyghurs are. I probably couldn't find Hong Kong on a map.

We had a saying when I was a kid, I told her. That if you dug down deep enough—or fell in a well deep enough—you would fall all the way to China. That's what you did, Amanda. You fell to China.

I don't know what you're talking about, said Amanda. This is why I couldn't read your book. Everything's metaphors. I hate metaphors.

I'm proud of you, I told her. That's not a metaphor.

She jumped off the well and threw her arms around me.

Thanks, Gramps.

Can I smoke a cigarette now?

No!!!

Now it was my turn to sit on the well. My legs were getting tired.

Amanda climbed back on and we sat facing each other, she with her legs crossed, me with my long legs dangling over.

Tell me what to do, Gramps.

About what?

About everything.

That's a tall order. You know how to run a marathon?

Is this another metaphor? Because if it is, I'm warning you in advance I'm probably not going to understand it.

You run a marathon the same way you run to the corner. One step at a time. I've always found that when I'm overwhelmed with choices the best thing is to make just one decision. Just one. Of course, in my case that decision is usually to have a drink. I'm not recommending you take the easy route.

So I should make one decision? It can be about anything?

Yes. But it has to be now.

Now? You mean right now?

It can be about anything. The million-dollar contract from Babylon. Or what you're going to wear tomorrow.

Those are both hard, said Amanda, and laughed.

She sat there thinking.

Don't try so hard, I said. Take your time. Close your eyes. Let your mind wander over recent conversations and messages, anything at all.

Messages. Emails! shouted Amanda.

Sure, emails...

I know! exclaimed Amanda with sudden energy.

She opened the emails on her phone and scrolled through. She found the one she wanted and held up her phone so I could see.

A publisher in New York wants me to write a book.

But you complain about writing papers for English class, I told her.

Not me, silly. You!

Me?! But what kind of book?

About my life, duh!

But you're only sixteen. No sixteen-year-old who's ever lived deserves a memoir—

Gramps, hellooooooooo! This is business class calling. This is the beach with all the rum and Cokes you can handle. Sometimes I think you're the one who's sixteen, you're so stubborn!

OK.

OK, what?

OK I'll write it. I'll try. But I'll need to do research. I'll need to talk to people.

Not a problem.

She extended her hand. Deal?

Can we do this without your attorney present?

She shook my hand enthusiastically.

But you have to promise to tell the truth. As insipid as it is. I know you have to make up conversations and stuff. But tell the truth as best you can. Tell people I'm not a hero and I don't know where Hong Kong is. And don't say anything bad about my parents, or about anyone—except Black Hat Ned. I don't care what you say about him. And don't put down social media and technology just because you hate it yourself. And don't use big words and long sentences with lots of commas and dashes like you did in your other book. Promise?

Promise.

ACKNOWLEDGMENTS

I want to thank Lauren Grosskopf and Jack Estes for their labor of love and literature that is Pleasure Boat Studio. Also to Lauren for her stellar design work. And to my friend Dr. Siegfried Kra for connecting me to Pleasure Boat Studio.

I'm grateful to Galya Gerstman, Kay Sloan, Jacob Appel, Rebecca Austin, my parents and everyone else who read the book in draft or advance copy and gave valuable feedback. To my sister, Ellen Schreiber, who convinced me to publish this as a young adult novel and helped me with promotion. And to my sons, Jorge and Jael, who got me up to speed on influencer culture.

MARK SCHREIBER was born in Cincinnati, Ohio in 1960, graduated high school at age fifteen and began writing novels full-time. *Princes in Exile,* which explores a prodigy's struggle to accept his own mortality at a summer camp for kids with cancer, was published in 1984 and made into a feature film in 1991. It has been published in ten countries, received two awards in Europe and was shortlisted for the Austria Prize. *Carnelian,* a fantasy, was published by Facet in Belgium. *Starcrossed,* a rebuttal to *Romeo and Juliet,* was published by Flux and translated into French and Turkish. His illustrated science book, *How to Build an Elephant,* was published as an Apple app by Swag Soft. He has written over forty books and received two State of Ohio Individual Writer Fellowships. For the last seven years he has been a digital nomad, living on four continents. He currently resides in Costa Rica.

CPSIA information can be obtained
at www.ICGtesting.com
Printed in the USA
FSHW021619250821
83976FS